DIE Back

RICHARD ALLEN

Richard Allen is a retired senior police officer who, in addition to uniform duties, saw service with the CID, the Vice Squad, the Drug Squad and Special Branch.
Richard is the author of two best selling works dealing with police management and leadership,
which were listed as recommended reading by both the US Department of Justice and the Police Staff College.

'DIE Back' is the second in a series of
Mark Faraday adventures.

By the same author

Non-fiction:

Effective Supervision in the Police Service

Leading from the Middle

Fiction:

DIRTY Business

To our daughter,
Suzi

Chapter 1

Sunday 29th July.

California, USA and Bristol, England.

SHE PRESSED just two keys. 0.11955 seconds later the solar cells of the wing-like panels of the 21 ton Multi-Bird 4 glistened in the sun's rays as the satellite's Attitude Control System adjusted slightly so as to regain its station keeping, disrupted by the unusual solar winds and increase in radiation pressure. Dr Mary-Beth Howard relaxed into her command seat for a few moments, her eyes apparently flitting from orange data display to orange data display, but her eyes were like those of the beautiful Peregrine Falcon, dark and alert, observing every aspect of her domain at Lawrence Vandenberg Air Force Base, California, analysing all before her. Then she relaxed a little more, if Dr Howard was actually capable of relaxing, satisfied that the MultiBird, travelling at a little over 7,000 miles per hour, had regained its perfect geosynchronous orbit 22,237 miles above the Equator.

MultiBird 4 would continue to orbit the earth, linked by a laser data inter-satellite link to three other smaller satellites, these in low asynchronous orbits, one 87 miles above the Earth's surface, the others, 733 miles and 927 miles, providing 'footprint' images as they passed over their target area. Together, these satellites would now begin to gather data via their multi-spectral sensors capable of distinguishing ground features as small as one metre square. There was never enough time, thought Dr Howard, but her people at least had until the Fall before they must perfect and co-ordinate this data collection and use it in earnest.

Satisfied that for the moment her job was done, Mary-Beth Howard allowed her thoughts to wander as she imagined Multi-Bird 4 traversing the heavens. Soon the satellite would pass in front of Scorpius, one of the oldest and brightest constellations known, located in the centre of the Milky Way galaxy, the home of our own solar system. For Dr Howard, it was not only the size of our solar system with a diameter of 100,000 light years that was breath-taking; it was also the sheer beauty. A smile creased her face at the thought, particularly of Alpha Scorpill, 600 light years from Earth, glittered with an unusual metallic red while the entire region was bathed in a red nebula.

***

David Collins saw what appeared to be a thousand red stars trailing out in front of him in a long, graceful curve, mirrored by a parallel approaching stream of a thousand, pure white stars. He frowned, peering forward, the red and white stars sparkled, a distracting explosion of light as the wipers of his truck battled to clear the torrents of rain that cascaded against the windscreen. He didn't mind the rain. He had experienced far worse and this job would be a walk in the park. Safe and risk-free, unlike some of the others. The others, he thought. The others had always involved risks, the risk of being caught, being killed even – and poor food. Now there was only seven miles to go before he reached Bristol, a straight run down the M5 to Avonmouth.

Like Dr Mary-Beth Howard, David Collins had other thoughts too. He was thinking of the other drivers, Simon and Shaun. On all their jobs together, Collins had always been protective towards Simon Mooney. A skilled driver and good humoured, Simon was a dreamer with a walrus moustache. He imagined Mooney in the pristine cab of an identical Mercedes-Benz Actros, covered in pieces of cake and surrounded by crisp packets and chocolate wrappers. The other man on this job, Shaun Walker, was a lot different. A powerfully built, handsome womaniser; aggressive behind the wheel, handy in a tight corner but sometimes too ready with his fists. Shaun, he knew, would be pounding along the M4 towards the M4/M5 interchange at Almondsbury at the maximum limited speed of 54 mph, whilst Simon would be eating another cake as he approached the junction for the M32 on the outskirts of Bristol. They would all soon gather together at Avonmouth to continue the job.

Chapter 2

Wednesday 1st August.

Police Headquarters, Bristol, England.

AS SOON as the little orange light went out on her telephone display, the chief's personal assistant spoke to Chief Inspector Tait: 'The chief constable is off the line now'. In response, the assistant staff officer tapped on the redwood door and walked into the chief's office without waiting for a reply. The chief constable was seated behind his wide desk in full uniform displaying his seven medal ribbons above his left breast pocket.

'Do we have a full house?' asked Sir Hastings Perry looking up from his papers.

'Full house, sir', replied Tait, 'and if I may remind you, sir, that it will be the first attendance by Mr Stayer and Miss Craven in their capacities as substantive superintendents.'

'Yes', replied the chief, thankful that Tait had reminded him, his usual meticulous preparation having been interrupted by the local Member of Parliament demanding to speak to him 'out of courtesy' before he spoke with the Home Secretary.

'Thank you for that, Richard. And', he continued as he rose from his chair, 'we have a full agenda, which is good.'

No reply was necessary as the chief constable walked towards the full length mirror and adjusted his tunic belt, making absolutely sure that the buckle was perfectly in-line with the buttons. A well built, impressive looking man with jet black, wavy hair and a contented smile, the chief was nevertheless not arrogant, although maybe a little vain, but he realised that as the chief constable of the Severnside force and over nine thousand staff he was always 'on stage.'

Both men walked out through the secretariat and to their right, along a short carpeted corridor towards the double doors. Tait slowed his pace, the chief maintained his and pushed open both doors to the conference room. It was all theatre and had the desired effect, four assistant chief constables, twenty seven superintendents and chief superintendents and eight principal civilians moved in their chairs as the chief cheerfully announced: 'Good Morning, everyone.'

Sir Hastings walked towards the centre of the conference room before moving to his chair behind what everyone affectionately referred to as 'the headmaster's high table'. As he did so, the chief pointed towards one of his senior officers who had recently returned from sick leave, smiled an acknowledgement to another and nodded to a third, then took his seat immediately below the carved grey granite coat of arms of the force. He opened his burgundy coloured leather folder, so carefully prepared by his staff officer, as Tait appeared at his side and silently placed a cup of black coffee near his chief's left elbow.

'Right-o', said the chief in a positive and business-like tone. 'We have a very full agenda today and so we had better get on, but, before we do, I want to welcome Mary Craven and Robert Stayer to this, their first meeting of the Strategic Command Group'. Mark Faraday looked across towards Superintendent Stayer, now commander of Bath District. At 39, Stayer was a little older that Faraday and smiled as if pleased to be there. Quite a different personality, thought Faraday, than that of Superintendent Mary

Craven of the South Gloucestershire District. Flaming red hair, hard faced and cold, her effort at a smile was such that she gave the impression that her promotion had been long overdue and it was a privilege for everyone that she was there amongst them. 'I shall rely upon you both, as I rely upon all of my district commanders, simply because I just cannot run this force alone and because time and time again it is you, all of you, who have provided the solutions to the issues that confront us. It is good, Mary and Robert, to have you as part of this team. This team work, this corporate approach, has never been more important than it is now'. The chief paused as the staff officer, on cue, displayed on the screen a series of bar charts, the content of which did not make for good reading.

'Here we are,' the chief continued. 'In the first quarter of this year we had 19 murders. This is more than our usual yearly average. In the last month alone, there have been three more. The CID is overwhelmed with current cases, let alone the successful reopening of so many cold cases. Now it seems that we have exhausted suitable venues for fully equipped MIRs', he said, referring to the suite of rooms especially equipped and set aside for murder enquiries and other major incidents. 'The budget for the forthcoming year was fixed, since which time I have argued with the Home Secretary and HMI for a modest increase, but to no avail. The bottom line is that the budget represents, in crude terms, an increase of only 1.7%. It is anticipated that the current national pay negotiations will result in a 2.9% pay increase across the board. As 83% of our budget is expended upon staff salaries, we don't need to be Oxford dons to realise that our budgetary allocation will not cover these anticipated pay increases, let alone the hike in fuel costs'. Sir Hastings paused, and then continued. 'Therefore, we will need to make some hard choices. Derek,' he said, referring to his Director of Personnel, 'will be looking again at the recruitment profile. Bob will be taking a long, hard look at our real estate, maintenance and refurbishment programme and you, John, I know are examining our vehicle replacement programme. These three wise men', he said as he looked at the three principal civilian officers in turn, 'will be presenting papers by the 28th with options for discussion. For now, I need to be sure that you are all signed up to the new policy regarding the investigation of suspicious deaths'. The chief looked around the assembled senior officers. They all nodded in agreement.

'We all seem to be in agreement then', said Sir Hastings but, as was his custom, asked: 'Can I just test that out? What about you, Carole. Do you have a sufficiency of trained and experienced staff to undertake the screening?'

'I am fortunate, sir, to have some ex-RCS detectives on district, whilst others have been able to gain experience in connection with the Frome and Shepton Mallet murders last year', replied Superintendent Beckley. 'I think we will be OK.'

'And you, Mark,' probed the chief, 'are you as confident in the middle of the city as Carole is in a more rural area?'

Superintendent Mark Faraday leaned forward slightly in his chair and placed both hands flat on the blotter in front of him. At 32, Faraday was one of the youngest BCU commanders in the UK. 'We can never be sure that a new policy will work, sir', the commander of the Bristol Central District replied. 'What we can be sure of is that our previous policy did not work and I believe that the new policy gives us a fighting chance of screening effectively. Like Carole, I am lucky to have some good people and you've given me a sound replacement in DI Yin'. A number of the male superintendents discreetly glanced towards Faraday with a knowing, or was it an envious, look at the mention of Kay Yin's name as Faraday continued. 'And, of course, we have the advantage of the new headquarters' helpline as a long stop.'

'But we shouldn't be simply using the helpline as a long stop,' interrupted an owl-like Chief Superintendent Wynne-Thomas. 'If I can suggest, Sir Hastings', he said peering over-large, heavy-framed glasses balanced on a small, pointed nose, '*some* district commanders may need to consider the use of the helpline throughout the course of the,' he paused deliberately, then continued: '*more complex* enquiries.'

Some of those seated in the conference room would be grateful for the opportunity to seek really experienced investigative advice from HQ CID, as indeed would Faraday, but, the underlying barbed meaning of the comment was not lost on many, including Faraday and Sir Hastings.

'Thank you for that, John,' observed the chief. 'You are quite right, of course, that we should all avail ourselves of the helpline, but I have confidence in you all not to overburden HQ and know that you will only use the helpline when you judge it necessary to do so.' The chief look towards his ACC (Crime). 'David?'

As David Comer took up the theme, the chief constable absorbed what had already been said. Carole Beckley was an experienced former member of the Regional Crime Squad and CID school and so he valued her views, but it was Faraday who always impressed him. Determined and resourceful; thoughtful, yet capable of swift action when circumstances demanded, he was charming as well as handsome. His staff respected his undoubted abilities, in fact, he guessed that many were probably quite fond of him, but these strengths, his recent successful part in foiling a terrorist plot and his overall abilities, generated envy amongst his less able colleagues and some of his seniors. Faraday, reflected Sir Hastings, had few faults, although he could be outspoken and did have a tendency to be ruled by his heart and not always his head and, maybe, this was the reason for one failed marriage and a series of female admirers.

Superintendent Guy Hamilton of HQ Ops, seated next to Mark, pointed his pen at a note he had written: 'If looks could kill'. Faraday rearranged some papers on his blotter and drew a little sketch of an owl's head, then sat back in his chair and casually looked to the left of Wynne-Thomas, panning to his right towards the chief constable. As he did so, Faraday's eyes met those of Chief Superintendent Wynne-Thomas. They seemed to be filled with smouldering resentment. Faraday lowered his gaze, unable to fully comprehend why a man in the position of a chief superintendent should act as he did. He certainly would never do so. Faraday, unwisely, merely dismissed this attitude as unfortunate and irrelevant, instead concentrating on the presentation by the ACC (Crime).

During the buffet lunch, Faraday spoke with some of his closest colleagues. As lunch was drawing to an end, Guy Hamilton saw Wynne-Thomas approach. 'Careful, Mark, Wynne-Thomas is approaching at ram speed right behind you.'

'Faraday,' said the Welshman. Mark turned around and faced the chief superintendent whose thought processes seemed to falter as he stared bitterly at the single, rose pink and pearl grey edged medal ribbon above Faraday's left breast pocket. 'The transfer of DI Yin to the Bristol Central District is, as far as I am concerned, in the nature of a secondment, Faraday. I will be monitoring carefully, in my capacity as the chairman of the Strategic Tasking and Co-ordinating Group, the use to which you put the force's scarce resources.'

At that moment the chief constable returned to his chair below the granite crest and the superintendents began to make their way back to their seats. Of necessity, Wynne-Thomas and Faraday walked a very short distance together to their respective seats but, as they parted, Wynne-Thomas gently squeezed Faraday's arm and spoke quietly in his ear. 'It might help you to focus your thoughts if I remind you that my group's short title is "The Oversight Group". My view remains that you are a loose cannon. Let me assure you, Faraday, that your activities will attract plenty of oversight from me.'

The conference resumed, issues were raised and matters discussed, options considered and decisions made until, at 4.35pm, the chief finally concluded Any Other Business and the conference drew to a close.

In the Force HQ car park, it was a rather amusing sight akin to a ballet performance, as all the superintendents seemed to crane sideways in unison, mobile phones at their ears, making their quick calls to their district headquarters before they drove home. As Faraday finally made his way to his black Volvo C70 convertible, he spoke with Guy Hamilton and Robert Stayer.

'It was good to see you here today, Robert,' said Faraday, 'A heavy day and a lot for all of us to take in.'

'Head's reeling a bit with Police Performance Assessments and KPIs', replied a tired looking Stayer.

'My head's throbbing too', said Faraday. 'These models and measures can be really useful tools, Robert, although I keep feeling that we can easily get comfortably bogged down with the window dressing required by the Home Office. The important thing to remember is that Bristol and Bath are not too far apart, traffic permitting, and Guy and I are only a phone call away.' They shook hands and drove their separate ways home, Faraday to Avon View Court.

Twenty-five minutes later, Faraday turned off into Julian Road, leaving the Downs behind him. After only another quarter of a mile he finally turned into Avon View Court. As he drove into the grounds of this modern and exclusive apartment development, across the red brick paving, he touched the button on the dashboard and, further on, a double garage door silently rose, the interior automatically illuminating. Of course, the garage was completely empty. His car parked, Faraday, removed his brief case and jacket carrier from the boot, then walked towards the foyer, glancing over his shoulder as he did so, checking that the garage door had closed down securely. He swiped his card in the security lock and entered the warm and plush interior.

On the second floor, he stepped out of the lift and walked along the carpeted corridor, glazed on the right-hand side, thus providing a clear view over the subtly illuminated gardens below. Faraday used his swipe card again and entered number 16, quickly tapping in his alarm security code. He turned on the hallway light and his thoughts drifted back to the previous year when the beautiful Helen Cave of MI5 had stood under that very same light. But now, like the garage, his apartment was empty.

Chapter 3

Monday 6th August.

London, England.

THE BLACK taxi stopped outside the Queen Elizabeth's Conference Centre, just across the road from Westminster Abbey. Although within easy walking distance of their offices at Horseguards, the driving rain compelled them to take transport. In any case, it would be much more appropriate for them to arrive by taxi like the others.

The two occupants quickly alighted as the cabby pocketed the crumpled bank note. They bent their heads against the rain and, with measured step, approached the large, automatic glass doors. Inside, they shook the rain from their Barbour's and then collected their conference packs and identification tags from reception.

Colonel Jeremy House-Layton fixed his ID tag to his hacking jacket: 'Jeremy Lawrence, Department for Environment, Food & Rural Affairs'. His younger colleague from Military Intelligence, Captain Andy Chappell, became Andrew Charman from the same government department. Both were about 5'9", and dapper, although House-Layton was immaculately groomed, confident and relaxed, whereas Chappell wasn't really confident at all, his movements less smooth, less natural and less assured.

They passed through the security checks and made their way towards the attractive young hostess who offered coffee. As they sipped the bland liquid, House-Layton glanced casually about the foyer whilst Chappell glanced at the hostess. House-Layton was faintly amused by the 41 year old's preoccupations, although not concerned – not there at any rate. But, reflected the colonel, the captain had a key role to play in the operation, no 'daring-do' of course, very much an organisational task, but today would serve to remind the captain that his task was critical, timing essential, and his promotion to the rank of major rested on the successful outcome of the operation.

The bell sounded and a hundred or so delegates made their way unhurriedly forward to the lecture theatre. The series of presentations under the auspices of the Environmental Protection Agency was about to begin.

House-Layton and Chappell settled into their comfortable back-row seats and patiently waited the twenty minutes until the second speaker took her place on the rostrum.

'Good morning, everyone', said the speaker. 'I am Doctor Kimberley Gill and standing in for Doctor Robert Evans who, as some of you may know, was a native of Gloucestershire, and this I believe accounted for his particular interest in Dutch elm disease.'

One could imagine Dr Gill as a headmistress, in command of her subject, at ease in her role, not overbearing but confident and enthusiastic, addressing her audience as if recounting a great adventure.

'Here we are,' she said pointing to the screen, 'the Dutch Elm, a wood of great utility, used over the centuries to make wheel hubs and wagons, coffins and chopping blocks, ships' keels, ammunition boxes and cheese moulds, water pipes and water wheels, yet,' she paused as she looked around the audience, then continued, 'virtually destroyed as a result of the activities of a little beetle'. The picture of this beetle now on the screen did *not* look quite so small.

'The disease, first discovered in France in 1818, but not formally identified until 1919, is a fungal: *Ceratocystis ulmi*, probably of Asian origin, and carried by the bark beetle'. She looked up from her notes before continuing. 'A particularly virulent form reached the British Isles in the late 1960s and by 1974 had killed 4.5 million elms, with well over 50% of the elms in Gloucestershire being wiped out'. Kimberley Gill was in her stride. No need for her notes now. 'Once the disease had taken hold, no elm was safe. *Ulmus Americana* was very susceptible. *Ulmus parvofolia*, the Chinese elm, was thought to be immune, but sadly this was not so. In particular, *Ulmus procera* was very badly affected.'

The doctor pressed the remote control button and vivid, panasonic pictures illustrated her presentation. 'The fungus is rather like yeast in the sap of the tree', she continued. 'It contains a toxic that produces a bulbous, gummy blockage to the tracheids. The fungus is usually brought to the tree by *Eurpea Scolytus scolytus*, or maybe the smaller *Scolytus multistriatus*'.

She peered over her Dior glasses. 'These beetles breed under the bark of recently dead elms, the female tunnelling into the sap wood where she is joined by the male. Tunnelling continues with the laying of little white eggs. Once the larvae emerge, they too begin tunnelling.' She shrugged her shoulders. 'Thus, the destruction continues.'

She paused and took a sip of tonic water as if to signify the end of one significant chapter and the commencement of another. 'Between May and October,' she continued, 'the young beetles emerge, fly off, sometimes many miles and, upon finding a new tree, give off a scent to attract others. In their travels of course, the new adults carries with them the fungus *Ceratocystis ulmi*'. A glance over the glasses again. 'All is not lost, however, for we will now consider parasitic wasps, predatory larvae and beetle-eating birds….'

***

House-Layton whispered to his colleague. 'I have something else to consider now as well. Stay here. I won't be long.'

The younger man assumed that his colonel would visit the toilets, but he did not. At the reception he saw Grieves, the deputy manager of the centre. No words were exchanged. House-Layton merely following Grieves to his office. Once the office door was closed, they shook hands warmly.

'How is everything, Dennis?' asked the colonel.

'First class, sir. Busy of course,' he replied as they both peered at a computer screen. Each delegate's photograph, taken at reception, as well as the organisational details of each delegate, flashed across the screen. The colonel's expression was tense, full of absolute concentration as he quickly assessed the photographs and details of each individual as they appeared. Grieves remained silent throughout, just looking at the colonel and waiting.

'Can't see anything of interest so far', said the colonel, 'but we'll keep going.' After a few more minutes the list and photographs were exhausted. 'Well, 107 altogether,' he smiled at Grieves. 'As you say, pretty busy.' And then, 'If you don't mind, Dennis?' said the colonel, producing the memory stick from the inside of his jacket. He quickly inserted the stick into the port and pressed three keys in turn. The process only took a matter of seconds.

'Thank you, Dennis', said the colonel. 'We can always rely on an old hand. Couldn't see anyone that I should know, but I will look again later when I have more time.' They shook hands and the colonel returned to the lecture theatre and slid unobtrusively back into his seat.

Captain Chappell pointed his pencil towards an item on the programme and whispered: 'We are now on defoliation of plants by photophasgus insects and parasitic fungi'. The colonel nodded in reply and settled more comfortably down in his seat. Another twelve minutes passed.

'....and so we find that *Operophtera brumata* is able to denude *Quercus robus* as can the chnysomelid beetle, *Gastrophysa viriderla*, decimate *Rumex obtusifolius*.'

Doctor Gill returned to the rostrum. 'Are they any questions at all before we take coffee?' There was silence. 'Then I think this would be a good time to take a break and when we return we will consider the question of pesticides.'

There was a babble of conversation as the lecture theatre doors swung open and the delegates made their way to the tables. As both men queued, House-Layton engaged in a continuous, one-sided conversation with Chappell regarding his recent sailing holiday off the Balearic Islands, designed to discourage conversation with others. They both sipped their coffees, information packs under their arms, biscuits in hands, the packs to drop, the biscuits to munch should they be asked any inquisitive questions.

Shortly, a bell sounded again. Some conference delegates discarded cups and saucers onto tables, others onto the reception desk, clearly to the annoyance of the young ladies working there. A few lingered near the remaining chocolate biscuits or hurried to the toilets.   As the foyer cleared, House-Layton and Chappell collected their coats.

Outside, the rain had stopped and the sun shone onto the Purbeck stone of Westminster Abbey. They crossed over Abingdon Street to Old Palace Yard and passed the equestrian statue of Richard Coeur de Lion.

'Any questions from the floor when I was out?' asked Colonel House-Layton.

'No, none at all.'

'And you, Andrew, do you have any questions?'

'Not questions', he replied rather sullenly.

'Come on, man. What?'

'I was hoping for something a bit more … significant, that was all.'

'OK. Come on. Let's pop in here', said the colonel, gesturing towards the Royal Entrance to the Palace of Westminster, immediately to the side of the Victoria Tower. 'You don't think this operation is … significant?' he asked as he nodded to the uniformed police constable at the door and discretely revealed his identity card in the palm of his hand.

'To be frank, sir, Nixon tried this once. I think this operation is likely to go tits up, that's all.'

'Along with your career?'

'OK, that is in my mind. But didn't the Americans abandon it because they feared it would get out of hand?'

They climbed the imposing staircase inlaid with marble and turned into the Robing Room, only used by Her Majesty before she opens Parliament.

'Quite so,' replied the colonel dismissively, and then he pointed around the ornate room adorned with mosaics, the gilt statues and profusion of carvings depicting the legends of King Arthur. 'The ceiling is marvellous, don't you think' he continued rhetorically as they both stared up at the richly coffered work, 'but the Royal Gallery, through here, is very much better.'

The captain had never been here before. The 110-foot long galley would be inspiring to most. The colonel wandered towards a group of rich, red buttoned-backed leather chairs. He sat in one of the chairs, hands steepled, relaxed as if at home, his back deliberately against the vast painting by Maclise depicting the death of Viscount Nelson at Trafalgar.

'Andrew, you mentioned Nixon. When elected president he did speak of "a war on drugs". He established the Special Action Office for Drug Abuse Prevention, an Office of Drug Law Enforcement and an Office of National Narcotics Intelligence. But the main activities of these departments were directed against Nixon's real or suspected political enemies. As far as drugs were concerned, these departments achieved very little. There was an interesting and imaginative operation, *Operation Screwworm* it was called. The plan was to develop a nasty little beetle, which had a well-developed taste for the opium poppy and then to release it in the *Golden Triangle*. But they had what Baroness Thatcher would refer to as "a wobbly". Understandable, of course. They reasoned that once this beetle had eaten all the opium poppies it would satisfy its vast appetite by devouring the world's rice and wheat.'

'But, sir,' persisted Chappell, 'this sort of things has got out of control before, hasn't it. What about the Brazilian killer bees?'

'Yes, nasty little fellows. The difference this time around, Andrew, is that science has moved on since then. DNA, gene introgression, that sort of thing. We have been able to genetically engineer strawberries with fish cells so as to introduce cold resistant qualities into the strawberry in order that they can be grown all year round. Now we have successfully produced new varieties of rice and cotton that are resistant to disease. Everything is so much more predictable and controllable now. It will not be too difficult for our people to ensure the controlled destruction of *papaver somniferum*, "the poppy that produces sleep".'

As Colonel House-Layton rose to his feet, so too did Captain Chappell. The colonel stared for some moments at the huge canvas. As he spoke, he didn't take his eyes off the slight, fallen figure in the centre.

'He fought a war, Andrew. True, a different war to the war that you are now part', said the colonel, who turned to face the captain. 'He won his war and England, and the world, where very much the better for it'. He allowed his words to sink in. Chappell nodded as if fully appreciating what the colonel had said but, as they both turned, the colonel walking briskly towards the Prince's Chamber, the captain followed, slouching with both hands in his pockets, mouthing silently 'What a load of fucking bollocks.'

They passed through the Prince's Chamber and then into the Chamber of the House of Lords itself. It was magnificent. At the far end, past the red leather seats, could be seen the gilded canopy above the throne.

'You said, sir,' asked the captain, his thoughts still with his career prospects, 'that it should not be too difficult to ensure controlled destruction?'

'Yes', said the colonel now standing near the Clerk's table as if to address the House. 'A poppy field of only about 25 square kilometres is sufficient to supply the entire US market. What was needed was precision in design. We have that now but, rather like a missile, we also need a stable delivery platform so as to ensure that our little beetle acquires its target.'

'I understand that some people are not as confident as you are, sir?'

'There is not the slightest need for anxiety, but it is a delicate issue that needs to be handled expediently, carefully and cautiously – that's all', said the colonel who then drummed the box on the Clerk's table and continued. 'Not many people realise, Andrew, but most of Churchill's greatest and most inspiring war-time speeches were made here, not in the Commons at all. The Commons was so badly damaged by bombing on the 10th May, 1941, that the Members of the Commons moved into the Lords and the Lords sat in the King's Robing Room.'

They walked along the Peer's Corridor and into the splendour of the Central Lobby, the lierne vaulting sweeping upwards towards the enormous brass chandelier, and then the short distance to the Common's Lobby. The archway that leads into the Commons Chamber intentionally retains some of the damage sustained as a result of the blitz. Appropriately, just to the left of this archway stands the statue of Sir Winston Churchill, determined and pugnacious. The colonel paused at the statue.

'Andrew, this operation is of the highest importance. The Prime Minister and the Foreign and Defence Secretaries have been briefed and are excited by the potential outcome. The Americans are whole-heartedly backing the plan. You are part of that plan, a very pivotal part so do not underestimate your role'. The colonel probed Chappell's silence. 'You are not convinced?'

'If you say this operation is important, then it's important but, on the face of it, it seems to be an admin job that a bloody good staff sergeant could undertake.'

'OK. Let me see if I can help', said the colonel, completely disguising his disappointment and concern. 'So far you have done an excellent job with the planning and logistics, particularly taking into account the weather and 120 day operational window. The last phase is the difficult bit and, in many respects, things haven't improved much since 1842, but your "home stretch" planning has been first class, sound yet imaginative. I particularly liked your use of Kempler. The Turks are being difficult again, of course, and want more movement on EU membership as payment, whilst the Australians are being very helpful as usual. In fact, I shall be popping down under for a face-to-face liaison very soon. You have done well, Andrew, and I am very grateful. The one thing you need to have constantly in your mind is that security is paramount.'

'And my accommodation, sir?'

'Yes. Umh. You will be in Shirehampton. A very nice apartment there, modern, of course, and secure... And my local base will at Abbeywood.'

'And the completion date this end remains Friday, 12th October?'

'Absolutely, just the right time for the optimum effect at the target locations during December through to January. But let me remind you that the Foreign Secretary has declared that MI6 will lead with the military in support'. Captain Chappell pulled a face and the colonel responded. 'Look, this is to our advantage. If this operation goes well, we get a pat on the back for being so helpful and your promotion to major is in the bag. If there's a foul-up, we sit back and MI6 gets a well deserved kick in the pants. For this operation, we are in support, nothing more. You have finalised the complicated planning, all that remains is for you to tie up the few remaining loose ends. Straight forward from now on, but I get the impression that you are still unhappy about this operation, Andrew?'

'I'm fine with it, sir. You've helped me to refocus' he lied. 'I don't have any problems with the operation now.'

'OK, that's good,' said the colonel as he glanced at his watch, 'Have to meet a friend,' he said and winked, 'Must go. See you back in the office.'

Both men walked their separate ways. Captain Chappell's thoughts tilting back and forth. One moment he thought of his promotion to the rank of major, an achievement he had thought impossible when he joined the army in the ranks. Then his darker thoughts drifted to his contempt for officers like House-Layton, their privileged backgrounds, family connections, life style and their convenient and romantic attachment to figures like Nelson and Churchill.

Colonel House-Layton was also deep in thought. He had always had reservations regarding the choice of Chappell imposed upon him. The captain was ambitious and industrious and had a good track record in respect of meticulous but flexible planning as well as security work in Northern Ireland, but a bitterness regarding his humble background and quite unjustified resentment of others had been revealed at least twice during his service resulting in ridiculous confrontations with others and errors of judgement, one of which had been a childish incident with other squaddies in the London Underground fourteen years before. The colonel reminded himself that he would need to be alive to the potential for the captain making an operational error of judgement at this final, critical stage.

Chapter 4

Wednesday 15th August.

Bristol, England.

IT WAS Barry's fault. He had been fussing about again and then dropped it. It smashed to pieces but, at least, hadn't broken the kitchen floor tiles. Bosch had said that it was now in stock if he would like to collect it, anytime between 8.30am and 5.30pm. Barry wasn't scheduled to be on the road today so he drove his 1992, 3-litre metallic gold Ford Grenada along Kings Weston Lane towards St Andrews Road, the details of the glass door written on a neatly folded piece of paper in his pocket just in case.

Barry had assumed that the Bosch depot would have been situated in the more prestigious Cabot Park on Poplar Way West with its wide roads and neat grass verges, but the depot was temporarily located on a road to the right, one junction before Poplar Way, a road full of pot holes and hardly any street lighting at all. As he drove into this grubby road, past a tyre depot, a plant and tool hire company and marine chandlers, he could see Ma Brown's café and the commercial unit with the four tall blue coloured roller doors a little further on to the right. Today these doors were closed down. He drove on, parked, walked into the Bosch depot and lazily waited for the assistant to return to the counter. Barry was in no hurry and from the reception area he was able to see if any vehicles drove onto the forecourt in front of the blue roller doors. He was quickly served and carried the heavy glass oven door to his car. As before, he didn't drive straight back to his home but parked his Ford, a big car for a 5'4" rugby hooker, outside the café. Seated in the window, Barry had a clear view of the blue roller doors.

Barry was prepared to be patient. What he had glimpsed three days before he was sure would provide him with an opportunity – his 'annual little earner' he called it. Barry wasn't a greedy man of course, or so he reasoned. He was single, lived alone in a small council flat, helped the old lady next door and disadvantaged youngsters who showed an interest in rugby, ran an old car and worked hard. And he did work hard, but, once a year his very carefully selected 'redistribution of resources' as he called his criminal activities, allowed him enough funds to gamble at the Palazzo Vendramin-Calergi in Venice for three days, twice per year, and also indulge in his other innocent vice – the annual cruise. Last year it had been on the P & O liner *Arcadia*, 63,000 tons of floating luxury. He had flown from Gatwick to Barbados and boarded the Arcadia during a gloriously sunny afternoon to set sail at 6pm sharp and during the following sixteen days he had sailed to St Lucia, Antigua, St Kitts, the British Virgin Islands, the Dominican Republic, Jamaica, the Grand Caymans and the Dutch Antilles.

Next year, Barry smiled at the thought, would be the best ever, twenty one days on the *Aurora*, leaving Southampton on the 7th January and sailing across the Atlantic to Ponta Delgada in the Azores, then on to Granada before skirting the coast of South America to enter the mighty delta of the Amazon and visits to the villages of Alter do Chao and Boca do Valerio and then the city of Manaus, one thousand miles inland.

Barry smoked little, but he lit another cheroot and allowed the blue-grey smoke to drift upwards to linger for a few seconds before being ushered away by the rising dry heat of the convector fan. In truth, Barry was looking way beyond the drifting smoke, through the café's glass window and across toward the blue roller doors. The commercial unit, a two-storey building, with reception and haulage-cum-loading bay on the ground floor with vehicular access at the side and additional office space on the first floor. Barry noticed the 'To Let' sign fixed to the concrete block walls below the blue prefabricated corrugated steel of the first floor and roof. With his plastic *Bic* ball-point pen, he scribbled down the phone number of the letting agency in the margin of the sports page of the *Daily Mail*.

He looked up as his breakfast arrived, eggs, sausage, bacon, tomatoes and beans. As he stabbed an egg with his fork and cut into the bacon, Barry had time to reflect. His little haulage business was efficient. MBA students could have studied his operation on the basis of efficiency, effectiveness and economy. They would have also had an insight into entrepreneurship. He had embraced change – he had been driven to. The demise of the Welsh coalfields, the rise in fuel prices, the increases in taxes and the operator's licence fee and competition from the big boys, all impacted upon his operation. Back in 1986, Barry Atkins had started his business with a tired Bedford 3 ton truck. Later, with the aid of a bank loan, he had bought a third-hand Foden articulated flat-bed. This vehicle had worked well and he had hauled everything around the UK from factory machinery to concrete blocks, but the flat-bed restricted his operation and he found it increasingly difficult to compete with the main players. Barry realised that his operation needed to be more flexible. He toyed with the idea of buying a tanker unit but, again, this would prove too restrictive. The solution was so simple and had come to him by chance at the quayside in Venice.

He had scrimped and saved for three years to afford this, his first cruise. He had flown to Marco Polo Airport, to take the short coach drive to the Bacino di Martittima where the P & O cruise liner *Victoria* had berthed. Later that evening the elegant liner cast off as Barry and the other 703 passengers crowded onto her lido desk port-side and a band played 'A Life on the Ocean Waves'. The passengers waved from the streamer festooned deck to friends on the dockside. Barry waved too – to smiling strangers – but his real attention had been attracted to the P & O refrigerated articulated trailer drawn by a tractor unit of a private haulage company from Kent. That one lorry on the quayside had provided Barry with the key to operating a more flexible haulage enterprise as well as provided him with the germ of an idea that would allow him to embark upon a less lawful, in fact totally unlawful, activity.

As Barry pushed aside his plate and began to butter his toast, a black Audi A6 estate car arrived on the haulage way in front of the blue roller doors, as did a second steaming mug of tea at his table. It was 9.10am. There were three men in the vehicle, the ginger haired one remaining in the driver's seat as the other two strode towards the reception office door. They were agile and lithe, although Barry did not particularly notice this. He should have, of course, and would later regret that he had not done so but, for now, he was concentrating upon their method of entry and the fact that as one opened the door with a key, the other looked up and down the road, particularly towards the café. When the door was opened, both men entered the building and, within minutes, the ginger haired driver stopped drumming his fingers on the steering wheel as one of the roller doors slowly raised open. The driver edged forward before the door had fully opened, eager to get inside the dark interior. As he did so, the driver switched on his headlamps, just for an instant, illuminating at least one Mercedes-Benz Actros truck before the blue door rolled down again. But it was enough to confirm what he had seen when he had placed his order days before.

Barry smiled then sipped his tea as he studied the building. There were five security lights, one above the reception office door, and one above each roller door. There were no security cameras at the front or covering the drive-in access at the side. Nor where there any security cameras in this road, unlike Cabot Park. That was good. He noted at the entrance to the drive-in access, the steel barred double gates topped with barbed wire, locked together by a heavy duty padlock and chain. Easy enough if it became necessary, he thought.

He returned to his tea as he glanced up and down the road. Most of the other units had large rubbish skips, but not this one, just some old tyres against the side of the building and a heap of wooden pallets against the boundary wall. Barry put his empty mug down on the Formica table and checked his watch. 9.23am. He would have to go, he reasoned. To stay longer would invite attention.

Barry Atkins, 41 years of age, driver-owner of 'B. B. Atkins Road Haulage of Bristol' drove to the end of the road and stopped before pulling out onto the busy main road. As he waited he read the sign at the entrance to this pot holed road:

City and County of Bristol
This road is not a road within the meaning the Act
Section 31 Highways Act 1980

Barry had never noticed the sign before, but he knew its meaning. Very convenient, he thought as he realised that this road was essentially private property and therefore not maintained by the local city council or highways authority, thus, rarely visited by patrolling police officers.

Chapter 5

Monday 20th August.

Bristol, England.

WHAT THE weather forecasters for the previous few days had described as 'scattered showers' had turned out to be torrential rain again, but Barry Atkins had had a good trip. He had driven his gleaming metallic pale blue 4x2 1848 Actros to Avonmouth and collected the hired articulated trailer unit, driving the six miles north-bound on the M49 before turning west onto the M5 into the principality. At junction 32, Barry had turned off into the Welsh valleys and towards the vacuum cleaner factory. Soon after his arrival his trailer had been loaded and, just over seven hours later, he finished his journey at the distribution centre on the outskirts of Antwerp.

Barry had taken his statutory rest break of nine hours before collecting another trailer, this time a refrigerated unit containing Belgium confectionary bound for London and, whilst there had been a minor delay in the ferry crossing to Ramsgate, he had still been able to take a Marks & Spencer trailer for the next part of his contract, a 282 mile journey to Exeter, where he collected an empty ship's container destined for the King Edwards Dock at Avonmouth.

Barry was pleased. Virtually every leg of his journey had been profitable and all had been achieved within the driver's hours of work regulations and AETR agreements. As he drove out of King Edwards Dock, he thought of his 'annual little earner' waiting for him less than a mile away and the promising phone calls he had already made. But first, he had to return his Mercedes-Benz V8 tractor unit to his garage under the stone-built railway arches at Avon Street.

These arches had carried some of the greatest steam locomotives England had ever known, all part of a railway network laid down by the famous Victorian engineer Isambard Kingdom Brunel as part of the Great Western Railway. Two of the railway arches spanned two roads, Avon Street and Gas Lane, whilst a further five arches carried the railway line towards Temple Meads Station. The first deep arch was empty and the old oak doors long gone but the others were all individually occupied as workshops or garages. The second belonged to Barry Atkins.

He drove his Mercedes-Benz alongside the first archway on the right and stopped a short distance from the great fifteen foot high wooden doors enclosing the second archway, dropped down from the cab, unlocked the Judas gate and entered the cavernous interior. Inside, Barry eased the wooden beam that secured the doors together from the iron hasps and, as he did so, the great doors swung open easily on their greased hinges. With the doors hooked open, Barry drove the Mercedes further up the gravelled road past the gates and reversed skilfully into the archway. Inside, there was the slight smell of oil and paint. Against the full length of the left hand wall was a deep, sturdy wooden workbench made of reclaimed railway sleepers and equipped with a large vice. At the rear was a floor-to-roof wooden partition wall, against which was a grey metal locker, some oil drums and above, about ten feet from the dusty, smooth concrete floor, was a wall-mounted electric heater which blew hot air down towards the work bench. Under this heater was fixed a horizontal wooden pole over which hung a towel. Barry was particularly pleased with the positioning of the heater – it helped with what Barry considered to be his 'camouflage'. A gleaming stainless steel sink unit was fixed neatly into the corner where the stone wall met the wooden partition, immediately above which was an electric water heater and coffee mugs hanging from hooks. Major servicing, of course, was carried out at the main Mercedes-Benz garage, but small repairs and re-spraying was carried out here, the slight dampness aiding the process.

Everything was orderly, three clip boards hung from equally spaced hooks, a pin board contained a year planner and tools were neatly laid out. The only sight that looked a little out of place was the pale blue paint on the back wooden wall where Barry would test and clean his paint stray gun. Barry would be using the spray gun again very soon. For now, everything was in readiness, the paint, the rolls of masking tape and neatly stacked paper under the work bench.

Barry checked his clip boards, turned off the bright ceiling lights, secured the great doors closed again and walked for ten minutes to his council flat. Once he'd read his post, Barry called in to see his next door neighbour, 82 year old Doris Fudge. It was 7.32am. The six mile journey from the docks to Avon Street had taken less than 25 minutes.   On Monday his bike journey back to the commercial unit with the blue roller doors would take much longer, 50 minutes he had calculated. He planned to arrive at 4am and then back at the railway arches no later than 4.45.   His movements at this time would attract little attention.

But it would be tricky. Atkins already had haulage contracts to meet in Hereford and Dublin, but Dublin had been good to him before. He would have to try and negotiate a satisfactory deal at short notice from a position of weakness, but he was sure that there was still a good profit to be made.

Barry Atkins showered and climbed into bed, but his sleep was fitful. Normally, he was able to give himself plenty of time to plan but he had had to act quickly. So much could go wrong. He would have to wait. A phone call was scheduled for 3pm.

***

Superintendent Mark Faraday MBE stood at the corner windows of his office on the second floor of his modern District Headquarters and looked across the Floating Harbour through the autumn drizzle towards Redcliffe Wharf and the church of St Mary Redcliffe beyond. It was 8.15am and 'morning prayers' with his senior district team members would be at 9 o'clock as usual. Meanwhile, prisoners on the ground floor where finishing their breakfasts and would soon be transported to the Bristol Magistrates' Court by a private security company. In the front office, more akin to the reception area of a building society, a defence solicitor shook hands with a detective, a member of the public produced her driver's licence and certificate of insurance whilst another answered his bail. In the report writing room, some constables wrestled with different coloured proformas, whilst in the locker room three constables prepared for patrol. On the floor immediately below Faraday, some CID officers made preparations for court, others sat at their desks deep in concentration with phones pressed close to their ears and others scurried about, preparing to interview two prisoners arrested in an early morning raid.

Jane Hart, Faraday's secretary, stood at the open door leading from her office to his and tapped on the door. She was wearing a floral green, short-sleeved, print blouse, apple green skirt and *Very Irresistible* by Givenchy. Faraday turned around and smiled. It was a natural response. Jane's smile was infectious. She was what Faraday would describe as 'dinky', about 5' but stunningly pretty with lovely teeth and great big brown eyes. He always thought that she looked like the twin of Audrey Hepburn and should wear a big hat as the actress did in *My Fair Lady*. Big hats and *Breakfast at Tiffany's* were always an in-joke between them.

'Your coffee and some more post', she said as she rolled her eyes and handed him the cup and saucer.

'And how much is in your waste bin?' he asked raising his left eyebrow.

'Oh', she replied with a conspiratorial smile and wink, 'the usual amount. Nothing you would want to see.'

Since his promotion to superintendent seven months before, he had grown to rely completely upon Jane.   Soon after his appointment, he had found it easy to confide in her over a particularly personal issue. At the time Faraday had asked if she had been comfortable with the knowledge of this revelation, to which Jane Hart replied firmly: 'It can't be a problem, Mr Faraday'. When Faraday asked why, she simply replied: 'Because, I am your *personal* secretary'. From then on, it was easy for them to become close and for him to rely upon her more and more.

At 8.25, Jane appeared at the open door again. 'DI Yin for you', she said, silently mouthing 'a little early', but Faraday had already heard the newcomer in her office and was stepping towards the door.

Detective Inspector Kay Yin was about 5'3" and wore a well cut, dark grey business trouser suit. She was trim with the movement of a cat-walk model. Maybe, men would not describe her as pretty or beautiful, but her short, raven black hair, pale olive skin, wide mouth, full lips and dark eyes made her alluring. 31 years of age, this officer had been a direct entry in the rank of sub-inspector with the Royal Hong Kong Police, but resigned in 1997 when Hong

Kong was returned to China in accordance with the 1898 Second Convention of Peking. Kay Yin came to the UK with her mother and father who had been the assistant commissioner in charge of, amongst other departments, the Special Branch. DI Yin had joined the Severnside Police as a constable under the fast-track scheme. She exuded confidence, her head held proudly, even slightly arrogantly thought Faraday. Maybe it was this confidence and not her striking good looks that had impressed the HPDS selection panel, the national system designed to identify constable and sergeants for the highest ranks in the service. The Bristol Central District would be a defining test of her abilities and potential.

'It's Kay isn't it?' asked Faraday as he extended a hand. Her handshake was not firm, thought Faraday, but somehow positive whilst gentle.

'Yes it is, sir', she replied, her eyes holding his, both assessing the other.

'Well, I'm delighted that HQ Personnel got it right and posted you here', he said as he pointed to an easy chair, then called: 'Jane.'

'Coffee for Miss Yin will be with you in a second', she replied from her office.

Superintendent Faraday took the seat behind his desk and shrugged. 'My secretary is a mind reader as well', he said then, turning to Miss Hart as she entered his office with the coffee, continued: 'Aren't you?'

'Whatever you say', she replied with a false bemused looked.

Faraday nodded in agreement to his secretary in acknowledgement of some unspoken words, then watched her as she left his office in silence, then spoke. 'I wanted to say hullo before "morning prayers" and I know we have an hour long meeting, just the two of us, this afternoon at 2.30. But, I thought I would take this opportunity to say a few preliminary words to you … ', he paused as his secretary entered the office and silently moved around behind Faraday's desk placing at his right hand a buff coloured briefing file and immediately in front of him what appeared to be a colour-coded file on top of which she placed a black desk diary. DI Yin noticed a series of coloured tabs neatly protruding from the pages. The secretary opened this diary and pointed to an item on a page. No words were spoken although smiles were exchanged, then the secretary left the office, Faraday watching her as she went. When Jane Hart had left the office, Faraday continued his conversation with the detective inspector, explaining the peculiarities of the district, the senior officers and crime trends. Plainly, DI Yin had already undertaken her research and was fully aware of the district crime trends, the National Intelligence Model and the PPM manual. She glanced over the content of the buff coloured briefing file handed to her by Faraday, but what impressed her was the elegantly written personal endorsement on the first page: *'Kay, you are very welcome here. Good to have you on board. Mark Faraday'*.

The superintendent and detective inspector discussed briefly their understanding of Neighbourhood Policing, then, as this preliminary meeting was drawing to a close, Faraday said: 'It is only fair to say to you that my way of managing is not universally approved, either by my superiors or by some of my subordinates'. Kay Yin didn't interrupt, she sensed that Faraday, for all outward appearances, was essentially a shy man and this part of their meeting was one of his set-piece presentations. 'I operate on the assumption that all police officers are intelligent people who, for years, have not been allowed to use their initiative and judgement. In my view it is actually getting worse. The government, for all that it proclaims, does not encourage leadership in the police service. I think the thought of a gathering of imaginative, independently-minded chief officers frightens them. Instead they seem keen to create a nation-wide cabal of mandarins obsessed with figures and statistics. My approach is to trust staff and allow them a huge amount of latitude within wide parameters. Some subordinates are not too comfortable with this independence and responsibility either. I will discuss these strict parameters with you this afternoon …'

Faraday closed his eyes as if to block out the voice in his secretary's office. DI Yin could sense his frustration.

'Good morning, sir', said a smiling and bespectacled Inspector Gordon Trench who had appeared at the office door.

'Good morning, Gordon. I thought you were at court this morning?'

'Absolutely, sir. Just passing through and collecting up some exhibits', he said whilst leering at Kay Yin.

'Have you met DI Yin. Gordon?'

'Saw you at a Federation meeting in June, didn't I?' asked Trench as he stepped forward to shake Kay Yin's hand.

DI Yin stood to face Trench. 'Yes, I'm sure we did', she confirmed with an engaging smile, assessing him as she had Faraday.

'You've moved into those apartments near St Oswald's Road, haven't you?' persisted Trench.

'That was some time ago', she replied abruptly.

The slightly dismissive reply was lost on Trench, although Faraday speculating that this young lady would not tolerate fools easily.

Jane silently returned to Faraday's office and said quietly to Faraday as she nimbly collected up the two coffee cups from his desk, 'They are all here now', Trench diverting his leering attention from Kay to the departing Jane.

The inter-play and body language was certainly not lost on DI Yin who noted Faraday's hardened look towards Trench then the more protective, or was it affectionate, look towards Miss Jane Hart as he said: 'Give us one minute, Jane, please'. He then turned towards Kay Yin and continued. 'I said that I trusted staff. It is as well that you are aware now that I trust and rely upon Jane absolutely. If Jane asks you to do anything for me, you can be assured that she will be acting on my behalf. If you have to get hold of me urgently or have to pass on to me a delicate issue, you should feel confident to do this through Jane. Are we clear?'

'Of course', she replied, realising that there would be no negotiation on this point.

Faraday nodded to Jane Hart in the doorway, then his deputy, the DCI, the head of admin support and the Duty Inspector began to gather in his office. DI Yin remained as Inspector Trench left to slouch against a filing cabinet in the secretary's office as he now directed his leering attention towards Jane Hart. As Faraday's team made themselves comfortable around the coffee table, Faraday looked through the open door at Jane's lovely profile, then looked down at his colour-coded 'morning prayers' papers as he thought of the research he had read whilst at university that argued that the human body is actually a powerful transmitter and receiver of electromagnetic energy, thus the reason why we feel so attracted to some, often overwhelmingly attracted, in a manner that defies logic and reason. Maybe that was it he thought, then took a deep breath and called the meeting to order.

***

Barry Atkins took the call at just after 3 o'clock from a phone kiosk at Tallaght, near Dublin. It was good news. His contact there would buy the Mercedes-Benz Alcros but at a much lower price than usual. Clearly, the Irishman had sensed Barry's urgency and had driven a hard bargain. They agreed a delivery date of mid-day the 6th September which would allow Barry to keep to his contracts to transport Japanese cars from Avonmouth to Hereford on the 4th, then cattle to Holyhead and across the Irish Sea to Dublin by mid-day the 6th. Barry would return to Bristol by Ryanair that same evening.

Chapter 6

Monday 3rd September.

Bristol, England.

BARRY ATKINS silently closed the front door of his first floor, one bedroom council flat, pushing against the door to check that it was locked, then walked along the shadowy external walkway hardly illuminated by weak bulkhead lamps, rucksack on his back and carrying his Brompton as easily as a light-weight flight case. At the foot of the dank concrete stairway he stopped and, with four quick movements and the tightening of three wing-nuts, the Brompton cycle was ready to ride, a comfortable, robust, lightweight and portable machine which would take him to Avonmouth. He breathed in the crisp morning air as he checked his watch. 3.10am.

It took 43 minutes of steady cycling to reach the commercial estate at Avonmouth but Barry didn't waste the time. As he cycled, as if with all the time in the world, he rehearsed in his mind what he would do. The details of the two-storey commercial unit where clearly in his mind. He had gone over the letting agency's plans and the details of the reception area, the four bays behind the blue roller doors and the access at the side of the building through the metal barred gate topped with rusting barbed wire. The greatest bonus was the fact, confirmed by the letting agency, that the premises were not alarmed.

He was alert now as he approached the building across the pot holed and dimly lit road, ever watchful. The road was deserted, one parked vehicle unattended and the buildings, idle and silent, as he glided up the slight incline of the haulage way and into the early morning shadows of the boundary wall. He was safe here and, unseen, he reduced his Brompton cycle to the size of a small case again. He carefully selected, then carried, a sturdy wooden pallet up the haulage way and placed it against the concrete block boundary wall close to the metal gate. He picked up his Brompton and mounted the pallet as if climbing up a broad ladder and sat astride the wall. Barry edged forward along the wall past the iron gatepost and barbed wire, then dropped the ten foot to the ground the other side of the gate. With the Brompton in one hand and rucksack on his back, Barry stumbled a little and fell back against the wall, but safe again in the dark shadows. For a few moments he remained absolutely still, taking deep breaths to steady his racing heart then, with a dozen brisk strides, he was at the rear of the premises and a small plywood door. Barry removed a pencil torch from his rucksack and held it between his teeth as he inspected the lock, but the collection of keys and picks did not trip the mechanism. He examined the wooden door frame, poked about in his rucksack again and found the jemmy which he inserted near the lock. Gentle but persistent pressure was enough to increase the gap between the door and jam for the door to fall open. Barry stepped inside with his Brompton and pushed the door shut.

Immediately in front of Barry Atkins were three grey Mercedes-Benz Actros 1848 tractor units, together with their grey coloured tanker articulated trailers. His torch light scanned along the sides of these 20,000 litre tanks to reveal what looked like motorway barrier-type reinforcements. Barry stopped as the beam from his torch illuminated a black on white skull and cross bones symbol staring back at him. He moved the light beam along the side barriers and the other diamond shaped warning symbols, the '683' of the Kempler Code and the UN identification number. He was, of course, familiar with the Hazchem and the European Kempler codes that governed the transportation of hazardous chemicals on the roads, but it was unusual to see toxic, flammable and corrosive plates on one vehicle. He pointed his torch to the skull and cross bones again and, for a moment, seemed fixated by the grinning, empty stare. He let the torch's beam drop to the floor and walked quickly and carefully on around the building, the torch pointing to the floor a few feet in front of each step. His reconnaissance revealed a door leading to a toilet and washroom, whilst another opened into a kitchen, all of which seemed surprisingly clean and tidy. A further door led to the reception area and a metal staircase.

Barry returned to the vehicle bays and with his back towards the blue roller doors, he looked up at these stone grey vehicles. He liked Mercedes-Benz but, as he looked at them, he shivered. It was cold, of course, but these impressive vehicles looked silently sinister. He checked his watch again and realised that he would get behind schedule if he lingered longer.

The vehicle to his right was directly inline with one of the roller doors and it was this one which he approached, pulled open the door and hauled himself up the three steps and slid into the driver's seat which automatically adjusted to his weight. Barry made further adjustments to rake and reach at the same time looking around the cab for the keys. Barry searched in the overhead storage space, the net storage bags at the rear of the cab and lifted the lids to the three under-bunk compartments. The keys were there. He closed down the lid and fitted the key into the ignition. As he turned the key to the first position the dashboard instrument panel with its array of yellow, green and red warning lamps illuminated. Barry waited until all the data appeared confirming that this Mercedes-Benz was ready for the road. He looked at the digital clock and noted that he was now about five minutes behind schedule as he swung out of the cab and backwards to the floor.

At the side of the trailer, Barry cranked down the trailer supports and locked them in place. With the trailer now supported on it rear axles and front support struts, Barry would be able to move the tractor unit forward, but first he retrieved from his rucksack front and rear number plates. His mouth ached from gripping the torch between his teeth and he needed to wipe the dribble from his face as he fixed the front plate in place my means of double-sided tape and the rear plate he slid into the square container above the off-side mudguard. Once clipped in place he leant over the chassis and pulled the fifth wheel dual-release lever which would allow the tractor unit to be driven forward leaving the trailer behind. Finally, Barry placed his Brampton in front of the passenger seat then, guided by his torch, he stepped towards the control panel on the wall to the side of the roller door.

Barry Atkins knew that the door would make a metallic rumble as it opened. He paused. He switched off his torch and gingerly peered around the door into the reception area. He could see no lights or movement in the road beyond. Satisfied, he returned to the roller door, the only sound the pounding of his heart. He shone the torch onto the three buttons of the control panel: 'up', 'down' and the red 'stop', hesitated, then pressed 'up'.

The noise seemed horrendous in the still night. The door didn't seem to move smoothly at all but rattled as it rumbled slowly up the metal guide rails. Barry quickly stepped back toward the vehicle, pulled himself into the cab again and waited as the door rolled up exposing an ink-black night sky. As the door clattered to a stop, Barry turned the ignition key and the 16 litre V8 engine burst smoothly into life. Engaging gear he edged forward and, leaving the tanker trailer behind, emerged onto the haulage-way where he slowed to a stop, swung out of the cab and walked quickly back to the roller doors, leaning inside to press the 'down' button. By the time the door had clattered closed, Barry Atkins was already in St Andrews Road heading in the direction of the railway arches.

***

In the pitch black darkness, Shaun Walker fumbled again with the bedside alarm. It was 4.17am. For a moment he could not understand why the alarm had sounded when it had been set for 7 o'clock. He turned on the bedside lamp and grabbed his mobile phone but the screen simply displayed the words: 'no messages'.

He stumbled into Simon's bedroom and turned on the light, ignoring Simon's mumbling protests as he made his way towards the open laptop on the table near the window. The screen glowed with a map of the greater Bristol area, in the right-hand corner of which was what he dreaded – a bright red pulsating dot.

'Oh, shit', he cursed then shouted: 'Simon, get your fucking arse up'. He didn't wait for an answer but thumped his fist on David Collin's bedroom door as he rushed back to his own bedroom.

'What is it?' asked a confused David Collins peering around the door.

'One of the units is on the fucking move', replied Walker as he pulled on his jeans over his Tommy Hilfiger boxer shorts and grabbed a red sweat shirt and his shoulder holster.

'On the move!' asked an anxious Collins. 'What do you mean on the move?'

'How in the fuck do I know, but she's fucking moving', he rasped as he thrust his automatic into the Arratoonian holster. 'Get that lazy bastard up and be outside in two minutes with the three-day packs and make sure knuckle brain in there brings the laptop.'

Walker, now fully alert, had sprinted to the detached garage and was waiting impatiently in the Audi outside the kitchen door of their isolated, rented bungalow at Pilning. Four minutes later, Collins and Mooney clambered into the car and belted-up, Mooney in the rear, computer on his lap. Walker gunned the 2.7 litre engine of the Audi A6 Avant and the front drive wheels span on the gravelled driveway leading to the road as Mooney gently touched the green cursor button and spoke in a precise voice.

'Right, right, right, boss. Target is at a steady 40 on the A403 towards Avonmouth, distance 4.3 miles.'

The Audi burst out onto the B4055 spraying gravel from the front wheels, the rev counter already in the red zone.

As Mooney pressed another set of keys and rotated the map of the map of Bristol on his screen, he was able to bring into sharper context the red pulsating dot of their target and the equally bright blue pulsating dot which represented their Audi.

'Shaun. Listen to me', said David Collins, firmly and calmly. 'It's just four miles and we will overhaul him shortly.'

'300 and we will be taking a left', interrupted Mooney, warning of the junction 300 yards ahead.

'I shall fucking kill him', blurted out Walker angrily, his eyes bulging with rage.

'Left, left, left', said a mechanical voice from the rear as, almost immediately, the occupants of the Audi lurched to the right.

'Ease off a bit, Shaun', encouraged Collins.

'Ease off. Ease off', roared Walker as if the request was totally unreasonable. 'If I loose that truck, they'll do me. They'll finish me off.'

'300. Roundabout.   Exit at 12 o'clock', said Mooney, his instructions short and accurate.

'If you don't ease off, *you will* lose that truck, Shaun.'

'Target is now 3.6 miles ahead and stationary at junction with the A4', said Moody as they screeched around and through the roundabout. 'Target entering the A4, heading for the city. 300. Roundabout. Exit at 9 o'clock.'

The Audi lurched to the left at the roundabout, the rear wheels crabbing, as Simon Mooney, engrossed in his screen spoke again: '300. Roundabout. Exit at 2 o'clock and short dual carriageway'. They lurched again, this time to the right, as Mooney continued to seemingly talk to his computer screen: '300. Roundabout and lights. I repeat lights. Exit at 10 o'clock'. The traffic lights were green in their favour as Mooney shouted, 'Speed camera, camera, camera.'

Walker applied the brakes and the accelerating Audi's speed dropped dramatically from 73 mph to 28.

'Don't screw up, Shaun', cautioned Collins. 'The last thing you want is Mr Plod all over us like a rash', then turning to Simon Mooney asked: 'Distance and Contact Time?'

Mooney checked the multitude of figures displayed on a bar to the right hand side of the screen. He pressed a few keys and then spoke: 'Target has entered a 50mph zone and is keeping at a constant speed of 42. Target speeds through the 30 and 40 zones have been well below these statutory limits. We are just nudging the limits. We should have visual in about six minutes'. Then, preferring to direct his remarks at Collins, continued: 'But, Dave, according to the latest up-dates, there are three speed cameras on this road.'

They drove on in brittle silence, along the dual carriageway that snakes its way alongside the River Avon until, as they entered the Avon Gorge itself, they could see in the distance the illuminated Clifton Suspension Bridge. 245 feet below this bridge, stationary at the traffic lights at the junction of the Portway and Bridge Valley Road, was their target.

For a moment the tension was gone and Collins and Mooney seemed relieved. But when they looked at Walker they saw the cruel smirk that crossed his face, just for a second, only to vanish as his eyes narrowed – he had become a predator.

***

For Barry Atkins, the journey from Avonmouth had been uneventful and he had pretty much kept to his schedule, arriving back at the arches at 4.56am. It was a little lighter now although sunrise would not be until 6.14, as he drove the Mercedes-Benz off the road and alongside the arches, past the great wooden doors. Once the doors had been secured open, Atkins deftly reversed back into the arch, pleased with the latest version of the *Telligent* electronic gear shift.

The three men in the parked Audi were able to see the great doors pulled closed. They knew who he was now and where he was.

On their journey from Avonmouth, Mooney had entered the 'VE' code for vehicle enquiries and the 'VRM' requesting details of the registered keeper of their vehicle now bearing Barry Atkin's number plates. Mooney had also used code '2' signifying a 'moving vehicle' enquiry. The response from the computer was instantaneous, giving Barry's address correctly as 22a New Kingsley Road, Bristol and confirming that he had been the owner of the Mercedes-Benz for the previous two years.

'Well, Mr Atkins might have been the keeper of his vehicle for two years but he has only been the keeper of my vehicle for …', said Walker as he checked his watch, 'the last 39 minutes and the little turd won't be keeping it for much longer. I'm getting my truck back.'

'Hang on a minute', said Collins, pulling Walker back as he leaned to get out of the car. 'You can't just go up to this guy and ask for the truck back.'

'Why not?' replied Walker. 'He's a thief. He knows he's a thief. What's he going to do, go to the police? I don't think so.'

'Won't he think it a bit strange that we haven't gone to the police?' queried Collins.

'What, so the police can impound it for evidence. No, he'll understand. We are all business men aren't we and we have businesses to run', he said, shrugging. 'We will tell him that we want our truck back so that we can get it back on the road again.'

'And we just shake hands and walk away, do we?' asked Collins.

'No. We have to … what can I say … put a bit of realism into it. He'll have to have a smack for being a naughty boy, won't he?'

'Boss', said Mooney who had spotted a couple of young women who appeared to be wearing nurses' uniforms under jackets being picked up by another young woman in a Peugeot 107. 'If you haven't noticed, there are a few more people mooching about and it will be sunrise in less than an hour.'

'You stay here with your computer and warn us if Plod or any other do-gooders appear', Walker said to Mooney, then turned to Collins: 'OK. Come on, we're going to knock on his door'. And, before Collins could reply, Walker had stepped out of the Avant and was striding towards the arches.

Collins followed and, by the time he had caught up with Walker, Walker was at the wooden doors, raising a hand to silence Collins. Walker scratched at the door with his finger nails and made an impressive interpretation of a cat's meow. Collins started to smile and, as Walker began to develop his cat's repertoire, Collins had difficulty in stifling a chuckle.

Walker didn't stop his performance, although he could hear Atkins unlocking the Judas gate. As the gate opened slightly inwards, Walker pivoted on his left foot, leant forward and drove his right leg backwards with such force that one of the hinges broke and the gate hit Barry Atkins in his right knee and upper chest. Atkins stumbled backwards against the Mercedes-Benz and, before he could recover, the two men were standing over him.

'You've been a naughty boy', said Walker pointing at Atkins as if he was holding a gun in his hand. 'And we've come to collect our truck', he continued in a matter-a-fact way, then drove his right foot skilfully into the peroneal nerve of Atkin's right thigh.

'It was a … mistake', said Atkins in his naturally high pitched voice, made higher pitched because of the searing pain in his leg. 'I … I … I made a mistake'.

The sound of Barry Atkins' slightly effeminate voice, his size, his vulnerability on the dusty floor and his audacity in stealing the truck, seemed to anger Walker – Walker, the bully.

'Your mistake, you poofy little turd, was to piss me right off', spat Walker as he took another step towards Atkins and kicked the prostrate figure again, this time in the ribs. Atkins winced as the spiteful pain seemed to reach every part of his body.

'No one … pisses … me … off', said Walker slowly, amused at the suffering of the man on the floor. But the man on the floor had experienced pain before on the rugby pitch; he could cope with that sort of pain but, he was frightened now. Atkins had met men like this before, men who enjoyed inflicting pain upon others. He looked up at Walker's head silhouetted against the bright roof lighting, darkened hollows for eyes. For a moment he thought he saw the skull and cross bones on the side of the tankers and he tried to clear his mind. Walker's ponderous words gave him time to think. The pain was real enough. Soon the pain would be disabling and he realised that he was in danger as Walker slowly continued his mocking rebuke.

'Those that do piss me off have to be punished.'

As he spoke, he drew his leg back to deliver another kick. As he did so, Atkins rolled to his right and onto his feet, grabbed the heavy shifting spanner and lurched at Walker. If Atkins had been on the rugby field, his studded boots would have dug into the turf and provided the stability he so desperately needed, but here, on the dusty, smooth concrete floor with his right leg failing to respond as it should, his movements were clumsy. Walker stood his ground, gauging every movement, his upper body twisting sideways as his right arm shot forward, punching Atkins in the right jaw. In what appeared to be one continuous movement, Walker grabbed the back of Atkins' neck with his left hand and thrust his exposed forehead into the vice bolted to the work bench. The noise was like the crack of a pistol shot. Death was instantaneous and Atkins collapsed on the floor like a doll dropped by a child.

Walker and Collins both knew. They stood there, looking down upon Barry Atkins, 41 years of 22a New Kingsley Road.

Collins knelt besides the body and felt for a pulse although he knew there would be none, only Atkins' marble-like eyes starring upwards confirming his death.

'Hey, come on. You saw him', said Walker, initial panic now lacing his voice. 'He tried to kill me.'

'But you killed him, Shaun.'

'We're all in this', said Walker through gritted teeth, 'up to our fucking necks'. Collins pushed the Judas gate shut as best he could, as Walker continued: 'Get him up into the cab.'

'Are you mad?'

'No. If we leave him here, someone will find him. We have to put time and space between him and us. Get that plastic bin liner.'

Before Collins could respond, Walker grabbed Barry's legs and dragged him over the concrete floor to the near-side of the cab, then searched through his pockets. There was nothing.

'Open the door and get up in the cab', he barked.

Collins did as he was told and, as Walker lifted Barry's limp body in an embrace, he spoke again: 'Get the bin liner over his head.'

Collins learnt out of the cab and covered the bloody head with the bag.

'Now see if you can get hold of him under the arms and I'll push.'

It was no easy task. They both struggled. Eventually, they managed to get his head and torso into the passenger foot well, Collins pulling Barry's left leg upwards.

'Tuck his left leg under his arse', snapped Walker impatiently as he pushed the right leg upwards and then under the corpse so that, in death, Barry Atkins assumed the position of an Egyptian crouched burial.

Breathing heavily from the exertion, Walker stood silently in front of the cab with the fingers of his right hand pressed into his forehead. Then, his decision made, he walked across to the bench, his eyes searching the surface. He quickly found the keys to the Mercedes-Benz and what appeared to be front door keys. He removed an anorak hanging from its hook and searched through the pockets and found Atkins' wallet containing his driver's licence, two credit cards, Air Miles and breakdown recovery cards, as well as thirty five pounds in notes, all of which he returned to the pockets. Walker then turned his attention to the clip boards hanging neatly from their hooks and compared some details on one of the boards with a Sasco wall planner. He ran his finger over the writing neatly inserted into the little squares denoting the 4th, 5th and 6th September and nodded to himself.

'Perfect', he said to Collins as he returned to the cab and threw the anorak into the cab and contemptuously slammed the passenger door shut. 'Use some of those rags and clean the vice and get the broom and get rid of all our footprints'. He pulled his dual-band radio from his pocket, keyed in one number and waited for his call to be answered. He didn't have to wait long, Mooney was waiting. 'OK, knuckle brain. Dave is staying with the truck and I need to go to 22a New Kingsley Road. Direct me.'

Mooney consulted his computer screen and provided the simple directions, back along Avon Street for 700 yards and first left. For Walker, the time passed quickly. For David Collins, his absence seemed to be for an eternity. Walker had easily gained access to Barry Atkins' flat. Although furnished cheaply, the flat was spotlessly clean, everything arranged neatly. In the single bedroom, near the foot of the bed, was an overnight bag already packed for his journey to Ireland. Walker rummaged through the bag and, satisfied, took it into the bathroom. He removed the only tooth brush, a tube of toothpaste, deodorant can and the electric Braun shaver and packed them into the bag. In the kitchen was another calendar identical to that in the garage as well as a passport and a print out of a pre-booked ferry ticket near bottles of drinking water. He looked around the rooms again, only to sniff contemptuously at the six, perfectly spaced, identical picture frames on the lounge wall.

Walker left number 22a as silently and unobserved as he had entered. Within ten minutes he was with an anxious Collins still clutching a bloodied rag.

'Right', said Walker cockily taking the rag from Collins. 'I'll drive the truck back to Avonmouth, you go with knuckle brain and follow me at a discreet distance.' Walker climbed up into the cab and leaned out through the open window. 'Hang on. Don't rush off.

Use the broom and remove the footprints first.' Collins methodically did as he was told and propped the broom against a wall. 'You haven't finished yet. Turn the lights off and open the bloody gates. Once I'm out, get rid of your footprints, close up and get out through the little door.'

'What about the broom?'

'Christ, do I have to think of everything. Chuck it back in and slam the door.'

Three minutes later, Walker was driving the Mercedes-Benz into Avon Street, then Temple Way towards Temple Circus and Temple Gate, directed by Mooney via his radio earpiece. They crossed Bedminster Bridge, past Bathhurst Basin, along Cumberland Road, Hotwells Road and onto the Portway again, the Audi following the truck at a distance of about 400 yards.

There was much heavier traffic now, the earlier commuters already beginning to congest some of the junctions as Mooney called Walker and reminded him of the 50 mph speed restriction on the dual carriageway ahead. Walker needed no reminding, he kept carefully within the speed limits and, as they approached Shirehampton rail station, Walker dropped his speed to 38 mph in response to entering the 40 limit zone just as Mooney called a warning.

'Blues and twos at 6 o'clock, boss', said Mooney, but Walker had noticed what appeared to be two police vehicles closing on them rapidly.

'Do nothing', he said through clenched teeth and without lowering his head to the concealed microphone. 'Keep … as … we … are', he said slowly and deliberately, although Walker's mind was racing.

There were two of them, one behind the other, a Mercedes-Benz estate and a Range Rover, blue roof and strobe lights pulsating, headlamps blazing. Collins and Walker kept their vehicles to the near-side lane as the police vehicles maintained their outer lane position. At about 800 yards from the Audi, the lead police vehicle sounded its siren, just twice, and within seconds had raced by. The police vehicles did not slacken speed, their only deviation was to move slightly to their left as they took the right hand curve. Then they were gone.

'Boss, if we're going to be stopped by the police, it will be 1000 at the roundabout. Last exit option. 300. Left to Portview Road,' said Mooney.

'We go on', said Walker sternly. And he was right. There were no police vehicles to be seen, not at the roundabout, nor at any other point on the journey back to the commercial estate.

When the Mercedes-Benz and Audi had been manoeuvred into their allocated bays and the blue doors had rolled down shut, Walker spoke to a sceptical Collins and an apprehensive Mooney.

'You know we've got a stiff in the cab, don't you?' he said to Mooney.

'Yes, boss.'

'Now listen in, both of you. The stiff in the cab was a thief and stole our truck. We went to get our property back and, as Dave will confirm, he took a shifting spanner to me. In the tussle he unfortunately hit his head. We couldn't do anything for him. It was an accident, that's what it was. What's happened, happened. There's no going back. Nothing can change. OK?' David Collins and Simon Mooney nodded in agreement to this reasonable argument. 'Neither of you need to concern yourself and', he paused and fixed his eyes on each man in turn, 'no one else needs to be concerned. We've got our truck back. You just get on with your work here and I'm going to take the stiff to his final resting place.'

'What if anyone asks where you are?' ventured Collins.

'Tell them I had a take-away and have the shits. If they want to speak to me, then they can get me … in my sick bed …on my mobile.'

'But, boss, somebody will miss him. What if the police start sniffing around?' asked Mooney.

'Why should they think we're involved? But they might. OK, so our story is that we were all nicely tucked up in bed and you both know nothing. OK?' Collins and Mooney looked at each other, their nodding again in agreement was the cue for Walker to continue: 'Meanwhile, I shall be laying a convincing paper trail for Mr Plod to follow if he gets nosey. That should keep them busy for a few weeks and by then we will be out of here. Job done.'

***

At a little after 11am, a blue roller door clattered open and Shaun Walker drove the Audi Avant out towards St Andrews Road, the M5 and the wild bleakness of Bodmin Moor. As he drove, Walker played the 'Still Sexy' CD by Errol Brown, although his passenger, Barry Atkins, his body completely sealed in a plastic bag under the luggage cover, would not appreciate the melody.

At the Sedgemoor motorway service area, Walker stopped and used his mobile phone.

'It's Walker, sir,' he said, like a confidence trickster about to rip-off a gullible householder. 'You have a problem, which I am sorting out for you.'

'Problem?' he asked anxiously. 'What type of problem?'

'Unfortunately, some bloke tried to break into our place of work', he lied. 'Nasty bastard. Of course, we tackled him, but he must have had a dickey heart. He croaked it.'

'Cro ... Croaked it!' he stuttered. 'Where is he?'

'You don't want to know, do you? How about I deal with it?'
His mind raced as he considered the options then asked eagerly: 'Can you?'

'I always have, haven't I?'

'Deal with it', he said sharply and added with great emphasis: 'Nothing, nothing must interfere with this operation. Do you understand?'

'I always understand, sir. Don't I?'

'I'll leave it to you then', said Captain Andrew Chappell.

Warrant Officer Shaun Walker replaced his mobile in the holder and started the engine again.

Chapter 7

Tuesday 4th September.

Bristol, Portishead and Bodmin Moor, England.

FARADAY LIKED the harbour, or more accurately, the sight of the sail boats and cabin cruisers on the water, particularly today, as they gently moved in response to the very slight breeze and the passing of a yellow-painted water ferry. It was a restful sight, the only other movement, the whirling of some black-headed gulls. He stood there looking out from his office, across the water, sparkling in the bright, early morning sun light, his thoughts drifted back to his happy childhood holidays in Cornwall, the …

Jane Hart appeared in the open doorway. She wore a pretty pale yellow dress with large black pokka dots. 'Everyone is ready, Mr Faraday', she said, gently interrupting his thoughts.

'Quiet this morning', he observed with a grin, alluding to the absence of Inspector Trench, but the grin faded from his face as he looked at his secretary.

'Mr Trench is delayed on an enquiry. He'll be here at about 9.15'. Jane winked although, this morning, there was no disguising her anxiety and preoccupation.

Inspector Gordon Trench, reflected Superintendent Faraday as he returned to his desk, was a heavily built, noisy and clumsy fellow. Intelligent and well educated, but not particularly able, he tended to look down on others. The others bustled into his office.

'Good morning, folks', welcomed Faraday breezily as his deputy, Chief Inspector Alan Moore, took his usual seat to Faraday's left. The other comfortable chairs around a large coffee table were quickly occupied by Helen Hemmings, the head of admin support, the duty inspector, David Taylor and Detective Chief Inspector Geoff Fowler, with DI Yin taking the chair to the right of Faraday's desk.

Jane Hart brought in the usual tray of coffees but, before she left, she pulled the black diary from under her arm and placed it on Faraday's desk, opening it at a page. DI Yin noticed their easy manner and the interaction between them, intrigued at the multitude of coloured tabs protruding from the pages.

The DCI and Chief Inspector Moore were able to give details of overnight prisoners and incidents. There was none of the nonsensical point-scoring between them that plagued so many districts and they worked well together. The DCI up-dated the group on the first day of a Crown Court trial that had implications for the Bristol Central District, although he had phoned Faraday the previous afternoon as soon as the court had risen. The DCI invited Kay Yin to speak in respect of a series of burglaries and reminded everyone that he would be taking two weeks annual leave on Friday the 7th. They discussed two welfare issues; a late morning appointment with the Lord Lieutenant regarding the forthcoming visit by the Duchess of Gloucester to a special needs school and an afternoon meeting with the Neighbourhood Policing Partnership.

Everyone heard Inspector Trench – in the corridor, in the secretary's office. He seemed always to manage to bump into doors and cabinets or bang his brief case down onto a desk and make an unnecessary fuss moving his chair about. This morning, Trench seemed to be fussing more than usual. A smiling Miss

Hemmings raised both eyebrows in mock disbelief whilst Faraday simply nodded a good morning as he continued to hand around the revised agenda for the Partnership meeting, then turned to Inspector Trench.

'Useful enquiry this morning, Gordon?'

'Not really, sir', he replied as if his time had been wasted but delighted to have the opportunity to impress his colleagues with his experiences. 'An old lady', he continued, flicking open his pocket book, 'Doris Fudge her name, of 22b New Kingsley Road, reported her neighbour, a Mr Barry Atkins, missing. She had a key to his flat, you know, sir, those rather dismal council flats on The Dings. Had a look around. Typical lorry driver's pad. Nothing untoward.'

'What do you mean, typical lorry driver's pad?' asked Faraday, his irritation showing.

'A single man and the place is a bit down at heel', blustered Trench before he got into his condescending stride again. 'Atkins is a lorry driver and owns his own lorry which he garages under the nearby railway arches. Found a key in the flat and went down there. Had a good look around, of course. Again, nothing untoward. The lorry isn't there but it wouldn't be', he concluded slapping his book closed with a satisfied flourish. 'According to the calendar in the flat, Atkins is on the road to Hereford today, Holyhead tomorrow, Dublin on the 6th.'

DI Yin looked quizzically and was about to speak, but didn't.

'So why was Mrs Fudge concerned?' probed Faraday.

'Something about Atkins promising to collect her prescription yesterday morning, but didn't. She agrees that she may have misunderstood and is forgetful. She *is* 82.'

'And what's his route after Dublin?' Faraday asked.

'Straight back to Bristol', he answered rather too quickly and dismissively thought Faraday. 'There was nothing on his calendar until Monday, the 9th. I think he must be having the weekend off.'
'Do we know anything about Mr Atkins?' said Faraday.

'I wouldn't know, sir,' he replied as if the question was foolish.

'Well, I need to know, Gordon. Check on Mr Atkins and Mrs Fudge, if you please. See if we have any record of him missing before, convictions or movements of interest and of Mrs Fudge making this type of call before and get someone to see him on the 9th.'

'Of course, sir', he replied eagerly with a sheepish smile.

There were no other items for discussion and so the meeting broke up, Inspector Taylor and Miss Hemmings collecting up the coffee cups, taking the tray out into the secretary's office whilst the DCI and DI Yin finalised arrangements for cover whilst the DCI was on holiday.

As they moved into Jane's office, Faraday spoke again. 'Helen, Jane and I will be popping out for twenty minutes. Is it OK if we divert calls to your office?'

'No problem, Mr Faraday', she said beaming.

'I will be on the air, Helen', he said as the two ladies left the office. 'Thank you.'

As Helen Hemmings and Kay Yin walked away down the corridor, DI Yin asked: 'Where are they going?'

'Oh, I don't know', she replied evasively. 'He calls it *Breakfast at Tiffany's.*'

***

Abbeywood, situated to the north of Bristol at Filton, is the headquarters of the Ministry of Defence's Procurement Executive. The buildings, surrounded by an ornamental lake, are situated in 98 acres containing 5,000 trees and 28,000 shrubs. Abbeywood's international, diplomatic and business connections made it an ideal temporary location for Colonel Jeremy House-Layton. His presence there amongst 6,500 other MOD employees attracted little, if any, attention at all.

After a very pleasant coffee, the colonel drove the short distance along Station Road to the A38 and Gloucester Road North until he reached Junction 16 of the M5. This wasn't the most direct route to Portishead, but it was the quickest and he arrived as scheduled at 11.30am.

The colonel had spotted the Ford Mondeo estate parked, as were all the other cars, in echelon along the Esplanade facing the grey sea. Most of the pedestrians where walking briskly, taking full advantage of the clear sky and prevailing salty sea air but, Captain Chappell, walking a little further on in the direction of Battery Point, was not enjoying the moment. He walked with his hands angrily stuffed into his pockets, a walk best described as sullen. House-Layton drove his Rover 75 slowly past Chappell and pulled into the kerb further along the road. He stepped from his car and stood near the door.

'Andrew,' he called.

'Hullo, Jeremy', replied Chappell, the colonel pleased that he was at least alert enough not to call him 'sir'.

'Let's take a stroll along here,' he said cheerfully as he locked his car with the remote.

They walked on back towards Chappell's vehicle talking aimlessly about the weather, the Severn Estuary with its second highest tidal range in the world and another government scandal. As they neared the Ford, Colonel House-Layton spoke again, this time in a clipped voice.

'I see you have the Mondeo'. It wasn't really a question, but the insecure Captain Chappell viewed the comment as one.

'It was convenient for today, Jeremy. I do use the Audi', he replied as both men stepped into the car.

'Andrew', remarked the colonel as he made himself comfortable in the front passenger seat. 'Rank does have its privileges, you know.'

'It's nice to think so, sir.'

'You've worked hard, Andrew. You deserve a few of the extra comforts. And I'm sure there are more to come.'

Chappell smiled appreciatively but made no reply, waiting for the colonel to speak as he knew he would.

'Always nice to get out into the fresh air', resumed the colonel as he pulled down the hinged sun visor and attended to his wind-swept hair in the illuminated vanity mirror. 'You know, the sound of water, the waves and the wind emit large amounts of life-enhancing ions. Makes you feel much better, much happier'. He closed the little cover across the vanity mirror and pushed the sun visor up and looked at Chappell. Their eyes met. 'Are you happy that everything is progressing according to the plan, Andrew?'

'Yes, sir.'

'So. No problems then?'

'No problems, sir'. Then, after a slight pause, he ventured. 'Walker's always a potential problem, but I have worked with him before so he'll be OK. And I know that any little problems that might crop up, you would expect me to deal with.'

'Do we have any *little* problems, Andrew?' queried the colonel.

'None, sir.'

'You are on schedule and can foresee no delays?'

'We are about three days ahead of schedule and I don't anticipate any delays at all.'

At that moment, from behind the headland, emerged the bulk of the 56,000 tonne, roll-on, roll-off, *Kitakyushu,* leaving the Royal Portbury Dock homeward bound to Japan.

'Well, that's very good to hear, because on Friday the 12th of October, our three tanker units will be aboard a similar vessel', he said pointing at the *Kitakyushu,* 'the *Santo Stefano,* en-route to Palermo and Istanbul.'

Warrant Officer Walker knew that, statistically, bodies were more likely than not to be disposed of by their killer in an area familiar to him. The disposal of the body of Barry Atkins would be no exception.

Walker had explored this particular part of the boulder-strewn Bodmin Moor when he had been an army instructor, but had dismissed it as being far too dangerous for recruit training, riddled as it was with the multitude of vertical shafts necessary for tin mining. Many of the mine shafts were easy to identify by their eerie, stone-built engine houses which had long ago contained the steam engines, machinery and the pumps. Other shafts had been fenced off by the National Trust and local Cornish Rotary Clubs, but many remained to trap the unaware. Barry Atkins was, of course, unaware.

Now, at a little before mid-night, Walker strode forward just as he had done when yomping across the East Falklands in '82. In the light of a full moon, he dropped to one knee with ease, Atkins balanced across his back in fireman's lift fashion, as he consulted his map and his Silva compass. He smiled with satisfaction, not unlike a buccaneer of old, his eyes and teeth glistening. He was nearly there he realised, only another thirty yards or so ahead, and to the right of a small granite outcrop, should be the gapping mouth of Shaft 2217 in the register of the Mines Research Group.

The broken fences marked the opening but Walker carefully scanned the immediate area with the powerful beam of his Maglite. He was well aware of how treacherous the old mine entrances could be, unstable after decades of ravaging by the harsh elements of the moor. Satisfied that all was secure, he stepped around the granite outcrop, the full moon shining down upon the gorse and moss. The White Fork Moss is, in particular, distinctive in features and common on damp moors, its form is large and cushion-like and easily dislodged. Walker was hunched slightly forward so as to bear the weight of Barry Atkins when he felt a clump of moss dislodge and his left foot slip. For a heart beat he froze, then he attempted to regain his balance by throwing his head and upper torso backwards but, as he did so, this movement only served to ensure that Atkins' body fell forward and more firmly around his neck, the dead weight of his victim propelling him 4,000 feet down to the bottom of the shaft, a shaft not scheduled to be fully surveyed by the Exeter-based Royal Commission on Historic Monuments in England for another seven years.

The laws of gravity will determine that any object dropped into Shaft 2217 would reach the bottom in 17 seconds. In the case of Warrant Officer Shaun Walker, his body took a little longer, in fact 32 seconds, as he tumbled through the pitch blackness, his direct fall impeded by the uneven sides of the shaft, decaying wooden supports and debris. However, his lonely cries of real horror in the darkness and the agony of rapidly accumulating multiple injuries lasted only 11 seconds.

Chapter 8

Thursday 6th September.

Bristol and Shrewsbury, England.

IT WAS very early morning when Captain Andrew Chappell drove the grey Ford Mondeo off the winding B4055 and up the gravelled driveway to turn in a large arch so as to park at the kitchen door of the detached bungalow.   Immediately behind the Ford was Sergeant David Collins driving the phantom black Audi.   Light flooded out from the kitchen as the door was opened by Corporal Simon Mooney.   The two men entered the kitchen and, almost immediately, the outside of the bungalow was plunged into darkness again as the door was quickly close.

Mugs had already been set out by Mooney in preparation for their return and now the hot coffee was drunk eagerly by the two men who had driven continuously through the late afternoon and evening.

'Well, I'm not very impressed', said Chappell who had decided to go through the ritual of giving his subordinates a lecture, although it was an exercise that only managed to make him feel slightly better and clear his mind. 'Nor are those at the top. None of this reflects well on you as a team. Fortunately, GPS had the Audi on the plot but where Walker is, I haven't a bloody clue, so he is now posted as AWOL.'

'I think he ...' said Mooney, but his comment was cut short.

'I think it is best we don't know,' said the captain sharply.

'Your very first job, corporal, is to make another brew, tea this time. Then get your head down for a few hours because there's still work to do.'

'Yes, sir,' replied Mooney.

The two other men looked at Mooney in total silence and so the younger man, understanding the unspoken instruction, collected up the mugs and walked into the kitchen.

Once Mooney was out of ear-shot, Captain Chappell continued. 'There is no need for Mooney to know too much. You are in charge down here now, David. You are ahead of schedule. All the crush barriers need to be fixed which will take some time but, after that, all that remains are the trackers, the cosmetics and double-checking the routes and timings. However, your first job, once you've had some shut-eye, is to have the Audi comprehensively cleaned – and I mean cleaned. It's in shit order. It looks as if Walker went for a drive in an Irish bog!'

'Right, sir.'

'Can I ask what you will be doing, sir?'

'I will call in most days and can help out. I don't mind getting my hands dirty, but not today. I shall be doing what I think Walker had intended to do.'

***

Captain Chappell had returned to his apartment at Shirehampton, across the road from the petrol station. He had managed to get four hours' sleep and had already been on the road for about 50 minutes when he spotted a telephone kiosk at Hethelpit Cross on the A417.

He pulled into the lay-bye and checked his pencilled notes, the details obtained from the tourist website, listing accommodation deals. In the kiosk, his first calls had been unsuccessful but, at his third attempt, he had been able to book bed and breakfast for that evening in Sutton, north of Dublin. Chappell volunteered to pay in advance. The proprietor gladly accepted his offer and noted the 12 digit number of Barry Atkins' Visa card.

***

Faraday switched off the lights in his luxury en-suite, removed his blazer from the valet stand as he swiftly walked through the master bedroom to the hall, slipping on his blazer over his uniform shirt and trousers, and entered the kitchen. He glanced at the clock – it was 7.13am – as he took two small bottles of Buxton Still from the fridge and put these into his brief case that he collected from the study.

For all the luxury and comfort of Avon View Court, the hollow sound as he pulled his front door closed, reminded Mark Faraday of how lonely he really was.

***

At 11.40am, Chappell's Ford Mondeo estate approached the outskirts of Shrewsbury along the A49. He was selective. He chose a service station that was busy, one with a supermarket, a shop, a fast food outlet, coffee shop, restaurant, motel and, most importantly, toilets. Without hesitation, he parked near a cluster of trees amongst a group of vehicles. He peered into and double-checked the contents of Barry Atkin's overnight bag. Completely satisfied, he left his car and walked in the direction of the restaurant. If he was observed, if anyone even bothered to do so, he would have been seen as wearing a dark green anorak and cloth cap and carrying a non-descript overnight bag.

He entered the extensive rest facilities, browsed around the shop and purchased a *Daily Mail* and *The Telegraph*, then entered the restaurants and ordered a chicken salad and chips. He was in no hurry and, at the end of a rather unappetising meal, ordered another pot of tea.

At 12.35pm, Chappell left the restaurant, walked the short distance to the toilets. He checked the notice listing the toilet cleaning schedule. Satisfied, he entered a cubicle, removed his anorak, placed Barry Atkins' bag on the floor and sat on the toilet. After reading another few pages of *The Telegraph*, Chappell was sure that all the people that had been in the toilets when he entered had now left and, of new arrivals, maybe only two remained. Once he had placed his cap into his coat pocket and folded the anorak so that the brown lining was all that was exposed, Chappell left Atkins' bag at the rear of the cubicle and walked from the toilets straight to his car.

Of course, the car park surveillance cameras may have recorded Captain Andrew Chappell returning to his car. If any of them did, the significance of a respectable-looking man wearing a green jacket and cap, carrying a bag, leaving a Ford Mondeo and an equally respectable-looking, bare-headed man, carrying only a brown jacket, returning to a Ford an hour and a quarter later was very unlikely to register with the operators. With hundreds of vehicles and thousands of pedestrians appearing on a multitude of CCTV screens in any one hour, these movements would undoubtedly be viewed quite innocently: a man parking and entering a service station wearing a coat and carrying a bag, whilst a different man, more casually dressed, left the services. In any event, within seven days, the surveillance tapes would be wiped clean and all trace of his visit would be lost.

Chapter 9

Monday 10th September.

Shrivenham, England.

IT HAD been MI6's show, but they had been very careful to be inclusive and demonstrate their appreciation of the co-operation they had received from other agencies.

Gerald Casey had headed up the MI6 team on the 12th June. He had been careful to pay due deference to the representatives of MI5, the Home Office, the Foreign and Commonwealth Office, HM Customs, GCHQ and the military, the latter represented by the Deputy Director of Military Intelligence, who was in attendance with Colonel Jeremy House-Layton.

Greenhill House had been an ideal venue for the briefing. A part of the Royal Military College of Science at Shrivenham, Greenhill House also hosted the Disaster Preparedness Centre and, as such, routinely attracted a host of anonymous visitors, including those from the Foreign and Commonwealth Office.

The silver haired and distinguished House-Layton had surveyed the assembled officials in what must have originally been an orangery, but now beautifully decorated and furnished, air-conditioned and with views over equally beautiful gardens, although these views were slightly obscured by the backs of military policemen standing outside the orangery, themselves, looking steadfastly towards the gardens.

MI5 had looked decidedly bored during that first briefing. He had thought he had heard it all before and knew that any new initiative would inevitably result in turf wars with the police and HM Customs and squabbles with foreign agencies. For the FCO, the only prospect had been of a great deal of tedious negotiations; placating the Turks whilst deploring their actions against the Kurds; supporting governments of the Commonwealth without being criticised for being paternalistic; and giving aid to the Far East whilst expressing reservations regarding their record on human rights.

Miss Ormerod, representing the Home Office, had seen credit for tackling the menace of illicit drugs shifting away from her department. She had decided to be attentive for appearance sake, of course, and had hoped to have been able to salvage something of advantage. And then there had been HM Customs. Their representative, delighted to have been invited to the briefing for the first time, had initially fiddled with the end of his embossed pencil that he had probably taken home for his young son.

During that earlier briefing, the *IMAX* world screen had glistened with the criss-cross of lines indicating the drug trade routes. 'As can be seen', had said MI6 as the territories of Amazonia came into sharper focus on the *IMAX* screen to his left, 'Bolivia, Peru, Ecuador and Columbia all have a critical role to play. Whilst for some individuals the rewards are high, for most the price is too high'. The blank screen to his right had rapidly showed a series of stills illustrating the grotesque murder of those who challenged the drug cartels, or merely got in their way. The 'neck tie' murders were the worst, the pulling of the tongue through the gaping hole in the slashed throat of the victim. The age and sex of the victims afforded no protection, young men, elderly women and children were included in the grizzly display. Customs had thought of his son and had stopped fiddling with the pencil.

'The drug trade', continued MI6 as the blank screen had glowed again to reveal the statistical data, 'equals half of Bolivia's GDP and represents four times its legal exports'. The screen had blinked again. 'Columbia has a population of 28 million. Last year there were 28,000 murders there, much more than those of the United States which has a population ten times that size.'

MI6 had neatly returned everyone's attention to the world screen again, firstly the *Golden Crescent*, an arc across Iran, Afghanistan and northern Pakistan, then the *Golden Triangle* of north eastern Bangladesh, Burma, Thailand and Laos.

'Much of the *Golden Triangle* is inaccessible', he had said as the screen had exploded into a montage of stills. 'It is jungle occupied and often controlled by hill tribes. In some areas the only currency is opium, certainly the predominant currency throughout Afghanistan, where the terrain in mountainous and unforgiving'. The pictures on the screen had faded to blackness and MI6 had sounded virtually dejected, but it had all been part of a carefully crafted brief to attract, and then hold, his audience's attention.

'Internationally, the drug trade is worth $500 billion', continued MI6 as he had paced for effect as the world screen illuminated again to highlight a variety of nation states. 'That is more that the GDP of the seven richest countries in the world'. All screens had been blank as MI6 had looked particularly at the government representatives. 'This trade is undermining currency, undermining economic stability, undermining legitimate trade, and, it's killing our people. It creates a fertile environment in which corruption is tenderly cultivated. What we do know is that the drug trade funds Middle East terrorism, as well as creating opportunities for crime to flourish world-wide. This is happening now, here. Automatic weapons and machine carbines have been used on the streets of Birmingham, Cardiff, Bristol, Manchester, Leeds, Plymouth,

Newcastle, Glasgow and London. All of these activities have been drug related.'

MI6 had moved from the lectern to a small table. He had poured himself a glass of water and had taken a sip, then resumed his place behind the lectern.

'The UK still attracts vast inward investment', he had said as government ministers had nodded supportively. 'Our country relies upon that investment. Our financial institutions are stable and as such play a huge part in maintaining a healthy balance of payments. We know, and that knowledge is confirmed by our colleagues in GCHQ, that France and Germany would shed few tears if our financial institutions failed only to be established in Bonn. We cannot allow that to happen.'

This last comment had brought an eager interruption from The Right Honourable Harold Staines, the Secretary of State for Foreign and Commonwealth Affairs.

'Hear, hear. A very pertinent observation indeed.'

There had been universal agreement with the sentiment expressed by MI6 – irritation with France and resentment of Germany – indicated by simultaneous and vigorous nodding.

'Our government institutions,' MI6 had commented, 'are essentially corrupt-free, which in turn creates confidence abroad. If our financial and state institutions remain so, then *Ukplc* remains solvent. If they are in any way endangered or that confidence is eroded, then we will surely decay.'

MI6 had moved slightly to his right in order that all would have a clear view of the *IMAX* screen as the world map had appeared again. 'There is another aspect, too', he had said as little bright circles had appeared on the screen. 'Each circle indicates internal conflicts fuelled by drug activities which threaten our financial, petro-chemical, construction, mineral and strategic interests, or, represent conflicts into which we may be drawn. Parachuting into Burma or sending HMS *Invincible* into the Andaman Sea is not the thing to do. Our approach is more devious, more effective, more permanent'. He had paused as if to acknowledge the chorus of nodding. 'The United States and the United Kingdom are at one on this matter. We have agreed to act jointly against the drug barons. We are co-operating with each other and are sharing resources and intelligence, although the United States will essentially be concentrating their efforts in their own backyard – South America. Our operation will be focused upon the Far East. The code name for this operation is *Operation Dragonfish.*'

He had moved away from the lectern and had taken two steps towards the ministers. Words and smiles had been exchanged, then he had spoken again.

'Thank you ladies and gentlemen. The minister thinks it would be just the right time to draw this session to a close, unless there are questions.'

The briefing had been comprehensive and there had only been a few questions. There followed a general bustle and movement, some officials headed for the toilets, others quickly to their vehicles drawn up outside in readiness. Customs had collected another embossed pencil from the empty room. Two children then, thought Colonel House-Layton as he and the DDMI walked out into the garden, the door opened by an immaculate military policewoman.

'I assume', House-Layton had enquired, 'that the choice of the title for this operations is all part of the disinformation plan?'

'Absolutely. The Black Dragonfish is a member of the *Malacosteid* family of deep water fish that actually produce light by way of bioluminescence. The choice of the name serves to add to the authenticity of the operation', observed the DDMI, 'as does your little trip to Western Australia. The Australians only legally cultivate a small amount of opium, but your trip will all add to the kaleidoscope of disinformation. You will travel via Singapore. Our friends there will ensure that information is leaked to the Russians and the Russian mafia will undoubtedly leak it to the Afghans. My concern, however, is numbers. I suppose the ministers like to be kept in the loop and have an away-day from Westminster but, if we are not careful, too many people will be in the know. I just hope that this bloody party doesn't get any bigger.'

Today, the numbers had grown by one, a representative from the American NGA, the National Geo-Spatial Intelligence Agency out of St. Louis, Missouri, the organisation responsible for all imagery, mapping and geographic intelligence, whose representative was in deep conversation with our man from GCHQ.

DDMI and Colonel House-Layton were in attendance again, of course, as were the usual gaggle of officials, including the two ministers. MI6 took the lead as urbanely as they had thirteen weeks before.

'*Operation Dragonfish*, I am pleased to report, is on target, and proceeding well within the time perimeters set. This would not have been achieved had it not been for the excellent cooperation and liaison between all the agencies involved', announced M16 diplomatically.

'You will recall', MI6 continued, 'that *Operation Dragonfish* was to be undertaken in three distinct phases. Phase A was essentially disinformation'. As he spoke 'Phase A – Disinformation' appeared on the screen. 'The foundation of this aspect of disinformation was our active interest in the genetic engineering of a little weevil with an enormous appetite for the opium poppy'. More captions appeared on the screen.

'Whilst this classified work', he continued, 'has been secretly undertaken by the highly reputed laboratories of Pan-Universal of Illinois, we have ensured that our interests have become conveniently known more widely'. MI6 moved about, like an actor upon a stage as he continued his presentation. 'The second part of Phase A involves the Royal Ordnance Factory who have kindly made for us some rather nice little canisters, about the size of a cigar tube, and for these to be subsequently distributed by a variety of means'. More bullet points appeared on the screen.

'Can I ask,' said one of the ministers, 'the means of distribution?'

'Why, yes,' replied MI6, pleased to have the opportunity to explain some of the details of the clandestine operation, but also to emphasise the co-operation achieved under the leadership of the Secret Intelligence Service. 'Firstly, our old friend, a Queen's Messenger, took one in a diplomatic pouch to our High Commission in the Kingdom of Bhutan,' he said, pointing to the Indian protectorate situated to the west of Nepal, 'their arrival being made known to a locally employed member of the High Commission's staff. Secondly, a UN aid worker, formerly REME, has ensured that such a canister, marked "Batch 24, Number 19" was conveniently found in Iran', he continued, tapping the screen. 'And, a further canister was conveniently dropped by an ex-Royal Marine who was part of a climbing expedition to Nanga Parbat in

Kashmir, just here', he said, once again indicating the location on the world screen.

'The third and final part of Phase A concerns the disinformation regarding an insecticide. This information has already been leaked via other or similar conduits as in part one'. 'Disinformation – insecticide' appeared on the screen.

'Now to Phase B', continued MI6. 'This phase builds upon the legal cultivation of opium in both India and Turkey for the subsequent manufacture of codeine, morphine and other opium-based medicines. We will shortly be recommending to the agricultural ministries of India and Turkey the use of an insecticide as a precaution. In due course, we will be even more helpful to these ministries who will become aware of an insecticide that is capable of combating our greedy little weevil'. More text appeared on the screen as MI6 paused, then looked towards his audience with a mischievous grin and added. 'Inevitably, those engaged in the illegal drug trade will also become aware of the insecticide.'

MI6 slowly poured himself another glass of clear water.

'And now to Phase C', he continued. 'Phase C involves the theft of the insecticide by illegal drug producers. Unknown to the drug producers, the insecticide contains certain properties that would make the poppy fields and places of manufacture uniquely visible to bioluminescence and *far-red* sensors carried aboard a series of American military surveillance satellites.'

Looks of approval were exchanged between NGA and a minister as MI6 continued.

'Finally, Phase D, the destruction of the poppy field and manufacturing centres by drones and covert as well as regular forces as a result of satellite identification.'

'Could I ask a question again? ventured the minister, not waiting for any agreement. 'Can I ask how you know that the insecticide will be stolen?'

'Because it is there,' replied MI6 simply.

'Because it is there?' asked a sceptical minister. 'Is that enough?'

'Oh, yes,' replied MI6 confidently. 'You can be assured that the intelligence gathering abilities of the drug cartels are equal to ours. You can be equally assured that these cartels will protect their interests at all costs as, indeed, we would ours. Planting of the opium plant will take place at the latter part of next month with the harvesting of the opium itself, depending upon the exact location of cultivation, between the end of December and early February. We know that they have already heard rumours regarding the weevils and we will ensure that they will find out about the insecticide very soon. Oh yes, they will steal it. I have not the slightest doubt. Where and when? Not quite so certain, probably the latter part of October during transit through Turkey. But the location of the theft is of no real importance. The successful theft of the insecticide is.'

***

Papers were spread on the coffee table over which Superintendent Faraday and Detective Inspector Yin craned. Kay Yin had presented a clear strategy for trying to make sense of the new legislation and the government's intentions regarding prostitution and the management of brothels. It was no easy task. The working girls were in many respects their own victims, trapped in a world that society disdained and their pimp's grip upon them ensured there was little prospect of their escape.

'This is an excellent paper, Kay. Thank you,' said Faraday, 'but what worries me is that the sex trade will be driven even deeper underground. We know that many of the girls do their business in the backs of the punters' cars, where the punters feel more secure in side streets of their choice.'

'You are not happy with the paper, sir?'

'I'm happy with your work, Kay,' replied Faraday, holding aloft the comprehensive paper submitted by the DI. 'What I am not happy with is this ... government window dressing. These measures will not help the situation, nor will they help the decent people living in these areas. The location of the brothels will do nothing to enhance the reputation of the community or the pride of the residents. I doubt very much if an MP will be found living next to one of these *legitimate* brothels.'

'Would you like me to re-work the community aspect?'

'No. No, I don't think so. I just get extremely irritated with initiatives that just haven't been fully thought through. Anyway, we're at where we're at, so, please liaise with Jane so that I'm included in any of the forthcoming community meetings.'

Jane Hart had been listening, of course, her ears attuned to his conversations. She realised that the meeting was drawing to a close and so peered through their inter-connecting door.

'Mr Taylor', said his secretary with a smile which seemed to quickly fade.

'I think we're finished, Kay?' said Faraday, uneasily.

'Yes, we are, sir', she replied, noting again the exchange between her superintendent and his secretary.

'Thank you, Kay. A lot of work in double-quick time. Well done,' then turning to Jane, Faraday simply nodded.

'David', Faraday said to Inspector Taylor as he walked into the office, 'how are things?'

Inspector Taylor sat down as Kay Yin began to collect up her papers. David Taylor was a diligent and capable officer, about the same age as Faraday, with a smiling, open face. Faraday had known Taylor for over ten years and knew him to be a totally genuine man He had a 12 year old daughter, but his wife had sadly died three years ago of cancer.

'There was another call, sir, mid-morning, from Mrs Fudge', said the inspector, Faraday nodding for him to continue. 'Her lorry driver neighbour didn't apparently come home all weekend.'

Faraday glanced at the wall clock. 4.55pm.

'When did the call come in?' asked Faraday as he leaned back into his chair.

'At 7.50 this morning.'

'And what action has been taken since then?'

'Well, Gordon's group was on duty but Gordon is on leave today, so ... nothing really, sir.'

'Until you picked it up?'

'I was checking through the reports and noticed the name.'

'You didn't notice it by luck, David. You noticed it because you are committed. I wish others would be equally committed. I specifically asked Gordon to put someone on this', said Faraday. There was what seemed a long pause until, exhaling air through his teeth, he continued. 'What have you found out?'

'Nothing known on either Mrs Fudge or Mr Atkins. However, I recall Gordon saying that this lorry driver would be travelling up to Hereford last Tuesday, then to Holyhead on the Wednesday, I think', he said looking towards the DI.

'I'm sure Mr Trench said the Wednesday and then Dublin on the 6th', confirm Kay Yin.

'Then driving straight back to Bristol, as I recall. So, what's the problem?' enquired Faraday.

'The problem, sir, is that I don't think Mr Atkins went to Dublin. At least, I am sure his vehicle didn't.'

Faraday sat forward, elbows on his desk, chin resting on his knuckles, as he asked: 'Why?'

'I've been doing a little arithmetic, sir. I could be wrong but, if I calculate the distance and timings between Bristol, Hereford, Holyhead and Dublin, and add in rest periods, loading, unloading, that sort of thing, then Atkins would have crossed the Irish Sea in all probability during the 6th on the *Ulysses* of Irish Ferries. There are other ferry companies, of course, but I've checked with Irish Ferries' director of security, he's a former chief superintendent with the Garda Siochana. He confirms that Atkins had booked the crossing but there is no record of him having boarded the vessel. Irish Ferries are checking the security video tapes but won't have an answer for us until tomorrow morning'.

'Tomorrow morning?' queried Faraday without rebuke.

'The *Ulysses* is their largest vessel, sir, and makes two return crossings per day. Atkins could have exceeded his statutory hours or been delayed and so, to be on the safe side, I've asked them to check for the 5th and the 7th. The ship can carry thousands of cars and hundred of lorries, but it shouldn't be too difficult to identify a silver coloured Mercedes-Benz Actros. It's a big vehicle and top of the range, but it will take them until the morning'.

'Sleep on it?'

'I think so, sir. They promised me a reply by 8am'.

'OK', agreed Faraday, distracted by movement in the outer office. 'Good work, David. Thank you. And you too, Kay. I'll see you both tomorrow, excuse me'.

Faraday hurried out of his office, leaving the two inspectors to make their own way through the secretary's office. As they both emerged into the corridor, they saw Faraday some distance in front of them, his arm around Miss Hart's shoulder. They were both standing still, the police officer dwarfing his petite young secretary. He pulled her closer to him and it appeared that Jane Hart was sobbing. The two inspectors were uncertain as to what to do, so they merely stood there silently, spectators to a private drama until Faraday and his secretary walked away towards the staircase and the car park, hand in hand.

Chapter 10

Tuesday 11th September.

Bristol, England.

HELEN HEMMINGS and DI Yin were talking in Jane Hart's office as Inspector Trench blustered in wearing body armour and cap and banged his brief case down on the desk.

'No Jane?' he said and, without waiting for an answer, asked: 'Is he in?'

'No', replied Helen as Trench peered into Faraday's empty office.

'Were's David?' he asked, referring to Inspector Taylor.

'Having breakfast I should think', said Helen as she shuffled some papers. 'He was in at six this morning'.

'Where's everyone else?' he asked with a confused expression.
'I asked Sergeant Harvey to tell you that morning prayers had been cancelled, Gordon', replied the admin officer.

'No one's told me', he said as if annoyed.

'You need to take that up with your sergeant', came her unconcerned reply as some of her papers floated to the floor. Both women bent to scoop them up. Trench made no effort to assist them but leaned forward to leer at them both. As they sorted through the papers, Trench spoke again.

'When will he be in?'

'Later', replied Helen. 'Before mid-day.'

'Oh', said Trench ponderously as if it would cause him the greatest inconvenience. 'I was supposed to confirm the time and date for an appraisal interview.'

'I think Mr Faraday has pencilled you in for 10am on Thursday', offered Kay Yin as she thumbed through the pages of the superintendent's diary.

'Why do you have his diary?' demanded Trench aggressively.

'Mr Faraday rang earlier and asked me to make some alterations to his office diary.'

'But it's his diary?'

'It's no big deal, Gordon', she replied, annoyed at his pettiness. 'It's just a diary.'

'Anyway', persisted Trench with a mischievous glint in his eye, 'Where *is* the lovely Miss Hart?

'She's off today', said Helen.

'Ah', said Trench with a smirk as if he had just solved a crime. 'Both off then.'

'Gordon. I told you', she replied. 'Mr Faraday will be in a little later and Jane is off today and possibly tomorrow. Illness in the family, or something.'

'Well, I can't hang about. I'm due at HQ at 10.30', said Trench pompously as he banged his way out the office.

Trench collected his nine year old Vauxhall Astra from the car park and set off along Cumberland Road towards force headquarters fourteen miles away.   A little later, as he turned across the bridge at Merchants Road, Faraday drove towards him and flashed his headlamps in acknowledgement, but Trench pretended not to notice the black C70 and drove on resentfully.

When Faraday entered his secretary's office, DI Yin was there waiting for him, clipboard under her arm.

'Good morning, Kay', he said, clearly preoccupied and apparently harassed and, without thinking asked not unkindly: 'Is there a problem?'

'No, sir', and, before he had time to ask any further questions DI Yin continued. 'I hope you don't mind but I've cleared a number of your calls and put two appointments in your diary. There are four matters which I think you will need to deal with today. I've listed these together with the appointments on this slip of paper', she said pointing towards a folded piece of blue A5 paper protruding from his diary, 'but none seems to be urgent and David has some news for you. He's on his way.'

'How did you and David know I had arrived?' he asked as he hung his blazer in his wardrobe and fitted his epaulettes on to his uniform shirt.

'Just a little spy network I have', she replied with just the hint of a smile as Faraday took the seat behind his desk.

'I can't recall anything about you ever being a secretary on your CV'.   He paused as his mind pictured her personal file, a photograph, a reference from Sir Dick Lee, the first Hong Kong-

Chinese commissioner. Then he remembered. 'Not a secretary, but you were a staff officer in Hong Kong weren't you?'

'A junior staff officer, sir, and just for 12 months.'

Faraday was going to continue the conversation but David Taylor entered the office holding a carton of milk that seemed for a moment rather incongruous, a police inspector in uniform carrying a carton of milk. It was only then that Faraday realised that the kettle was already boiling and three cups and saucers had been laid out on a tray.

'I'm going to have to keep an eye on you two conspirators,' he said as they both made the coffees. 'On the other hand, I suppose I could just go home and leave it all to you both.'

'Oh, we couldn't manage without you, sir', said Taylor with an impish grin.

'OK. OK', said Faraday as he accepted a cup of coffee. 'You have some news?'

'I hope you don't mind, sir, but I have to be at the Crown Court, the affray case', he said as Faraday recalled the stabbings at the Midas Club back in May. 'So I need to rush through. Had a call this morning from Irish Ferries. They are 100% certain that Barry Atkins' lorry did not cross over to Ireland on either the 5th, 6th or 7th or make a return trip.'

'OK, but I sense there's an "and" lurking somewhere?'

'There is. I put a marker on the system so that any reference to Doris Fudge, Barry Atkins, their addresses or BB Atkins Haulage is fed to me. The front office had a call at 8.23 this morning from the police at Shrewsbury. An over-night bag was found in a service station on the A49 which appears to belong to Barry Atkins. I have a list of the contents here', he said, handing Faraday a piece of paper, 'and have told them to treat the bag and contents as a crime exhibit.'

'When was it found?' asked Faraday without reading the note. He knew that Taylor would tell him if there appeared to be any significance in the contents.

'Afternoon of the 6th by a toilet cleaner'. Faraday was just about to ask why it had taken so long to inform us, but he knew there would be no need as the inspector continued. 'The service station keep found property for 24 hours in case the owner's return. Then, anything unclaimed is taken to the local police station.'

'The 6th, when you believe Atkins would have been in Dublin?'

'When I think he should have been', Taylor corrected.

'OK, what's your take on this, David?'

'He could have had a road accident, loss of memory, involved in a fight, I suppose'.

'Kay?'

DI Yin got straight to the point. 'We need the bag, sir, and I think we need to check if his lorry is back under the railway arches.'

Faraday noticed David Taylor glanced at his watch. 'You must go, David, it would not do to upset the man in the curly grey wig. Thanks for this.'

Taylor stood up and was about to take his empty coffee cup into the secretary's office, but it was taken by Kay Yin, her movements graceful, her helpfulness genuine.

As Inspector Taylor reached the door, he stopped and turned so that by chance he and the DI stood together, their faces seemingly sharing a concern.

'I think I speak for Kay too, sir, but you seemed to be anxious earlier. If there is a problem, maybe, we might be able to help?'

Faraday thought for a moment and was unsure of what to say. He was thinking of Jane Hart and also these two loyal inspectors, one of whom he had know for years, the other he knew hardly at all. Both so different to that clown Trench.

'There is a bit of a problem, David, but at the moment, neither of you would be able to help. But thank you.'

'You always say to us that you are only a phone call away,' persisted David Taylor carefully. 'We are just a phone call away too, sir.'

'I know that, David. In fact, I rely upon it maybe more than either of you think', he said and, looking at each of them in turn said: 'And in this mucky world, I am grateful for your concern.'

'Is there anything I can set in motion with this Atkins enquiry?' asked Taylor, changing the subject, resigned to the fact that his superintendent would not reveal the reasons for his preoccupations.

'No. You are busy enough but, thank you. I will speak with the driving school and see if they have a car that is doing any cross-country journeys today. If there is, they can collect the bag for us. Meanwhile, I think I shall go and see Mrs Doris Fudge. It will do me good to be busy.'

The two inspectors left the office and Faraday could hear the slight clatter of cups and saucers in the secretary's office. He started to read the note DI Yin had left for him and cross-checked his diary as she peered around the door.

'Excuse me, sir, but Atkins lives in The Dings and I've never been on an enquiry to that part of the district,' she said. 'I'll take my case and get a car. How about I see you out the front in fifteen minutes?'

Faraday was tempted to argue, but then thought better of it. Miss Yin appeared a determined young lady. He nodded to her as he picked up the phone and called the driving school.

The journey to Barry Atkins' home at 22a New Kingsley Road was only a matter of a few miles, into Redcliffe Way and Temple Gate and a little further beyond, but the traffic was heavy, as one would expect of a city with a population of 400,000, and so the journey took them over 20 minutes.

Throughout the journey, Faraday was deep in his own thoughts as DI Yin drove the pool car in silence. He thought of the petite Jane Hart and her tears and agonised about what else he could do but, as they neared Lower Station Approach, these thoughts were interrupted when a pedestrian ran from behind a parked coach to vault over the central reservation barrier. The Volkswagon travelling two cars in front of them in the inside lane swerved, but Kay Yin had anticipated the danger long before and neatly manoeuvred without the slightest harsh movement or comment, to continue their journey into Cattle Market Road. Her driving, thought Faraday, was smooth and positive like that of Helen Cave, totally at ease, yet with a confidence epitomised by her calm, oriental profile. He noted her beautiful hands caressing the steering wheel, so like Jane Hart's. He wondered again what caused one human being to be so overwhelmingly attracted to another, and then his thoughts drifted back to his lonely apartment at Avon View Court.

'Next left at the lights, Kay', said Faraday quietly, 'then third turning on the right, I think. About 600 yards and 22a and 22b should be on the right.'

Two little gnomes stood sentry outside of number 22b adding brightness to an otherwise drab exterior. Mrs Doris Fudge answered her door. She was alert and agile for her age, clearly concerned for her neighbour and eager to help the police as she bustled along the communal exterior walkway to Barry Atkins' flat in her little tartan slippers with the red pom-poms. From the impression generated by Inspector Trench, the two officers had assumed that 22a would have been an untidy, poorly decorated place of utility, with discarded newspapers, a large television and a fridge bursting with frozen meals and cans of cold beer. But what Faraday and Yin saw was a neat, spotlessly clean, well-ordered and comfortable home.

'Mrs Fudge,' suggested Faraday. 'If you would care to take a seat and it may be easier if my colleague and I have a look around quietly by ourselves. From time to time, we might ask you a question if we find anything. Is that alright?'

Mrs Fudge settled into one of the easy chairs, her anxieties forgotten for the moment as she fulfilled her important role.

'I'll take the bedroom and bathroom, Kay, if you take the kitchen', said Faraday. 'And then we will both take the lounge.'

In the small bedroom, the bed was made and clothes hung in the wardrobe, the drawers clearly designated for their own specific items of clothing. Likewise, the bathroom was spotlessly clean and ordered.

The kitchen was such that it appeared to be awaiting a viewing by prospective purchasers, with its clean sink and uncluttered working surfaces. Crockery and cutlery were all neatly in place, tea towels hanging on their stainless steel rails. In the cupboards and the fridge, not one item was out-of-date and the calendar was neatly endorsed.

When Faraday returned to the lounge, DI Yin was already there, seated in an easy chair next to Mrs Fudge, her brief case by her legs and note book and the calendar on her lap together with four sets of keys, all labelled 'spare' followed by the registration numbers of the Mercedes-Benz and the Ford or simply marked 'front door' and 'lock up'. A glance from Faraday was enough for Kay to help him begin to methodically search the lounge. A Tiny computer, Lexmark printer and neat Neovo flat screen occupied a corner desk. Hard and paper back books nestled on shelves; the TV, DVD and tape controls were all in a little rack and a rug set perfectly in front of the electric log-effect fire in the mock fireplace.

The search was cursory although, as they finished, Faraday, took one of the six photographs off the wall and then sat on the settee, DI Yin taking the other easy chair at Doris' side.

'Doris, just a couple of things you might be able to help me with.'

'Of course, Mr Faraday. If I can help.'

'The bedside alarm is set for 2am. I am wondering why that should have been so?'

'I can't say, Mr Faraday. I think Barry was going to leave early in the morning, Tuesday morning it was. It was going to be early, but not that early. I'm sure of that'.

'This must be a picture of Barry?' he asked as he held up the photograph for her. Doris' bottom lip trembled a little and then hardened as she tried to control her anxiety. Kay Yin leaned forward and held Doris' arthritic hand gently.

'I'm sure Barry is alright, Doris', she said. 'We just need to make absolutely sure, that's all. And I know you can help us.'

Doris, sniffled and moved her head up and down in acknowledgement.

'I notice', said Faraday, 'that Mr Atkins is wearing an evening suit in all the photographs and the suit is in his wardrobe. When does he wear an evening suit, do you know?'

'He's not in any trouble, is he?' asked Doris.

'Mrs Fudge,' answered Kay. 'All that Mr Faraday and I are concerned about is that Barry is safe. That's our priority. That's why we are here.'

She lowered her head and thought for a moment, biting her lower lip, before answering. 'He gambles a bit. You know those casino places. That's his holidays, he says. He's not a beach man, all that sun bathing. Can't do you any good, all that sun, my mother used to say'.

'We all like a bit of a gamble. The Lottery. There's nothing wrong in that', remarked Faraday gently, then asked: 'Do you know where Barry would take his holidays?'

'Abroad', replied Doris. 'Foreign places. Spain and Italy, places like that'.

'Do you think that these photographs were taken in Spain?'

'Not all of them. I think some were taken here, you know, in England. Some were taken abroad. I don't know which ones. He'd bring me back little presents', she replied, then with a mischievous grin added: 'Little bottles.'

'I only have one other question, Doris. Barry's a lorry driver isn't he? I found a clean embossed set of overalls in one of the drawers but I can't find any working boots. Does he have boots, do you know?'

'Oh, yes. Barry was most particular. He does everything proper'.

'And what about his washing?'

'I does that. He brings it all round to me, either on a Monday or Tuesday most weeks'.

'That's fine, Doris. One last thing. Barry has a Ford car?'

'Yes, he does that. It's a gold one'.

'And where would that be parked?'

'Out round the back. I knows it's there 'cus I can see it from me kitchen'.

'And it hasn't been moved as far as you know since, when, the beginning of the month?'

'No, it hasn't been moved, I'm sure of that.'

'You have been most helpful', smiled Faraday as he turned to DI Yin. 'Do you have any queries for Doris, Kay?'

'Doris', she said, still holding her old hand. 'This seems a silly question to ask, but ...'

'I don't think you would ever ask a silly question, my dear', interrupted the old lady kindly, tears beginning to form in her eyes. Doris Fudge sat more upright in her chair and asked: 'You were going to ask me something else?'

'There are sixteen small bottles of spring water in the kitchen. Why should that be?'

'He likes his water. He takes it on his trips. Says it detoxicates him'. Doris looked directly at the Chinese officer. She didn't want to ask the question that had been on her mind but took a deep breath, inflating her frail chest, and asked. 'You think something has happened to Barry, don't you?'

'I'm a little concerned, Doris', she replied without reference to Faraday. 'We want to find him and make sure that he's safe.'

Doris patted Kay Yin's young hand and nodded, her lips trembling a little. 'You'll tell me what's going on, won't you?'

'Doris, we will, of course we will let me give you my details', she said as she removed a card and a biro from her pocket. 'I'll write another number on the back. If I don't keep you up to date every week without fail you call me on this number.'

Doris Fudge took the card. She starred at the numbers running her finger over them as if to derive some comfort. 'I expect you will want to look around a bit more', she said as she stood up. 'Just pull the door to as you leave.'

The old lady walked towards the little hallway, her steps not so sure now. At the door she paused and turned towards them both. 'See if you can find Barry for me … you see, he's the son I never had. I have no one else'. Then she was gone, the front door clicking shut behind her.

Emotions are contagious and both Faraday and Yin felt her sadness yet, without a word, they gloved, Faraday moving to the telephone and pressed the 'play' key. There were five messages, two from the Avonmouth depot of South West Vehicle Distribution Ltd and three from Sweet & Sons Stock Breeders of Hereford, all asking, then demanding to know, why B. B. Atkins Road Haulage of Bristol had fail to collect their trailers.

'Have you some exhibits bags?' asked Faraday.

DI Yin produced a plastic bag from her brief case into which Faraday placed the complete telephone. 'I need another', he said curtly and walked into the bathroom followed by his colleague. He opened the linen bin and pulled out the only item in the bin, a pair of Y-front underpants, and slipped these into a bag. 'That should provide enough DNA' he said as the DI wrote on the labels. 'Now I want something with his fingerprints on.'

'The kitchen, sir,' said DI Yin. 'There's a metal sugar container in one of the cupboards which I haven't handled.'

Both items were bagged and tagged but, before the officers left Barry Atkins' home, Faraday made a final visit to the bedroom, returning with a manilla folder and a framed photograph.

'His bank accounts', said Faraday as he slipped the file into Kay Yin's brief case. He raised his eyebrows. 'Bottom drawer, bed-side cabinet.'

'And his computer?' she asked, waiting only for the word to disconnect the hard drive and bundle it out through the door.

'Not yet', he replied simply as he scribbled down a note of the details on the name badges worn by three of the young ladies in the photographs on the wall.

Both officers left the apartment and descended the concrete stairs, walking to the end of the building and to the rear car park. Barry Atkins' beautifully kept Ford Granada was parked perfectly in a marked bay, but the search of his car revealed no clues at all to his disappearance, only confirming how methodical and neat a person he was. A duster was neatly stowed in the near-side door, two biros, a tyre depth gauge and tyre pressure gauge were found in the off-side door together with a small Woolworths torch. The owner's handbook was in perfect condition and neatly placed in the glove compartment, the servicing records punctiliously endorsed. Mark noted in his pocket book the details of the servicing garage before they secured the Granada and returned to their own vehicle.

At the pool car, they placed the exhibit bags, files and framed photograph in the boot and drove to Gas Lane and parked. They walked up the well trodden roadway along the side the arches and stood together looking at the old fifteen foot high wooden doors. A small plastic plate proclaimed the owner to be B. B. Atkins of Bristol, but what attracted Faraday's attention was that, although the great doors were grimy and water stained, the result of years of streaming rain, the Judas gate appeared to have been recently kicked, the heel of a footprint was such that the kick appeared to have been delivered backward. Faraday extended his open right hand and Kay gave him the bunch of keys. He tried a mortice key and was able to turn the lock with ease, then using a Yale key turned the second lock and attempted to push the Judas gate inwards. There was some give near the locks but the gate was stiff and difficult to open. Faraday pushed the door again, this time much harder and it flew inwards, Faraday falling against the door jam. The policeman bent through the opening into the empty arch and, as his eyes became accustomed to the lack of light, he was able to see and remove the great wooden bar that secured both doors together. He pushed open the right door, then the left, using the hooks screwed into the wall, he hooked them open. Faraday turned to walk back into the arch but stopped in response to DI Yin's sharp command.

'Stand still', she barked.

A startled Faraday stopped and looked down, but saw nothing. As he looked up and over the concrete floor, he realised what his young colleague had seen. Mark Faraday's footprints appeared to be the only footprints on the dusty floor.

'Well, Trench didn't have a good look around, did he?' remarked Faraday angrily.

'Barry Atkins was a meticulously tidy man', observed DI Yin, 'but there's only one reason for this tidiness – removal of evidence.'

'But, who ever it is', said Faraday pointing forward, 'some evidence remains.'

'You mean those footprints under where the lorry would have been?' she asked.

'They tell a story but, can you see,' he said, pointing to the far end of the archway, 'there are tyre tracks which stop where a lorry would have parked. Then … I can't see clearly from here, but there are other tracks that seem to disappear under that wooden wall at the back.'

Chapter 11

Wednesday 12th September.

Bristol, England.

THE CRIME Scene Investigation team, lead by Susan Tope, had worked until late the previous evening, preserving the scene, donning what Faraday always referred to as their 'forensic romper suits'. They took a series of general and specific photographs, used a tripod-mounted medium-format camera with macro lens for the tyre tracks, the images of which would later be compared with manufactures' tread design guides. The team used *flourescin* and discovered traces of blood on the vice and a pattern of blood splashes on the work bench and wall. A saline solution helped capture the blood which would later be analysed in the serology laboratory.

At about 7pm, Faraday had been called at his office, as he had requested, and both he and DI Yin visited Gas Lane again. Two white CSI vehicles were still there, as was a uniformed constable, although the white and blue police tape had been removed and one of the white vans had been reversed up the rough roadway and parked outside the archway opening. Inside, the oil barrels had been heaved away to one side. As Faraday and Yin entered, one of the CSI officers, using the innocent-looking wooden towel rail as a large handle, pulled the rear-most wooden partition wall forward that opened like a great single door to reveal the gleaming Mercedes-Benz Actros of B. B. Atkins Road Haulage of Bristol. Of course, Superintendent Faraday and Detective Inspector Yin need not have been there for what was in reality was an unnecessary pantomime, but, it seemed to them that it was worth it.

Now, thirteen hours later, they had both returned to Faraday's office, seated around the coffee table. As they both settled into their chairs, Faraday commented upon his immediate impressions at the crime scene before moving on to specifics.

'When Atkins' lorry was revealed, I thought it strange that there were no company logos on the front of the vehicle or the doors, but the registration, VIN and chassis numbers all correspond to Atkins' vehicle. I always assumed that the drivers of these lorries liked to advertise themselves and took a competitive pride in the appearance of their vehicles. Not to worry. Maybe nothing. So, how did you get on?'

'I was able to go through, briefly, the manila folder last night, said Faraday. 'All bank statements. There seems to be three building societies and three mainland bank accounts involved. The accounts cover the last five years. One of the building society accounts seems to be the one he uses for holidays and, from the figures, not the modest holidays assumed by Mrs Fudge.'

He handed the file across to DI Yin and picked up his cup of coffee as he continued. 'Although extensive, or should I say lavish, his holidays seem to be straight-forward. There are regular visits to Venice, as well as very expensive cruises, but what I can't understand is four one-way flights. One from Dublin, two from Cork, one from Belfast and one from Malta.'

'What's the connection, sir?'

'Haven't a clue at the moment. What we, sorry, what I didn't find was his trading account or tax returns. They could be with …'

The phone rang in the secretary's office. Faraday stretched back in his chair and reached for the phone on his desk, a return call from the ACC Crime's secretary. He waited until he was put through.

'Hullo, sir. Faraday,' he said as DI Yin began to get up from the table to leave, but Faraday waved her back into her seat. 'I thought I would give you a heads-up. We have a Misper, a single man, a lorry driver,' said the superintendent, his briefing succinct and to the point. 'An elderly neighbour alerted us to his absence. His scheduled trips over the last week have not been met. He garages his lorry in a railway arch in The Dinges. This was empty and seems to have been tidied up so I asked CSI to check it out late yesterday afternoon. CSI did find some blood splashes near and on the work bench. Could be nothing, of course.'

'The result of a fight, do you think?'

'Could be, sir. Or just as easily a minor work-related accident, but I doubt it.'

'Could he have been involved in a road accident somewhere, perhaps?' suggested the ACC.

'I don't think so', replied Faraday diplomatically. 'We have checked the local hospitals, but negative. If he'd had a road accident in another force area, we would probably have heard by now.'

'Do we know anything about him, Mark?'

'He runs a one-man haulage operation. Nothing known, not even a traffic ticket, which seems unusual. As I mentioned, he's single and takes exotic holidays, although I have a feeling he's also operating some sort of scam. We have to await forensics and, in the meanwhile, he could have simply run off with the vicar's wife. If CSI find nothing, then I'm probably wrong and it will remain a straight-forward Misper. Can I suggest, sir, that we await the results from CSI and I can leave DI Yin to oversee at this stage?' concluded Faraday.

'I'll leave it to you, Mark', replied the ACC. 'The course of action you propose is completely in-line with the chief's new policy. Incidentally, how is Miss Yin settling in?'

'Very well indeed, sir. I think that she will be fine.'

'OK. Thank you, Mark. Keep me posted'. Faraday replaced the receiver.

'Thank you, sir', she said softly.

'For … for what?' asked Faraday, looking up from his notes, genuinely confused.

'For your kind remarks to the ACC.'

'Oh', replied Faraday, as if the comments were of no consequence. 'It was just a remark, Kay. If I thought that you weren't up to it, I would have had to have said so. Now, let's visit Susan Tope.'

They walked down the stairs and onto the ground floor. Before entering the Forensic and Crime Scene Unit, they signed the register and walked along a secure corridor. To their right, behind a floor to ceiling glazed wall, scientists were already bent over bright exhibit tables. Miss Tope was standing at the head of the corridor against the double doors.

She was tall, thin, rather plain but with an engaging smile and humorous personality. 'We can't go on meeting like this, Mr Faraday. People will talk', she said with a laugh and, turning to DI Yin, commented indifferently: 'They will anyway.'

The two officers followed Miss Tope into her office. On a side table was a large brown exhibit bag. She checked her watch as she donned latex gloves. Faraday and Yin followed her example as she made a notation on a form before breaking the forensic seal.

'Right, we will leave it to you, Susan', said Faraday.

The forensic scientist carefully removed the overnight bag, unzipping the top so as to lift out each item within.

'Two shirts, Primark, medium size', she said placing each item neatly on the table. 'A pair of jeans with wide leather belt,' she continued examining the markings. 'Don Giovanni and pair of Clark's lace-up shoes, hardly worn and nice and clean. And, three pairs of Y-fronts'.

'About what you would expect for three days away from home?' asked Kay, but Faraday thought she was making a observation and so she asked again. 'I was asking, sir. You're a man, is that what you would think he would take?'

'Sorry. Probably', replied Faraday, engrossed in other items on the table. 'He would need a coat, a sweater or something. It's pretty chilly in the Irish Sea, even on board a ship, so probably wearing or carrying them. And the toiletries, Susan?'

'You've noticed something?' she asked.

'It may be nothing, but he's packed a hand towel but not soap', observed Faraday.

Miss Tope picked up each item in turn, the tooth paste, tooth brush, electric shaver and deodorant spray can. She made a further notation and turning back to the table, nudged the deodorant can that wobbled, then rolled off the table top to clatter on the floor.

Faraday stretched forward and with index fingers only, lifted the can and replaced it on the table on its side.

'It's nearly empty', he said.

'But there were two full cans in his bathroom', remembered DI Yin.

'So why didn't he pack a full can?' asked Faraday, 'or soap?'

'And I'm sure there was a toilet bag in his bathroom.'

'But not one in this overnight bag', observed Faraday.

As Miss Tope began to itemise the contents of the wallet, Faraday became more uncomfortable. 'Maybe it is nothing, but I'm not getting the "feel good" factor with all of this. The wallet with a driver's licence, two credit cards, an AirMiles card, breakdown service card plus £35 – why is it in the bag? I might put my passport in my hand luggage but the rest, the rest would be in my jacket or in a trouser pocket'.

'Lorry drivers often wash in service station', suggested DI Yin.

'Yes, they do' agreed Faraday.

'But you're not convinced that Atkins just left it?'

'He could have, but I don't think so. It's all too ...'

'Convenient?' she said as they both burst out laughing.'

Miss Tope explained that the examination of the bag and contents would not be at the top of her priority list, but promised to complete the examination as quickly as she could. Faraday would have to be patient. He thanked Susan Tope and both officers returned to Faraday's office.

'Where were we, Kay?' he asked as they resumed their seats around the coffee table.

'You were going to say something about one-way flights, sir?'

'Ah, yes. Flights', said Faraday as he gathered his thoughts. 'Lost it. Give me a moment', he said as he closed his eyes, thinking of the context of his earlier comments. 'Whatever. There were those odd one-way flights. What the significance was, I don't know', he said impatient with himself as his short-term memory hindered him again. 'Anyway. We need Atkins' business accounts and tax returns. I can't quite put my finger on it but deposits seemed to be made every now and again, groups of them, to all his accounts. I've marked them with little yellow highlighter dots', he said, as he handed her the file.

'Now I remember', he said, picturing the pages marked with highlighter. 'One-way flights. Some of the deposits appear to tie up with his holidays and the one-way flights. Maybe the deposits represent his gambling wins but, we all know that punters invariably loose and the house inevitably wins. I had hoped that his business records would have been in the garage. I need you to go back to his apartment and search it.'

'I will call in on Mrs Fudge again.'

'OK. OK' said Faraday, his thoughts cut short by the noisy arrival of Inspector Trench.

Faraday raised his left hand towards the door to halt the interruption as he jotted down some notes. 'Right, Kay. At the moment, but we can talk after prayers, I need the video tapes from the service station. Any available tapes within two miles of Gas Lane. A Misper circulation and I need you to go back to Atkins' flat and find his business, his trading accounts, and tax returns. OK?'

'No problem, sir.'

'I also need the banks' and the AirMiles' people to give us times, dates and locations of any transactions during the past week. And see if you can get hold of the details of his vehicle insurance and breakdown service. If he's borrowed another vehicle, his absence might be all down to a busted gearbox or drive shaft.'

'And the credit note?' she asked by way of a reminder.

'Yes, the credit note... I have just the man for that', he concluded as he turned to the door and invited his senior team in.

'No Jane again today then, sir?' asked Trench as he dropped heavily into one of the chairs.

'On leave, Gordon', replied Faraday, as he and Yin exchange a short report for a file. Preoccupied, Faraday didn't notice Trench's raised eyebrow and smirk.

The meeting was a brief affair. The district performance figures were good and the priorities were, with a few exceptions, being met. A disciplinary matter was mentioned as was the disappearance of Barry Atkins. For once, Trench remained silent and looked decidedly uncomfortable. As the meeting broke up, Faraday asked Trench and Taylor to remain.

'David, you're off duty at two. Are you going straight home?'
'Yes, I was, sir. Did you want something?'

'You might be able to help me with a small, well, quite a large detour, if you could?'

'Tell me what you want me to do, sir', he said willingly.

'Could you call in on this company', asked Faraday, handing the credit note to Inspector Taylor, 'and ask them if they have seen Atkins. We will have a proper press release photograph before two o'clock. A long shot, but Atkins has obviously visited this company recently, so they might know something about him'.

'It's worth a try, sir, and only a few miles out of my way. I'll call back in for the press release at about 13.45, if that is OK?'

'Yes. If it's not on Jane's desk or mine, check with Kay, would you?'

'Of course', he replied and was gone.

'I could have done that enquiry for you, sir,' said Trench.

For a moment, Faraday wasn't sure what to say in reply. He wasn't sure if Trench was genuinely put out at not being asked to make the enquiry. But he reasoned that such an enquiry could have easily have been undertaken by a constable and Trench must have realised that. Faraday assumed that Trench was playing one his games again, pretending to be willing and helpful, but rarely achieving anything. Faraday's response was harsh, maybe unnecessarily so.

'I asked David to undertake a simple task because it would be convenient for him to do so but, also, because I am able to rely upon him.'

'Are you suggesting', said Trench hesitantly, pushing out his chest and looking around towards DI Yin as if challenging Faraday to question his ability in front of others, 'that I can't be trusted?'

Faraday resumed his seat behind his desk and steepled his hands. 'I'm glad you've raised that point with me, Mr Trench. Let me put a question to you', said Faraday staring past Trench and out of his window as he gathered his thoughts. 'You told me that when you visited Barry Atkins' garage lock-up that you had checked the garage, but you didn't step inside the garage, did you?'

'I could see perfectly clearly that the garage was empty.'

'But you told me that you had checked the garage'.

'I ... I said that I had checked his flat but only looked into the garage', lied Trench. Faraday tried to remember the words spoken by Trench, his anger at the inspector's dishonesty muddling his recollection.

'I recall what you said, Gordon', interjected DI Yin. 'You said that you had had a good look around the garage and you could see nothing untoward.'

'You must have misunderstood', he replied dismissively.

'I haven't misunderstood *you*, Gordon', she replied icily.

'If you had bothered to have entered the garage', continued Faraday, 'you would have noted that the floor had been swept clean around what must have been a parked lorry. That lorry has now gone to reveal a series of tyre tracks which led us to a concealed lorry.   As a consequence of your cavalier lack of attention we have lost ...', he said as he looked instinctively towards DI Yin.

'Eight days, sir', she replied quietly.

'Eight days', Faraday repeated. 'And I specifically asked you to detail someone to this case, didn't I?'

'Yes, but you didn't make it clear that it was a priority.'

'What do I have to do, spell it out for you?' retorted Faraday. 'A police officer's task is to obtain and secure information and intelligence; to thoroughly investigate cases. This you failed to do.'
'But, he's only a missing person.'

'Only a missing person!' exploded Faraday angrily. Then, controlling his exasperation, continued in a more level tone. 'Let us hope for your sake, Gordon, that Barry Atkins isn't only a dead person.'

Faraday bent his head over the papers on his desk. Trench remained where he was for a moment, looked around, not so much in embarrassment but annoyance at being ignored, then walked out resentfully, bumping into the door frame as he went.

DI Yin collected her papers. Faraday looked up from his papers then leaned back into his chair.

'I will always protect those who really try their best even, probably wrongly, when they have little ability. I particularly admire honesty and loyalty, but I get very impatient with people like Mr Trench', said Faraday, adding: 'Did it show?'

DI Yin did not answer the question directly. 'He's not very competent, but he's ambitious and he's weak. That means he is potentially very dangerous.'

'And you think I've made an enemy?'

'Maybe we both have, sir', she said with a careless smile but, as she reached the door, she turned, her face one of concern.

'Sir. In the absence of Jane', said Kay Yin, 'if there is anything you want me to do, you only have to ask.'

Faraday did not respond as she simply placed his diary on his desk and quietly left the suite. He thought for just a moment but realised that DI Yin probably already understood. She was a bright, perceptive young lady. She had read the signs. She knew his secret.

***

Inspector David Taylor turned off St Andrews Road and travelled the short distance across the poorly surfaced road to stop at the large display board detailing the road network and location of industrial units. Taylor checked the name against the credit note and saw the name of Avon Domestic and Industrial Electrical Suppliers, an authorised supplier and Bosch servicing depot. As Taylor engaged first gear, he glanced in his mirror and saw a number of approaching vehicles, including a black Audi. Initially, Taylor took no particular notice of the Audit until he pulled onto the forecourt of the Bosch depot and saw, across the road, a blue door rolling up to allow the Audi entry, at the same time revealing at least one Mercedes-Benz Actros vehicle within.

The Bosch receptionist was helpful and called a colleague to peer at the photograph of Barry Atkins on the newly printed press release. Whilst they could remember the reason for the credit note, no one could recall anything about Barry Atkins himself. Nevertheless, the receptionist agreed to post a copy of the press release on the wall in the customers' area. On no more than a whim, Taylor wandered over the road towards the blue roller doors and tried to open the reception office door which was locked. He would probably have walked away but heard a male voice say what he thought to be the words 'dick head'. Inspector Taylor thumped on the blue metallic doors which rattled at each thump. At first there was no response but after a few more hefty thumps the reception office door was opened by Simon Mooney.

Inspector Taylor was not old, but was an 'old school' type of copper. He wore his black Regatta civilian anorak opened so as to reveal a pristine white shirt and black uniform tie above black trousers with a razor-sharp crease and smart black shoes. These where his calling card and he simply stepped past Mooney.

'Good afternoon, sir. Just wondering if you could help me with our enquiries', he said as he walked on through the other door and into the bays containing the three grey painted Mercedes-Benz.

Collins and Chappell approached the officer. 'Ah' said the inspector, 'I was just asking your friend here, but I can ask you all to have a little look at this picture. Do any of you know this man?' Chappell made the pretence of looking at the poster, then asked Collins and Mooney: 'A missing person. Can't say I've seen him. What about you guys?'

'No, can't say I have', said Collins as he scrutinised the photograph. 'What about you, Simon?'

'Nope', replied Mooney too quickly and with hardly a glance.

'Oh,' continued Taylor disappointedly. 'I thought you might have seen him about here.'

Chappell looked towards his colleagues and shrugged. 'No. Not us.'

'OK. Let me just leave a poster with you', said Taylor as if to conclude the conversation. 'If you see him about, just call the number at the bottom there.'

'We'll do that', replied Chappell, as Taylor walked back out towards the reception office, then suddenly he turned. 'What are you blokes doing?'

No one replied, although Collins and Mooney instinctively looked towards Chappell. The silence seemed to last for minutes but in reality it was three or four seconds at the most before Chappell, his cover rehearsed, answered.

'We carry out specialist contract work preparing standard, commercial vehicles for carrying toxic loads. In this case, these vehicles will be transporting a derivative of *Trichloromethylsilane*.'

'And what's that then?' asked the policeman.

'It's colourless but very toxic', replied Chappell.

'And what's it used for?'

'It's used in the silicone chip and fibre optic business,' explained Chappell helpfully. 'It can withstand extremes of temperature apparently, so ideal for that sort of work, but nasty stuff in its liquid form.'

'I don't like nasty stuff,' commented Inspector Taylor, 'so I will leave you to it. By the way, who do you work for?'

'Intercontinental Bodyworks of Swindon', replied Chappell.

'Well, good luck Intercontinental Bodyworks of Swindon and give me a call if you see Barry Atkins', said Inspector Taylor as the sound of his voice trailed off through the door.

Chapter 12

Bristol, England.

THE NEATLY cut, lunch-time sandwiches, fresh orange juice and still water had been brought up to Superintendent Faraday's office about twenty minutes before Inspector David Taylor in shirt sleeve order and DI Kay Yin wearing a black trouser suit arrived. Faraday ushered both officers into his office as Jane Hart arranged the coffee cups that would later only need hot water to be added. Jane closed the door, leaving the three officers to sit around the low table, although Faraday's intimate concern towards his secretary had again not gone unnoticed by the two inspectors.

'You seem to have a big bundle there, Kay', said Faraday, pointing to the files. 'Do you want to go first?'

'Yes, I can', she said as she heaved four files onto her lap, on top of which was a clip board. 'Firstly, I found his trading accounts, together with his tax returns and an Italian bank account, hidden neatly behind his immersion heater in an airing cupboard. I have made a bullet-point breakdown for you but if, for the moment, I can summarise', she asked and continued in response to Faraday's nod. 'On five occasions and each in a different year, Atkins seems to have received payments into this Italian account of between £25,000 and £34,000, which then appears to be drip fed into his six legitimate mainland accounts. I say Italian account but it is actually into a bank in San Marino, the small republic that lies between Rome and Venice'.

'Any idea where the money comes from?' asked Faraday as he starred out of the window and across the harbour.

'None', she replied, now not disconcerted by his apparent lack of attention. 'But if I can leave this account for a moment and move to this one,' she continued, holding up a blue folder. This bank account is certainly his trading account. From this account it would seem that he runs a sound little business which should allow him a comfortable life. However, on four occasions Atkins purchased a ferry ticket to Ireland, once to Dublin, twice to Cork and once to Belfast'.

'One-way trips?' asked Faraday, still staring out of the window.

'Yes. One-way. But there were other trips. A Eurotunnel charge, then a one-way ferry charge from Reggio to Messina, followed by another one-way ferry charge for Porto Empedocle to Vittoriosa.'
'Vittoriosa?' asked David Taylor.

'Yes,' offered Faraday, 'the ferry terminal in Valletta, Malta.'

DI Yin pulled out another file, a green one, and continued: 'This file contained paperwork for his tax returns. They go back for seven years. Atkins is very methodical. He claims for every item of servicing, spare parts, fuel, meals, ferry tickets, bridge tolls. You name it, he claims for it.'

'But?' asked Faraday.

'There's a pattern. A few days after he has travelled to Ireland, he makes a return journey by a budget airline, yet, pays for it from his holiday account, not his business account. Not only that, within days of that journey he received a major deposit in his Italian account'.

'And Malta?' asked David.

'Yes. One-way flight to England with Air Malta', replied Kay Yin.

'But, why Malta?' asked David Taylor. 'What's the significance of Malta?'

'They drive on the left … as they do in Ireland', said Faraday, still looking out of his window and across the harbour.

'And you think?' asked the detective inspector.

Faraday slowly moved around in his chair and asked: 'What do you think, Kay?'

'It could simply be that he's shipping out illegal cargoes of some sort. Maybe using a hire vehicle and shipping out containers with top of the range 4 x 4s would be a favourite, that sort of thing. Or it could be the lorries themselves, either ones he has stolen or moving them on for a thief', she replied.

'Which do you believe to be the most likely?' he probed.

'If he's picking up 25 to 34K a time, then that's a lot of cash for acting as a temporary chauffer. My bet would be that he's a thief and, this time around, he could have stolen from the wrong people.'

'He dare not claim these return trips on his tax returns for fear of alerting the authorities so, he disguises them as holidays', suggested Faraday as he turned towards the window again with another sandwich. 'But, could these large amounts of money not be from gambling?'

'They could be,' responded Kay Yin. 'He does take his Italian holidays at about the same time'.

'He must be a very lucky gambler', commented Inspector Taylor light heartedly. 'When we find him, he'll have to tell us his secret.'

'I've got a horrible feeling that we will never find him alive', said Faraday as he reached around for his glass of orange.

'I think you are right, sir', said DI Yin.

'Why?' asked Faraday casually.

'Because, I've spoken to his banks and the Air Miles' people. Barry Atkins hasn't, apparently, made any fuel purchases since Friday, 31st August. We have his lorry and his car hasn't moved from its parking bay, so I think we can assume that he's not driving another vehicle.'

'Well, he could be', Faraday mused. 'For someone else. Or with someone else on a long haul who purchases the fuel. Whatever, we won't close down on that possibility yet. Anything else?'

'Not at the moment, sir,' concluded Kay Yin. 'Service station tapes should be with me tomorrow and David has loaned me one of his light-duty PCs to review security and highway tapes as we speak.'

'Well done, Kay. Over to you then, David.'

'Speculation, sir,' began Taylor, 'but having listened to Kay, things seem to fit. For what it's worth, I went down to the Bosch warehouse and they could not remember Atkins but I left the press release. What I did notice nearby was a Mercedes-Benz Actros truck. I only saw it for a few moments as a gleaming Audi drove into one of the industrial units. So I wandered across. The roller doors were shut down by the time I'd got across the road but I heard voices and I was sure I heard someone say "dick head", so I banged on the roller door a bit harder than usual. Made a dreadful din. Eventually a guy opened a side door and in I walked'. Inspector Taylor described the three men and the three Mercedes-Benz and the tanker trailers. 'I might be wrong, but these men are military or were military.'

'Oh. Why do you say that?' asked Faraday intensely, turning around to face his colleagues.

'As I say, I could be wrong, but two of them seemed to be too deferential to the third man. Everything was too neat and too orderly, laid out just as if it was a Transport Corp depot and I realise now, well I'm pretty certain at least, that they didn't say "dick head",. What one of them said was "dicker".'

'Dicker?' queried Faraday. 'There's a significance?'

'Oh, yes. "Dicker" is the term used by the military in Northern Ireland to describe a terrorist lookout.'

Faraday leaned back in his chair, looking out towards the dock again. 'Index plates?' he asked mechanically.

'Only on the Audi and the registered keeper is listed as Intercontinental Bodyworks of Swindon.'

'And who are they?'

'They apparently specialises in converting standard commercial vehicles to carry non-standard loads, particularly hazardous chemicals.'

'Why do you say "apparently"?' asked Faraday.

'I've discreetly checked the address, but it's in one of those managed office complexes.' Faraday visualised a similar complex near the Parkway that he had visited recently, plush offices for rental with secure access via a staffed reception suite plus use of conference and other facilities.

'But you think it's just a front?'

'It might be legit', speculated Inspector Taylor. 'The Swindon office could be where all the organising and administration takes place and the company has teams of engineers all over the country doing the conversion work.'

'But you're not convinced?'

'No, I'm not, sir', he replied firmly. 'They have a website with a few photographs of vehicles, but no client company names on display. Nor are there any photographs of the directors or engineers.'

'You said that the tankers at Avonmouth had Hazchem markings, so that should give us a company name for those vehicles?'

'No, not Hazchem, sir', corrected Inspector Taylor. 'The trailers were fitted with Kempler Codes.'

'What are Kempler Codes?' asked DI Yin.

'Hazchem are the UK markings displayed on a vehicle carrying hazardous chemicals, but Kempler are the international equivalent ... Sorry, David. I've interrupted, you're the traffic expert.'

'No, you are quite right. The Kempler Codes are very similar to Hazchem panels. Orange in colour as well as a UN substance ID numbers, that sort of thing', he said as he referred to his note book. 'The numbers "683" were on the plates. "6" indicates a toxic substance, "8" corrosive and "3" fire. Nasty stuff. A truck driver can use either the Hazchem or Kempler plates. Unfortunately, the drawback with the Kempler Code is, unlike Hazchem panels, they do not list the name and contact phone number of the company.'

'Very convenient again', remarked Faraday with a smile as he exchanged glances with DI Yin. 'Anything else, David?'

'No, sir', replied a bemused Taylor, unaware of the private joke between Faraday and the DI regarding toilets and conveniences.

'OK. This has been very useful but', remarked Faraday without criticism, 'we still have a very incomplete picture.'

'One question, sir' asked DI Yin.

'Yes?'

'Why did you also take the framed photograph from Atkin's bedroom?' asked DI Yin.

'Oh, yes', replied Faraday as he got up from the chair and walked behind his desk. He sat at his desk as he picked up the photograph frame, which he held up towards them both. 'All the photographs of Barry Atkins on his lounge wall show him in an evening suit with a beautiful girl, a different beautiful girl.'

'And that one?' asked Inspector Taylor, pointing towards Faraday's desk.

'This is Atkins, without an evening suit and with one of the same young ladies,' replied Faraday, 'but this one shows her holding a rose. And it is this photograph that was at the side of his bed'. He lowered the photograph to this desk and spoke to DI Yin: 'The holiday account you have there, Kay. Did Atkins holiday in Venice last April?'

Kay Yin thumbed through the papers. 'Yes. Yes, he did', she replied curiously. 'He took a flight out to Venice on Friday, 20th April, returning on the 27th.'

'Why do you ask?' said Taylor.

'It's just a piece of useless information I happened to have in my silly head because my name is Mark. You see, St Mark is the patron saint of Venice. The 25th April is St Mark's Day and on that day a man would traditionally present to his lover the *boccola*, the rose bud.'

'Maybe not such a useless piece of information', commented DI Yin, 'but could it not be Valentine's Day in England?'

'That could have been a reasonable explanation, but, I pulled the back off and the photograph was taken by Salvatores of Venice.'

'But what is the connection between Barry Atkins and Avonmouth?' asked David Taylor.

'There may be none at all', replied Faraday. 'But, at the moment, there is little else to go on. So, David, I need you to check on Swindon. Go there if you have to. Pretend you want to hire an office or something. I'll leave it to you, but I want to know more about Intercontinental Bodyworks of Swindon.'

'And me, sir. How can I help?'

'Not quite so exciting, I'm afraid. Go back to 22a and access his computer. Can you do that?'

'I think so', she replied with a knowing smile.

'And see how far we've got with the tapes.'

Chapter 13

Friday 14th September.

Swindon and Bristol, England.

HE PUSHED open the wrought iron gate and walked down the flagstone path, between identical park benches, to the front of the old building, once a gentleman's residence of some style, now the imposing centre-piece of the managed office complex. Inspector Taylor pressed the intercom button.

'Highridge Lodge. How can we help you?'

'I'm David Taylor. I rang you yesterday.'

'Yes you did, Mr Taylor. We are expecting you. Please come straight through.'

The inspector, dressed in blazer and open shirt and carrying a brief case, pushed open the glass door when the buzzer sounded and approached the reception area.

'I'm Amanda', said one of the smiling young ladies. 'Would you care to sign here, then I can show you around.'

Taylor endorsed the register and Amada pulled off a perforated strip and inserted the piece of paper into a little badge holder marked "visitor". Then she guided Taylor towards one of the conference rooms. Over coffee - very nice coffee - Amanda presented Taylor with a brochure and explained the reception process, the unique phone number for each office routed through reception, postal arrangements, typing services, conference facilities and the allocated parking. Taylor asked about telephone conferencing and parking for visitors before a short tour of vacant offices. There was only two, one smaller office suite in the former stable block and a much larger office in the main house. Taylor made a pretence of configuring the office and, finally, checking the communal toilets and washrooms.

The whole exercise, from leaving his home address to returning to Bristol Central, had taken Inspector Taylor a little over three hours. He was back at District headquarters by mid-day.

***

Just as DI Yin was about to brief Faraday, they heard Inspector Taylor speaking with Jane Hart in her office.

'David', he called. 'You made good time.'

'I could have been quicker', said Taylor as he appeared, silhouetted in the doorway, 'but, I needed to take my time as if I was an interested, prospective client.'

'You found what you were looking for?'

'Almost immediately and then more.'

'OK. The floor's yours.'

'Nice set-up', said Taylor as he settled into a chair. 'A very professionally managed facility and expensive too', he continued as he handed one brochure to Faraday and another to DI Yin. 'The bottom line is that International Bodyworks have an office there. It was simpler than I thought, their name was on a board in the foyer.' Taylor paused as the secretary entered the office with a coffee for him. Faraday and his secretary exchanged glances, not unnoticed by the two inspectors. Nor unnoticed was his almost indiscernible, gentle wink to Jane as she left his office. Taylor stirred his coffee and then continued. 'I was invited into a conference room and given what I suspect was the standard sales pitch by Amanda – and very good she was too. I asked to be shown the office units available and was shown two, one of which was on the same corridor as International Bodyworks. The entrance doors to each office have porthole-type windows and I was able to peer into International Bodyworks' office. The office was well furnished and equipped. The walls were hung with pictures of heavy vehicles, but it didn't seem to me like a working office at all.'

'No sign of occupancy?' asked Kay Yin.

'Yes and no', replied Taylor as Faraday scanned the brochure. 'There was a neat pile of unopened mail on a desk alongside a computer but the in and out trays were empty.'

Faraday leaned forward as he replaced his cup in the saucer. 'Did they explain the security arrangements to you?' he asked.

'Yes, they did, sir. The front entrance and the gated approach to the car park are covered by CCTV. Entry and exit is controlled by receptionists during the working day or a security guard between 1800 and 0800, weekends and Bank Holidays. Each office suite has it own swipe card and confidential waste is dealt with by a security firm. They say that all cleaning staff are provided by the same security company and vetted'.

'They explained nothing else?' continued Faraday. DI Yin relaxed a little as she realised that Faraday had also spotted what she had noticed in the brochure.

'No, sir.'

'They may have rumbled you, David', said Faraday, raising his hand indicating that no censor was intended. 'The brochure says that everyone, everyone, is photographed as they pass through reception. Now, I wonder why Amanda didn't tell a prospective client that important piece of reassuring information?'

'I don't think that that could have been anticipated, sir,' commented DI Yin protectively as she rose from her chair and endorsed a dry-wipe board 'confirmed' alongside 'Intercontinental Bodyworks address at Swindon.'

'No, you are quite right, Kay. Its good work, David', responded Faraday. 'The important thing is that another piece of the jig-saw is firmly in place. Now, Kay, your up-date, please.'

'Mr Faraday asked me to write up what we know so far on the board here'. She stood and pointed at a number of words circled in blue ink on the board. 'I was able to access Barry Atkins' computer,' she continued. 'There was a lot of e-mails traffic, holiday bookings for example. Significantly, there was confirmation with South West Vehicle Distribution and Sweet & Sons of his trips from Avonmouth to Hereford and Hereford to Dublin. There was also an on-line, one-way ferry booking for himself and his vehicle from Holyhead to Dublin for the 6th. There were also e-mails regarding contracts on the 8th September through to the 11th November'. Her finger moved to the words 'cell phone'. 'We are still checking his cell phone. There's a lot to check, but certainly no calls at all since Saturday the 1st. Lastly, tapes.'

DI Yin glided across the office. 'If I may?' she said as she approached the DVD/tape player on Faraday's desk, picking up some computer disks and checking her written notes. 'Your PC Blake has done an excellent job, David. Dozens of tapes have been checked by him and he has put the relevant details onto this disk', she said, holding the disk on her index finger. The disc was inserted and the screen glowed.

'This is the rear of Barry Atkins' vehicle, without trailer, at 04:38 on Monday the 3rd at the Cumberland Basin towards Hotwell'. There was a slight pause as the second and third set of images appeared on the screen. 'This is the same vehicle, 4 minutes later, at Cumberland Road, and the same vehicle at 04:49 at Temple Gate'.

In response to DI Yin's pressure on the pause button, the images on the screen froze. 'We had some luck,' she continued. 'The following are photographs taken by a speed camera at 06:51.22 and 06:51.24 on the Portway, activated by two police units responding to a major RTA on the M5. The first shows a police Mercedes-Benz estate, travelling out of the city towards Avonmouth, passing Atkins' lorry at 73 mph. The second shows another police unit, a Range Rover, passing an Audi estate. The registration plate is clear. The Audi is the one you clocked, David, with the Intercontinental Bodyworks' people at Avonmouth.'

Taylor had got out of his chair and was now kneeling in front of the screen. 'Re-wind, Kay, back to the beginning', he asked.

'Sorry, David. There's one more photo I need to show', she said, pressing the play button. 'PC Black was really diligent. When he saw the Audi, he recalled seeing an Audi estate before and went back over all the tapes again. This is what he found'. Clips of the Audi appeared again, this time at 04.42, in-bound at the approach to the Cumberland Basin, a matter of minutes behind Barry Atkins' vehicle.'

'They're not the same vehicles', said Inspector Taylor.

'Go on, David. What do you mean?' encouraged Faraday.

'Sorry. The Audis are the same, it's the lorries, sir,' replied Taylor. 'They are not the same. Can you rewind, Kay?'

DI Yin rewound the disc and the clips of the lorries appeared again, then she froze the screen to hold a perfect image of the lorry.

'They look exactly the same, David', said DI Yin.

'They would. They are the same basic models. But, give me just a few more seconds', he said as, still kneeling, he looked around for the exhibit photographs. 'The photographs, the photographs of Atkins' lorry in the arches. They were here'.

'Here they are', said Kay Yin as she retrieved the photographs from under some papers on the floor.

Inspector Taylor looked through the photographs and stopped at the picture of Atkins' vehicle, then pointed to the screen. 'Yes, here it is', he explained. 'You see, the Mercedes-Benz Actros range provide a choice of four cab configurations: the Premier Day, or maybe it's called the Premium Day cab, it's not important. Then there's the Standard Sleeper. The next in the range is the High Roof Sleeper followed by the top of the range, the Executive Mega Sleeper. The vehicle on the tape is the Standard Sleeper', he said, 'but these photographs', he continued as he waved the loose collection of CSI photographs, 'show Atkins' vehicle equipped as the High Roof Sleeper with the extra head room above the cab' Inspector Taylor placed the photographs on the coffee table like a poker player showing his winning hand. 'These vehicles might have the same registration numbers but they aren't the same vehicles.'

'And why should Atkins book bed and breakfast in Dublin if he could sleep comfortably in his cab?' asked Faraday.

'And we know, sir,' said DI Yin, 'that from his bank that he booked the B&B on the 6th for the evening of the 6th.'

'Which the B&B people tell us was not taken up and, in any case, would have been when he should have been back in the UK courtesy of a Ryan Air flight.'

'That's correct, sir', confirmed Kay Yin, adding: 'All of which is strange in itself.'

'Strange?' questioned Faraday

'Yes, sir. According to Atkins' business accounts, he has never stayed in a B&B before whilst on the road.'

'We seem to be left with a multitude of "whys?"' said Faraday, turning in his chair to stare out his panoramic window. 'Tapes. Are we sure that there were no other sightings?'

'PC Blake is diligent. I'm confident that there are no other sightings of the Audi or the lorry, or lorries. The speed cameras are static but the traffic and surveillance cameras could have been pointing in any direction as a vehicle passed. I've gone over the location of all the cameras and the one-way systems are such that movement of the Mercedes-Benz and Audi could easily go undetected.'

'OK, but the questions remain. Why was the Audi on the road at, what was it?'

'04:42 and 06:51', replied DI Yin. 'And why where the Mercedes-Benz on the road, trundling back and forth? Who was driving the Mercedes?'

'If Barry Atkins stole a vehicle from Avonmouth, how did he get there from his home?' posed Faraday.

'I'll get Blake to go through the tapes again and search for a gold coloured Ford Granada.'

'You've read my mind', said Faraday turning from the window. 'I'm sure you will, Kay, but make sure that he doesn't think he's failed'. He had seen Inspector Taylor's expectant look. 'Something on your mind, David?'

'We don't seem to have enough to arrest the men from Intercontinental Bodyworks or search their premises?'

Faraday turned toward the window again. 'I don't think so. If we look at this completely objectively, there is nothing at all to link Intercontinental Bodyworks with Atkins, other than the fact that Atkins visited a kitchen cooker company that happened to be situated in the same road as Intercontinental Bodyworks. Dozens of other people must be doing the same on a daily basis. Let me be the devil's advocate', continued Faraday. 'The vehicles seen on the tapes bear Atkins' registration number and he's missing. Agreed, Atkins' registration number can be seen on a vehicle that appears, in fact it may well be, a slightly different model. But, does the Mercedes-Benz seen on the film belong to Intercontinental Bodyworks? We don't know. The colour of the vehicles on the screen seems to be similar to Atkins and International Bodyworks, although we know that their vehicles are quite different colours. The offices of Intercontinental Bodyworks appeared to be empty when you visited, David. So was mine at 7 o'clock last evening and at 7 this morning. No, a magistrate would not grant a search warrant on what we have at the moment. They just will not do it. The courts don't like arrests or searches on the basis of hunches. That was what PACE was all about', Faraday turned away from the window and back towards his colleagues as he continued: 'But I would love to let CSI loose on the tyres of the lorries at Avonmouth. If any of their vehicles had been in Atkins' garage, they would have collected something from the dusty floor. In fact, that reminds me, Kay. Please chase CSI regarding the tyre tread patterns.'

'If Intercontinental Bodyworks move the vehicles on to the road', said Taylor gleefully as DI Yin scribbled a note, 'I can find all sorts of traffic legislation that would allow us to stop and examine them.'

'But there doesn't seem to be any immediate prospect of them moving', remarked Faraday as he rested back into his chair. 'So, that must be our long stop, David. Meanwhile, I had a call earlier from Chief Superintendent Wynne-Thomas'. He paused as he reached for his phone and taped one key. The phone bleeped in his secretary's office and was quickly answered. 'Jane, close your door would you, please. Thank you'.

For a moment, the two inspectors were surprised at the request, but as they heard the secretary's door to the outside corridor close, they exchanged glances. Jane Hart would always be trusted. 'The chief superintendent', continued Faraday, 'is aware of our enquiries into the disappearance of Barry Atkins and has made it clear that, in his *oversight* capacity, he is concerned that a superintendent and two inspectors are involved in this case, a case he feels should be handled more appropriately by Inspector Trench.'

'I wonder why?' commented DI Yin disparagingly.

'He has decreed that this is a straight-forward Misper', continued Faraday, raising both hands to silence any protest. 'I am not going to get into some sort of guerrilla warfare with him which will waste time and energy and therefore have agreed to hand a file to Inspector Trench. I say, a file'. Faraday turned towards DI Yin. 'Kay, compile a file with relevant Misper details, including NMPH and ESIS. Maybe I should have utilised these before', he reflected. 'In any event, Mr Trench may come up with something. When you've compiled the file, do not put your name on it', he said as he reached for one of his District Instruction notes. He endorsed the pale blue coloured paper and handed it to DI Yin. 'Clip this note to the file and put it in an envelope and place it all in his tray marked "urgent – for meeting with superintendent". If there is subsequently any criticism that the file was incomplete, it will be my responsibility.'

'I can do the file, sir, and I don't mind if my name is on it', she said. 'But I do', replied Faraday briskly. 'The chief superintendent is looking for any excuse to damage me and I don't want either of you caught in the cross-fire. You understand, Kay?'

'OK, sir.'

'It's five to one', he said looking at the wall clock. 'I have a meeting scheduled with Mr Trench for four-thirty. Could you possibly have the file in his tray before three?'

'Of course, it's only a matter of photocopying', she replied.

'Don't worry', said Faraday with a reassuring grin. 'I'm not letting this drop. I will ensure that Inspector Trench gives Barry Atkins the correct priority and, how should I put it, I will be keeping a weather eye on this case and may wish to satisfy my curiosity from time to time. I will keep you both in the loop. Meanwhile, I think David, you should pay Intercontinental Bodyworks one last visit and ask them why they were driving their Audi around the city on a sightseeing trip in the early hours of the 3rd.'

***

There was no need for Superintendent Faraday to check his watch. The clumsy, noisy arrival of Inspector Gordon Trench was precisely on time.

'Come in, Gordon', said Faraday without sarcasm, although the inspector was already about to take a seat.

'Good afternoon, sir. Just thought I would up-date you regarding the Misper.'

'Barry Atkins?'

'That's him, sir. There have been no sightings. The file indicates that there have been no bank transactions made since the 31st August. I thought it appropriate to involve other agencies, including the volunteers with NMPH', he said in such a tone as to suggest that this was his personal initiative to involve the National Missing Persons Helpline. 'Bearing in mind the Misper's travels abroad and the possible international dimension, I've now interfaced with the European Schedngen Information System', he continued, pleased to use the word 'interface' and pronounce Schedngen correctly. 'I've also ensured that the details are comprehensively recorded on COMPACT although I was a little concerned that DI Yin has been visiting Mrs Fudge.'

'Has Miss Yin's visits caused a problem?' asked Faraday casually.

'Not in so many words', he replied as if reluctant to criticise a colleague.

'In any words or manner at all?' asked Faraday, trying to disguise his mounting irritation.

'It's just a little disconcerting, sir. I wouldn't want there to be any crossed wires or unnecessary duplication of effort.'

'Mrs Fudge was distressed, apparently looking upon Barry Atkins as a son. Miss Yin and Mrs Fudge struck up a relationship of sorts and Kay promised to speak with her once a week. If you make sure that Kay is up-dated once a week, she will ring Mrs Fudge and reassure her, that's all.'

'Well, if you think it necessary', he replied with a sour tone.

'Gordon', replied Faraday to a morose Trench, 'it's not a necessity, it's simply a fellow officer keeping in touch with Mrs Fudge with whom she has established a rapport'. Before Trench could reply, Faraday changed tack. 'Meanwhile, could you explore the possibility of this case being included on Crime Watch UK.'

Inspector Trench beamed as Faraday had anticipated. 'Does this mean that, as the officer-in-the-case, I would appear on TV?'

'I would think that would depend upon what NMPH classification you have given Barry Atkins, but I'm sure that you would have recommended the priority to be "high" so, I should think that there would be a very good chance for you to appear on Crime Watch', said Faraday, Trench virtually beside himself with excited anticipation. 'I will leave you to negotiate, Gordon. Ring the detective chief superintendent and the press office before you go. Tell them that this initiative has my support. If they want a call from me, just leave me a note. We could work on a script together, if you wish, but it would, of course, be your show in more ways than one.'

'Excellent', proclaimed Trench as if his brilliance and ability had, at long last, been recognised. He stood, eager to make the calls before the weekend.

'One last thing, Gordon'. Trench began to deflate. 'You are on duty Saturday and Sunday?'

'Yes, I am. Eight to four both days.'

'Good, then, as officer-in-the-case, could you undertake the preparatory work for stop-checks to be in place between 02:00 and 07:00 Monday, one at Barton Road and Gas Lane, a second at Oxford Street and Avon Street'. As Trench remained standing, in a pose similar to someone desperate to visit the toilet, Faraday gestured to the inspector to resume his seat. 'You'll need to take a note, Gordon'. Trench occupied the chair noisily and extracted a pen from his pocket. 'Between two and seven, this Monday', repeated Faraday. 'Barton Road with Gas Lane and at the junction of Oxford and Avon. Get log sheets made up plus copies of photographs of Barry Atkins. The officers need to ask if anyone saw Atkins between two and seven on the 3rd September, or saw his Mercedes-Benz. There should be photos of his lorry in the file. They should ask if anyone saw a black or dark coloured Audi A6 Avant.'

'There's no picture of an Audi in the file, sir', remarked a perplexed Trench.

'Find one', replied Faraday, then added more lightly: 'The local dealer will let you have a couple of brochures, I'm sure. I want to know the identity of everyone stopped and where they have come from and where they are going. Regulars will know other regulars and so anyone stopped must be asked if they saw anyone loitering, the sighting of an unusual vehicle or a vehicle parked in an unusual place or a small group of men. Erratic or strange driving; squealing tyres; men shouting. That sort of thing. I want specific questions to be asked, Gordon. Not "did you see anything suspicious?" - a question which is usually utterly meaningless.'

Trench remained in his chair with the expectant look of a child on a potty. 'I think that will be all, Gordon. I'm leaving this completely to you.'

'Thank you very much, sir', he said, eager to leave and make his phone calls to the press office.

Chapter 14

Monday 17th September.

Victoria, Australia; Missouri, USA and Bristol, England.

THE OFFICES could not have been more unlike, but the purpose of their occupants was the same.

Fortuna Villa, so near to the old Bendigo Creek gold fields, was ornate, turreted and massive. First built in 1855 by the mining magnets, Christopher and Theodore Ballerstedt, whose ancestors had fought in Blucher's army at the Battle of Waterloo and had come to Australia via the 1849 Californian Gold Rush, Fortuna Villa had been taken over by the Australian army's Survey Corp in 1942 and was now the home of DIGO, the Defence Imagery and Geo-Spatial Organisation.

The phone rang. The call was expected. Assistant Secretary Drew, the head of intelligence, picked up the cordless receiver and walked towards the open window into the late afternoon shade of the front balcony. It was delightfully cool here as he looked out across the stillness of the glass-like lake, bounded by beautifully tended lawns, silver birch, eucalyptus and river red gum trees.

'G'day, John', said Philip Drew.

'Hi, there', replied John Lindner, chief of the InnoVision Directorate of NGA in St Louis, Missouri. 'Just a personal call to say that I have spoken to London and we are hooked up. All systems are go. We are just awaiting the confirmatory executive mid-October. How's it down there with you, Philip?'

'That's about the size of it here too', replied Drew. 'I'm getting together with my UK opposite number in a few days and looking forward to working with you guys operationally.'

The two men talked for a few minutes more. They knew little of each other although they knew the other's national characteristics well. Australia, casual, open and optimistic. The United States, generous-hearted and patriotic.

The courtesy call finished, John Lindner replaced the phone and remained at his desk in his ultra-modern plush office that reminded all who entered his office of his key position in the defence agency. He had gotten in early, his official car picking him up at 06:15. Now only 09:20 and the day hardly begun, he was already not at ease. It wasn't the Australians or the Brits who were troubling him. The problem was much closer to home. He knew that discreet enquiries had already been made by a Californian congressman. He knew the congressman and he didn't like what he knew.

***

Superintendent Faraday heard Inspector Taylor speaking with his secretary before peering around the door.

'Good afternoon, sir. Jane said that you were free for a moment.'
'I am, David. Come in', he said, tagging some papers and pushing them aside. 'How did it go this morning at Avonmouth?'

'They were locked down again so I had to thump on the door hard', he replied as he took an easy chair at the coffee table. 'Only one of them, Collins, the older man with the thick moustache, was there this morning. I asked him if he had any news for me about Atkins, but negative. No surprises there. I chatted to him about the three vehicles. He said that they are all for a company in Portsmouth.'

'Did he name the company?'

'No. I asked, but he said that they just carry out the work as instructed and that others deal with the paperwork. If I pressed him, he pretended to be distracted or to find some complication and crawled under or over the vehicles. At first it all seemed natural enough, but I casually persisted and a defensive pattern became clear. He was good, but not that good. I am sure that these were well practiced diversionary tactic. As I was leaving, I asked Collins why their Audi was on the road at twenty to five and at ten to seven on the 3rd.'

'And his response?'

'Too rehearsed. He said that they had been out for a curry and a pub-crawl the previous evening. He said that Mooney, that's the youngest one, had been sick and so they had gone to one of the late night, street coffee vendors to sober him up and get some fresh air'. Taylor halted his account as Jane brought in two cups of tea, discreetly ignoring the half smile and lazy wink exchanged between his superintendent and the secretary before he continued. 'It seemed to me that maybe like a lot of contractors, these men would be living together, so I asked where they had eaten their curry. They said the "Pahahar". It's a take-away. I've checked. The owners can't remember these men, nor are there any credit card receipts in their names or the name of the other man, whom Collins simply referred to a "Mr Charman". Taylor sipped from his cup and then replaced it on the table. Faraday didn't hurry his inspector, he knew Taylor was thorough.

'One of the lorries is apparently completed. The second is nearly finished and the third will be ready for the road in about a month.'
'What are they actually doing to these trucks?'

'The main work seems to be fitting elaborate side-crush barriers, steps and walkways, that sort of thing?' he replied with a slight frown.

'You have some doubts, David?'

'It's probably nothing, but I patted the side of one of the tankers. It seemed to be full. I would have assumed that the work they were doing would have been done when the tanks were empty. But, I'm probably wrong. These tankers are big beasts with double, sometimes triple skins so, difficult to be certain.'

'It may be of significance. We can keep it in mind', commented Faraday, adding: 'And other work?'

'The roof lining was out of two of the cabs, wires dangling down. They said that they were having problems with the satnav.'

'Do they seem to know what they're at?'

'Oh, yes. They appear to be competent mechanics. Collins clearly wanted to impress on me that they were mechanics and that drivers would come and deliver the vehicles to Portsmouth. Why he should want to emphasis that I don't know. Pride, maybe. Anyway, as I walked away, I fired a question at him. I asked where they were living. It caught him off guard and he sort of blurted out that it was an old bungalow on the B4055. I've check this out. There are a number of small farms there as well as four bungalows scattered about. An agency had let one to, you've guessed, Intercontinental Bodyworks until the 31st October. There's one other important development, sir. Kay asked me to update you. The tyre treads. We know the manufacturer and now we know the purchaser.'

***

Captain Andy Chappell's mobile rang, the ominous three dashes repeated. The call could only herald a problem – and it had. He had immediately pulled the Audi into the kerb and checked the display. 'Code 22' followed by a unique six digit reference. Now, twenty minutes later, he was standing, in bright early autumn sunshine, at the six digit reference location overlooking the grey, fast-flowing River Avon awaiting some startling news or a stinging rebuke from Colonel House-Layton. It would be a surgical rebuke and an ultimatum.

Whilst 'Code 22' was the top priority code, the colonel seemed in no particular hurry to get to the point, but Chappell knew that that was when House-Layton was at his most formidable.

Colonel House-Layton had arrived casually enough, seemingly more interested in the nautical activities on the bank opposite than talking to Chappell. But Chappell knew that the colonel was ever watchful, the location chosen, as all the others, so as to allow multiple ease of access and egress and, more importantly, privacy without attention.

Andy Chappell resented the calm confidence of Colonel House-Layton who, pointing up the river one minute and down the river the next, explained with effortless ease the significance of the Roman port at Sea Mills and recounted details of the disastrous wreck of the steam ship *Demerara* in 1851. His resentment grew as he began to get colder, the chill wind funnelling up the river, and he realised that his colonel's knowledge wasn't restricted to the historical. House-Layton had been prepared for this rendezvous, comfortably clad in a green Barbour, muffled again the chill by a Peruvian lama wool scarf whilst Chappell, in open necked shirt and light-weight pullover, shivered in what was for him the unexpected cold. House-Layton pointed along the bank.

'It was just here in years gone by', commented the colonel, 'that, as a safety precaution, sailing ships were required to unload all their gunpowder before proceeding up river to the port of Bristol. It was a sensible precaution, of course. The last thing the city merchants wanted was for a small fire on board one ship to get out of control and endanger the hundreds of other ships berthed at the quays alongside the warehouses, destroying their considerable investments. Their thoughts were that the gunpowder stored here would be in safe hands, to be collected when the ships return down stream to trade across the globe'. The colonel turned and faced the captain. Although the colonel appeared outwardly calm, Chappell detected the utter coldness in his eyes as he continued. 'I'm disappointed with you, Andrew. *My* thoughts were that this part of the operation was also in safe hands, but I believe that matters are slipping out of your control and endangering our global operation.'

'I can assure you, sir. Everything is under control.'

'I *know* that it is not under control, Andrew', replied the colonel, the uncertainty in the captain's voice confirming his thoughts. 'And I will tell you why. My office is automatically informed of any PNC checks made on our vehicles. I now know that the local police have been making enquiries regarding the Audi allocated to *your* team. I also know that enquiries have been made regarding Intercontinental Bodyworks at Companies House'. Chappell tried to remain composed but he was shaken and his discomfort continued as the colonel questioned his subordinate.

'There has been police interest at Avonmouth, Andrew?' asked the colonel, although he had no knowledge of any.

'Yes, sir', he said, thinking it better not to lie.

'And the nature of this interest?'

'A policeman came around to enquire about a missing person', he replied, conveniently omitting to describe the missing person as a lorry driver.

'What rank was he?'

'An inspector, sir.'

'Name?'

'Taylor. Taylor, sir.'

'Did this *Inspector* Taylor enter your premises?'

'Yes, he did.'

'That was a mistake, Andrew.'

'He just pushed his way past one of the men, sir,' blustered Chappell in a weak attempt to place the blame on others.

House-Layton ignored the response. 'So you didn't think on your feet, Andrew. You failed to use your initiative. You allowed this, this copper', he said condescendingly so as to humiliate the captain, 'to control the situation, yet you seem to consider yourself capable of holding the rank of major'. This last remark struck Cappell like a blow to the stomach, as was intended, but the colonel continued: 'You could have told him that there was heavy overhead equipment, that there were chemicals, that there were Health and Safety issues, in fact told him anything. You should have done what most competent policemen do: they ably talk their way in and out of problems. Instead, you allowed this copper to run rings around you. All you had to do, *captain*, was to be a little more clever than this … copper.'

'You are quite right, sir. I should have had a grip on the situation', said Chappell as he tried to recover.

'And what did this policeman do, once he'd entered the premises for which *you* are responsible?'

'He gave the men a copy of a missing person poster and just showed an interest in the lorries', he said but, in seeking to minimise the significance, drew attention to the nature of the police enquiry.

'For heaven's sake, Andrew. Policeman don't just show an interest because they have nothing else to do. My experience tells me that policemen suspect everyone and believe no one,' continued the colonel, then adding as if exasperated: 'I had hoped that you would have grasped the importance of this operation?'

'I did … I mean I do, sir.'

'I am not convinced that you have taken on board anything I said to you in the House of Lords', snapped House-Layton. 'This operation is sensitive in political terms and delicate in terms of execution. Like the Bristol merchants, we have made a huge investment with our partners around the world. The operation involves an array of foreign countries, including the United States and Australia. A number of satellites have been re-tasked as part of this tricky operation.   Do you have any idea at all what it takes to re-task one bloody satellite, let alone three?'

'No, sir.'

'It requires months of ball-numbing negotiations, gentle persuasion and lots of toadying.   The result has been that numerous agencies are cooperating in a manner previously unknown as are government departments and ministers.   Yet, what we have is a series of disturbing events, the first of which is that one of *your* men is AWOL.'

'I'm sure there was nothing in this visit, sir', said Chappell, in an attempt to divert attention away from the missing Warrant Officer, 'Just a copper being nosey.'

'The result of this copper "just being nosey" as you put it, is that the manufacturer of the tyres fitted to *your* vehicles has alerted me. An Inspector Taylor from the Severnside Police, phoned them early this morning. This inspector now knows that the tyres were part of a MoD consignment. I am also informed that a "Mr" Taylor visited Swindon enquiring about renting office space and the PNC checks on the Audi allocated to your team were made by an Inspector 2121 Taylor. As I see it, this operation is very likely to develop into the worst military cock-up since the British retreat from Kabul in 1842'. The colonel paused, then added: 'and that will put permanent pay to any notion you had of promotion, unless you get to grips with it.   On your present form, I'm just not convinced that you are up to it'

'I'm up to it, sir. I can get on top of this.'

'Right, you listen in', said the colonel as he jabbed his index finger at the captain. 'I will expect you to sort this mess out by all and any means appropriate. I am off to Australia tomorrow evening and shall be away for about two weeks. During that time, I will expect you to have slowed this inspector down. I don't care how this is done. Discredit this copper, discredit his boss, whatever is expedient. Use your imagination and arrange for him to be breath tested if you like or get him photographed with a hooker, but just do it. Use your ex-buddies from 14 Company if you wish. However, whatever you do must be plausible and deniable. I don't care what it is provided it deflects attention away from this operation until after the 11th October. Are you clear as to this requirement?'

'Clear, sir.'

'Secondly, it is very likely that between now and when you put the breaks on that inspector, the police will pull you in for a "routine" check. You better make sure that you have your cover word perfect and ensure that there are no documents on you or in your vehicle that will reveal anything about this operation or your true ID. Do you understand?'

'Absolutely, sir. The only documents I have on me are the driver's licence, certificate of insurance, the RAC card and two bank cards. All false, of course.'

'OK', said the colonel sternly, although both men knew that the RAC swipe card also gave access to a number of military and intelligence facilities.

Without another word the colonel walked away down the tow path to the main road and across the dual carriageway to his parked car, leaving Chappell to shiver at the river bank. He was satisfied that his caustic remarks would serve to motivate Captain

Chappell. In this, the colonel's assessment was correct, although he would not have anticipated the consequences.

For Chappell's part, he remained on the river bank, frustratingly kicking stones from the path into the grey waters below, now oblivious to the chill in the air. He was angry, an anger that would prove fatal.

Eventually, Chappell slowly sulked back to his car, hands thrust into his pockets. As he walked he brooded over this latest turn of fortune, the coveted rank of major slipping through his fingers and all because, he reasoned, of the snoopings of a nosey copper.

Chapter 15

Tuesday 18th September.

Bristol, England.

SHE WAS seated behind her desk dressed in a pretty, candy-stripped dress with puffed sleeves, starring up at him with those big Audrey Hepburn eyes. They were both facing away from the door and towards the harbour window, so engrossed in their conversation that they did not notice DI Yin standing in the carpeted corridor. Jane Hart was silent, full of concentration. Mark Faraday spoke softly and DI Yin could not hear the words but, whatever he said resulted in an outburst of giggling from his secretary. As if delighted for her happiness, he took her right hand in his and squeezed it gently as she mouthed a silent 'thank you'.

DI Yin tapped on the open door. 'Good afternoon, sir', she said cheerfully as if oblivious to the scene she had witnessed and holding up her laptop. 'Not any great breakthrough, but interesting and confirmation, I think.'

'I would be grateful for anything at the moment', said Faraday as he waved the DI into his office. 'The stop checks Monday morning didn't throw any light on Atkins at all, although there were two arrests. A disqualified driver and someone wanted for fine default.'

He took his seat behind his desk as DI Yin opened the laptop she had placed near his blotter. Her fingers glided over the keys and the screen quickly came to life.

'As you know', she said. 'details of stolen vehicles remain on PNC for only six years and these are the Mercedes-Benz lorries stolen six years ago', she said as she swivelled the laptop towards her superintendent.

She learnt over the screen and pressed a key. 'And five years ago', she said, pressing the key repeatedly, 'and four, and three, and two and one year ago'.

'Quite a few, Kay.'

'Yes, there are but, may I?' she asked as she moved to Faraday's side and pressed another combination of keys. 'I've been playing with this. You see, if we look specifically for Mercedes-Benz Actros lorries, the pattern understandably changes.'

'And just the tractor units?' he asked.

'Precisely,' she said with a beaming smile. 'If we look just for the tractor units, not the whole rig or rig and cargo, the number of tractor units stolen country-wide is very much smaller. If we then look at any location in the UK, Lancashire, for example, and display the thefts of Mercedes-Benz Actros tractor units for any of the six years, then display on the screen only those vehicles still outstanding', she said, pressing the keys again, 'and compare the data with similar thefts in the greater Bristol area, there are statistically more vehicles outstanding in a seventy mile radius of Bristol than any other similar area. I've tried this with Cardiff, Newcastle, Leeds and other similar-sized cities. The statistical pattern is clear. You will remember that Atkins' own vehicle was not fitted with a name board or painted with any company logo. Well, PC Blake has checked the details of the Mercedes-Benz Actros tractor units stolen in the greater Bristol area ...'

'Let me guess. None of these vehicles were badged?'

'Correct, sir. And it works out that every nine to thirteen months, for the last six years, a Mercedes-Benz Actros tractor unit has been stolen in our area – and not recovered.'

DI Yin stood back from the desk as Faraday turned to look out of the window. 'What this does …', he mused, then paused. Kay Yin realised that to interrupt would break his thoughts and so remained silent. '… is to confirm our suspicions that an individual or individuals may be methodically stealing a particular type of vehicle. But it brings us no closer to identifying this person or these persons. Nor does it provide a tangible links with Atkins'. He reflected again and smiled up at her. 'But, I would bet that there is a link somewhere. Nice work, Kay. And, Barry Atkins, wherever you are, nice work, too.'

She closed down the laptop and began to leave the office. 'I assume that there's no need to brief Inspector Trench on these statistics?' she asked with a raised eyebrow.

'I don't think they will help him with his enquiries, although we might have to alert the Stolen Vehicle Squad. If it is the case that most of the vehicles went abroad and with Atkins missing, the possibility of recovery or arrests is little better than nil at the moment… Let me sleep on it', he said. As she began to walk from his office, he added: 'And I'll pick you up at 9.30 tonight?'

***

Captain Andy Chappell waited impatiently for his call to be answered. When the call was answered no one spoke. He wondered where they were.

'It's Andy', he said at last.

'Yeh?' came the non-committal and indistinct reply.

'I need a *black knight* job done.'

'OK', the voice said as if the task was of no consequence at all.

'When?' the voice asked.

'ASAP.'

'OK. Call me: 79.'

***

Faraday had picked up DI Yin from her Redland address at 9.15pm. By 10.15 pm he was driving his C70 convertible up the long gravelled, tree-lined driveway illuminated throughout its length by ornate lamps, to the blue and white striped canopy outside La Rochelle Casino on the outskirts of the city of Bath. He pulled the Volvo to a halt at the foot of the sweeping stone steps below the main entrance. Coming towards him in evening jacket and bow tie was Winston, the Jamaican who worked security and also acted as one of the casino's car jockeys. Winston wasn't walking, he never did. He seemed to jive, perpetually in motion, as he went to the passenger door and held it open. Kay Yin took his extended hand as she stepped from the car, his eyes following her as she made her way up the steps towards the white glazed door opened by two men dressed as Regency footmen. DI Yin looked nothing like a police officer, dressed as she was in a beautifully embroidered, gold coloured, Malay *kebaya* – and that was her intention, an intention to appear completely un-police officer-like and to be on a par with the most glamorous of guests. On both accounts she succeeded.

Faraday drove his car a few yards further on and parked as Winston approached. They shook hands.

'How are you, Winston?'

'I ain't good. I'm a sufferin' from them wid-draaaal symptom. Every time I get out of one of them there cars it's always the same. Mercedes-Benz wid-draaaal symptoms is the worst, man'. He rolled his eyes in his head and chuckled infectiously. 'The little Chinese chick is working the tables and knows to expect your friend.'

'Thanks for preparing the ground.'

'It's no bother. I told the Chinese chick that she had nothin' to fear from you', he replied. Then he loped off and was gone as more cars streamed up the driveway, their headlights illuminating the great house and creating moving shadows behind the Doric columns, the arrival of other cars drawing the two men apart.

They knew each other well. Both had lost their fathers too early and both lived by their own codes. Each gave the other respect and a friendship had grown that neither abused. It had begun eight years before when Detective Sergeant Faraday had been part of the team that investigated the murder of Errol Langston, a pimp who had been lured to a telephone kiosk and, whilst taking a call, his throat had been slit. Errol Langston had been Winston's older brother. When Winston and his mother had gone to the mortuary to formally identify Errol, Winston had been an angry young man, seemingly ignoring the careful and reverent way in which Faraday had drawn back the shroud. He became even more angry when he saw Faraday comforting his sobbing mother. 'Hey, wha' you doin' man? That's my job', he had shouted but, when it came time for

Errol's funeral, Winston had gone to the police station and asked Faraday to attend.

The number of cars approaching La Rochelle lessened and Winston was able to take a break. He suggested that Faraday take a coffee in one of the lounges, but Faraday joined Winston in the staff quarters at the rear of the house, happier to be away from the falsehood and pretence above.

At five past eleven, Winston received a call on his ear phone – Detective Inspector Yin was just about to leave.

They drove back to Bristol along the A420 and, at Tog Hill, could see the panoramic lights of Bristol before them. But DI Yin did not notice the remarkable view, her thoughts elsewhere. She had prepared for the interview with Miss Jennifer Ooi, a Chinese-Malay croupier, but her enquiries only revealed Barry Atkins as a moderate spender who had modest wins from time to time. He was considered a quiet, inoffensive man, fastidious in his appearance and polite in the presence of beautiful women.

'I think he was actually very shy', said Kay Yin, 'but he certainly welcomed the attention of the girls.'

'What did they think of him, the girls?'

'He was a regular. Visited about once every two weeks, so most of the girls knew him and liked him. He wasn't arrogant or clipped his fingers at them like some. He didn't grope or leer. He just liked their company.'

'Did he ever boast, talk about money, that sort of thing?'

'No, he didn't, or so they say. Miss Ooi did ask him what he did for a living and he said that he was a lorry driver.'

'Did she believe him?'

'No. She thought he probably owned a small car showroom, a small garage somewhere, something like that.'

This was probably a reasonable assumption, concluded Faraday. Lorry drivers are not usually associated with gambling. Faraday's mind drifted to Barry Atkin's home.

'And the photograph?'

'No significance there. There is always a photographer on hand in the casino and they charge exorbitant prices. Good quality photographs, but pricey. You were right. Three of the photographs on the wall were definitely of girls from the casino and we know that two were taken on-board ship and another appeared to have been taken in a stately home. Photographs taken in the casino are put into cardboard presentation folders and are collected from cloaks as the punters leave.'

'So he must have had them all especially framed afterwards?'

'Yes', she replied, then added: 'and then perfectly displayed in his home.'

Faraday reflected upon what he had been told. It all seemed to describe a man who had created for himself a little make-believe world, safe and comfortable.

'Did Miss Ooi say that he was seeing any of the girls?' he asked as they drove into Kingswood on the outskirts of Bristol.

'Seeing punters is a sacking offence, although she says that some of the girls have dated punters. But, she is sure that none of the girls were seeing Atkins.'

'They thought him pathetic?'

'No, I don't think so', considered DI Yin. 'Atkins would always have a meal alone in the restaurant, so the girls fussed around him a bit.'

'Why?'

She thought for a moment before answering, drawing together the threads and innuendoes of her conversation with Jennifer Ooi. 'Because he was never a nuisance or a problem to them. I think they liked him because he was … harmless.'

Chapter 16

Thursday 20th September.

Bristol, England and Sentosa, Singapore.

IT WAS dark. There was no moon as they parked in The Ridgeway, an exclusive road of million pound priced homes. Number 3 was one such: vacant and for sale. The grounds of all these homes, for the most shrouded in black, impenetrable shadows, were extensive and the rear gardens long – ideal for ex-members of 14 Company.

The route taken by any normal visitor to the apartment block would have been along the side of the driveway through the pleasantly lit gardens to the front door but they had taken a different route, approaching the apartments via the long back garden of the vacant house and into the small but dense Sheep Wood. It was pitch black. They were unseen.

The apartments were three stories high but built on a gentle slope. As a result, there was a further floor at lower ground level for waste bins and utilities, reached from the communal hallway by a flight of stairs. The rear door here was also controlled by an electronic lock, but this presented no obstacle to these men.

They were good, these former members of a Covert Method of Entry Team. As they walked towards the front door of the policeman's apartment they appeared as two friends visiting a resident. The mortice lock provided only a minimal delay to entry and the digital alarm was by-passed within seven seconds. One of the men went to what appeared to be the study, the second to the bedroom. The first man carried nothing as he went about his work. The second man's task was much simpler, he carried only a thick A4 sized envelope.

By 12.33am both men were back at The Ridgeway. The whole operation had lasted 21 minutes.

***

Colonel House-Layton, travelling as Mr Jeremy Latimer, had had a pleasant stop-over in Singapore. He had stayed at the Rasa Sentosa, the country's only beachfront hotel, overlooking the sandy white Siloso Beach and the South China Sea beyond. In addition to shopping for Mrs House-Layton and taking afternoon tea at the Raffles Hotel, the colonel had, as planned, met with the British High Commission's military attaché in War Memorial Park, an innocent enough activity enjoyed by many – and observed by their Russian counterparts from their embassy near Lermit Road. That evening, at 7.25pm, he would board flight QF078 for Perth, Western Australia.

Chapter 17

Friday 21st September.

Western Australia and Bristol and London, England.

QF078 TOUCHED down in Western Australia at 12.25am local time. Mr Jeremy Latimer queued with the other passengers at immigration control and tediously moved slowly forward until beckoned to a desk.

'The nature of your visit to Australia?' the official asked.

'Conservations,' replied House-Layton without any pretension. Never good idea to be pretentious, thought the colonel, when visiting Australia. 'I'm doing some work with your Department of Conservation and Land Management.'

She smiled, but persisted. 'And where will you be travelling?'

'Down to the Fitzgerald River National Park, across to the Nullarbor Plain and then the Great Victoria Desert'.

She turned the passport one way then another as she thumbed through the pages and checked the black, green and red coloured circular, square and triangular immigration stamps 'Well, enjoy your visit, sir', the official said as, satisfied, she returned the passport to House-Layton.

House-Layton, carrying his hand luggage, collected his one suitcase from the carousel and then queued whilst his bags were scanned again and sniffed by two dogs, one attempting to detect illegal drugs, the other the illicit importation of food or vegetation.

Immediately outside the terminal, House-Layton waited for his car. He didn't have to wait long. Almost immediately, a silver grey Holden Commodore pulled into the kerb. The driver got out and made a pretence of examining a reservation print-out. The ID card within the folds of the paper were confirmation as was the driver's code name.

'Only one message for you, sir', said the driver as the Holden drove towards the Swan River. 'I was told to tell you: "Black Knight to White Bishop".'

***

Faraday chaired 'morning prayers'. Thankfully, it had rained heavily the previous twelve hours which had resulted inevitably in a reasonably quite night – more minor RTAs than anything else. The briefing had been principally concerned with the plans for the weekend and as the DCI, Geoff Fowler, had returned from his holiday leave, this would allow Faraday to take leave the forthcoming weekend.

The DCI, DI and Faraday huddled around the coffee table as the other officers left his office.

Once he heard Inspector Trench barge his way noisily out of Jane Hart's office and into the corridor, Geoff Fowler spoke to Kay Yin. 'Trench obviously didn't like the boss praising you', he said to DI Yin and, turning to Faraday, continued. 'He doesn't think he's likely to be promoted CI does he?'

'He's put his application in', replied Faraday diplomatically. 'The first to do so.'

'You better hurry up then, Kay', said Fowler as, in unison, the DCI and DI looked at Faraday.

'We've discussed it, Kay', said Faraday. 'I said to you that I was aware that Geoff would recommend you. Put in your application and we will support it.'

'But I've only been here six weeks.'

'But you've been an inspector for three years, that's long enough and you have your Hong Kong experience as well. In any case, I have spoken to your previous district commander. He is prepared to put on a joint report with me that we will both sign.'

For the first time, both men saw DI Yin embarrassed. 'I am grateful. There's a lot of good people out there', she hesitated. 'It's very good of you both. Can I think about it?'

'Of course', replied Faraday, 'you have to do what you are comfortable doing. Let me say this to you. There are good people out there, but we are thinking of the good person we have here and the closing date for applications is next Friday, the 28th. OK?'

'OK, sir.'

'Now, before we all go, Geoff', said Faraday, 'I had better update you on another aspect of Mr Barry Atkins.'

Superintendent Faraday briefed his DCI a little so that he would not be compromised, but Geoff Fowler, like a naughty schoolboy, wanted to know all the details. When Faraday had finished he posed one question to the DCI.

'Maybe, I am making too much of this. Atkins being some sort of serial lorry thief is pure speculation although I think we can say that Intercontinental Bodyworks have a connection with the military. Whether they have been involved with the disappearance of Atkins is just more speculation. I'm minded to let Trench run with the Misper angle. If Atkins is simply missing or even worse, we can't at the moment do any more than provide the extensive publication that's now in train.'

'We lost the moment with the delay in receiving the information that he was missing', observed Fowler. 'Any possibility of timely action was lost with Trench's lack of interest and dithering about when we did know the guy was missing and Wynne-Thomas sticking his fat nose in.'

'Well, we are at where we are at', said Faraday. 'What I propose, if you agree Geoff, is to leave this case with Trench, but I don't want to leave it alone. I'm sure that the lorries won't be moving for another month and I think I have a way of getting to them. It's better if I have a private ferret about, but I may need to utilise Kay from time to time.'

'Fine with me', agreed the DCI. 'I know Kay will tell you and me if this gets too heavy for her or interferes with her other duties.'

***

Detective Sergeant Jim Dow had been at work in the large, busy office at New Scotland Yard since 7.40am. The office was open-plan but as tight as a drum, certainly as secure as the Special Branch offices along the corridor. There was a single point of entry, a camera and intercom protecting the reinforced double doors. It was now nearly one o'clock as the FBI transmitted their early morning list.

DS Dow had been one of the Met officers sent to New York in the aftermath of 9/11, their prime role to assist in the identification of the bodies of UK subjects. It was in the nature of things that he should now be one of the detectives with a liaison role with the FBI. Jim Dow had collected the list and returned to his work station, one of a long series of identical, partitioned areas a little over five feet by seven feet, his own private and disturbed world. To his right was his computer screen which gave access to that world, but, immediately in front of him, on the pale blue baize partition, was his constant reminder of sanity, a picture of his wife, Ann, together with badges from the FBI and NYPD.

As with most of the suspects, they made little effort to disguise their identity and, consequently, were surprisingly easy to track down. DS Dow assumed it was contemptuous arrogance. But he didn't care. It just made a murky job so much easier.

Within an hour, most of the home or office addresses had been established. PNC and local intelligence checks were quickly made, but a routine reply to one of these checks meant that DS Dow needed to report to Detective Inspector Matthews immediately. The revelation was not unique but DS Dow thought it prudent to close the DI's door before he spoke.

DI Matthews examined the FBI printed list and the hardcopy responses from PNC and the Severnside Police. Satisfied, DI Matthews dialled a Bristol number.

***

Miss Baker was a rather rotund headmistress, usually jolly and full of optimism, but she was more distressed now than ever. She had taken the call shortly after her PA had brought in her afternoon tea.

She didn't drink her tea nor did she eat the Chocolate Hob Knobs biscuits.

The call had confirmed the anonymous letter delivered to her earlier in the morning, a letter she had placed in a desk drawer. The letter had been marked 'confidential' but was, nevertheless, opened by her PA. Miss Baker knew that once the contents were known, there would be disruption and distress. She thought, but only for a fleeting moment, to do nothing but her PA had read the contents and now there was the phone call. The caller's voice had not been loud, but it had been heartless.

It would be horrible, she thought, but she pressed a key. Her PA answered.

'Yes, Miss Baker?'

'Get me Mr Geoffrey Brittan on the phone', she said in a monotone voice. 'Then ask Mr Fowler to see me but, at this stage, not a word to anyone else.'

Chapter 18

Sunday 23rd September.

Bristol, England.

NORMALLY HE would be awake within seconds. This morning it was so different. Maybe it was because he knew he was not on-call as the senior duty officer. Maybe it was because he knew, for the first time in over a year, complete contentment.

'Mark', she said, shaking this bare shoulder gently, 'Mark, the phone.'

He began to wake from a deep sleep, confused both at the sound of the phone and the scent of *Amor Amor* by Cacheral, his mind dream-like at the thought of the previous evening and early morning. He began to turn around to face her and put his arms around her to hold her close.

'Mark', she said as she kissed him on the lips. 'You must wake up, darling. The phone. It might be important.'

He turned back towards the phone and gathered his thoughts. He looked back towards her once more then, reluctantly, threw the duvet off and swung his legs to the bedroom floor. He focused on the bedside clock and noted the time: 04:47. Mark Faraday picked up the cordless phone.

'Hullo', he said, not recognising the caller's mobile number displayed on the screen.

'Sorry to trouble you, sir', said Inspector Trench in a self-important tone. 'But Mr Wynne-Thomas asked me to contact you. You are to report to District HQ immediately.'

Faraday tucked the handset under his chin as he stepped into the en-suite, returning to the bedroom and began to remove a pair of boxer shorts from a drawer. 'What's the situation, Gordon. Brief me?' asked Faraday, assuming that a major incident was already underway and that Trench, as the night tour inspector, was informing his superintendent of developments.

'I'm afraid that I can't go into details now, sir,' he replied with the cockiness in his voice of someone who was in the know.

Faraday wondered if an MP or even a cabinet member had been arrested and Inspector Trench was concerned not to make an unguarded remark. 'Gordon,' said Faraday calmly. 'Obviously you can't talk, but I need to know what to wear. Plain clothes, uniform, riot kit or what?'

'Plain clothes would be appropriate, sir', replied Trench.

'I'll be there in fifteen minutes.'

Faraday arrived at his district headquarters at just before ten past five. With Chief Superintendent Wynne-Thomas in attendance and the apparent urgency, Faraday had assumed that he would have seen some indications of a higher than usual level of police activity, maybe crew buses parked in the road, handlers assembled in the police yard trying to keep their dogs quite or huddles of expectant officers talking and smoking, but there was nothing. In the station office, Faraday saw Sergeant Hodder.

'Good morning, sir', said the sergeant.

'Good morning, Jim. Where's Inspector Trench?'

'Oh, he's up in your office with the chief super', he replied with a troubled expression. 'It doesn't look good, sir. "Cold Call" is up there too', he said, referring to the nickname used to describe Detective Chief Inspector Malcolm Cole from the Professional Standards Unit.

'Any idea what's up, Jim?'

'I haven't a clue, sir. I'd tell you if I knew, even if they told me not to.'

'Well, I better find out. Thanks Jim', he said as he stepped up the stairs. The corridor was in darkness except for the light that shone from Jane's office. Faraday walked through his secretary's office into his own office.

'You better shut the door, Faraday', said the chief superintendent. The act of shutting the door at least served to give Faraday a few seconds to calm himself. He was irritated to find Wynne-Thomas sat behind his desk with Trench lounging in one of the easy chairs at the coffee table.   Trench wore the self-satisfied smirk of someone not in jeopardy but simply the spectator to events likely to cause ruin to others, confirming his thoughts that one of his staff was in trouble. Wynne-Thomas and Trench were both in full uniform and so Faraday felt under-dressed. DCI Cole, wearing a perfectly cut grey suit, was standing to the side of the chief superintendent, a clip board under his arm, his facial expression giving credence to his nick name.

'There's obviously a problem, sir?'

'You are absolutely right, Faraday,' replied Wynne-Thomas in a tone that suggested that it would be quite natural to assume that problems would habitually be associated with Faraday and his district. 'There is a problem. The problem is that one of your inspectors has been arrested.'

Faraday's mind raced with the possible permutations with thirteen inspectors. An inspector arrested for drunk driving would not necessitate the presence of a chief superintendent or Professional Standards, although a death by dangerous driving would, but the inspector's district commander would ordinarily have been called first.

'Would you care to tell me who the inspector is?'

'Taylor has been arrested', he replied gruffly.

'On what charge?' asked a stunned Faraday.

'He's a bloody paedophile, that's what he is', he said loudly, spitting over Faraday's desk, 'and you knew nothing about it.'

'Where's he being held?' asked Faraday, ignoring the veiled criticism.

'Southmead', replied Trench, emphasising that he was aware of facts before Faraday.

'I can't believe it', said a shocked Faraday. 'I just wouldn't have believed this of him. What was it, complaints from a neighbour?'

'His home was raided a short while ago and his computer seized', said Wynne-Thomas.

'And pornographic literature, hard pornographic material, was also found', added a gloating Trench.

'What about his daughter, Emily?' asked Faraday.

'She's with her aunt', replied the chief superintendent, although Faraday had not missed the slightest hint of a furtive glance between Wynne-Thomas and Trench.

'Who's dealing?'

'It's a crime and so Detective Superintendent Jarrett is dealing, with Mr Cole, of course.'

'Will he be released on bail?'

'Not for a while, I shouldn't think', replied the Welshman caustically. 'You should know what these paedophile rings are like. In fact, I can't understand how a former Vice Squad detective like yourself has allowed this to be going on under your nose.'

'How am I supposed to know what staff do in their private lives. Paedophiles are secretive and devious ...'

'Gordon here', interrupted Wynne-Thomas, 'had his suspicions.'

'Well it's a great pity that Mr Trench didn't share his suspicions with me', said Faraday to the chief superintendent.

'It was difficult to have the confidence to share my suspicions with you, sir, when David was known to be one of your favourites', sneered Trench.

'It must be an even greater pity that you did not have the confidence to approach Mr Wynne-Thomas with your concerns', retorted Faraday.

'The facts are, Faraday, that Taylor is in a cell where he belongs and he's off limits. You know the procedure. No one has contact with him. His only avenue of contact is Superintendent Jarrett and Malcolm here'.

'And who is acting as Mr Taylor's friend?' asked Faraday.

Wynne-Thomas seemed startled by the question. 'He hasn't asked for one and I can't imagine anyone wanting to be a friend to a paedophile. Can you?'

'The Federation should, nevertheless, provide a friend. If they won't, I will act as his friend.'

'Are you mad?' snapped the Welshman. 'You will do nothing of the sort.'

'I'm sorry. Why not?'

'Because there would be a conflict of interests'.

'How can there be a conflict of interest?'

'Because I say there is.'

'Then can you say why I am here?'

'You are here to search and empty out Taylor's locker and then inform the nigh shift when they go off at six and the early shift when they come on duty. So we better decide what you are going to say that explains Taylor's absence.'

At 5.50am, the night tour assembled in the briefing room as the early tour came on duty. Inspector Trench had deliberately added to the drama by creating a mysterious atmosphere by saying: 'Move on into the briefing quietly, the superintendent wishes to inform you of a serious disciplinary matter in progress'. As a result, there was a mixture of amused or detached interest and anxiety. Police officers don't like disciplinary enquiries which often degenerate into the investigating officers engaging in fishing expeditions, in which the slightest oversight is discovered. Faraday checked with Trench that all were present. Satisfied, he walked to the front of the briefing room.

'Good morning everyone', he said. There were a few muttered replies whilst Trench stood near Faraday concentrating on what he was about to say, waiting for an indiscretion. 'Some of you will be eager to get off to bed, so I will be brief. I have to tell you that Inspector David Taylor was arrested in the early hours of this morning'. There were muffled mutterings.

'Quiet', barked Trench unnecessarily.

'He was arrested', continued Faraday, 'as the result of information received from the Metropolitan Police and is being held at Southmead. I am confident that Inspector Taylor will be released very shortly. Meanwhile, Detective Superintendent Jarrett and DCI Cole are the officers in the case. Other than the fact that, for the moment, Inspector Taylor is no longer on duty, his absence should have no impact whatsoever on your daily duties. Are there any questions?'

'What was he arrested for, sir?' asked a young PC.

'I am aware of the initial reasons for the arrest, but as I am confident that this matter will be quickly resolved, I do not propose to add to any rumours at this stage.'

'But, sir', asked another PC, 'there will be rumours if we don't know.'

'I'm not going there', he said forcefully. 'If I told you that Mr Taylor had been arrested for theft, you would ask whether it was shop-lifting or robbery. If I said that it was robbery, you would ask whether it was armed robbery. If I said that his arrest was in connection with a sexual offence, you would ask if he had been caught with a prostitute or had indecently assaulted a male in the toilets. You know the score, so no further comment from me, other than where is PC Ross?'

There was movement to the left of the assembled group and a hand was raised.

'Good arrest last night, officer. Well done', said Faraday, referring to the young constable's arrest of youth who had threatened the officer with a knife.

The constables and sergeants shuffled out through the double doors leaving Faraday to reflect. He hoped that the mention of an arrest in connection with a sexual offence would completely deflect their thoughts away from sexually-related crimes. But Faraday knew that they would all soon know.

Chapter 19

Monday 24th September.

Bristol, England; Western Australia and Victoria.

IT HAD not been the easiest of days for anyone. Speculation regarding Inspector Taylor's arrest was rife. One rumour was that he had been taken, under high speed escort, to London. This was untrue. Another rumour was that the David Taylor was being detained in police custody for a further twelve hours in accordance with Section 42. This was true.

Chief Inspector Alan Moore, Faraday's deputy, had quickly got to grips with the organisational consequences of David Taylor's absence, not only in respect of Taylor's routine day-to-day responsibilities but also in connection with three future operations and five court cases involving the inspector.

The presence of DCI Cole at the district HQ, together with his unsmiling assistant, DS Grimms, checking and cross-checking Taylor's duty roster with the inspector's desk diary, pocket book, incident logs and vehicle log books, did nothing to lighten the atmosphere at the station.

At a little before 5pm., Jane put through a call to Faraday from the office of the Deputy Chief Constable. The news was worrying.

'I've just had a call from the Press Office', said the DCC, 'as a result, I have had a very difficult conversation with the editor of the Bristol Evening Post. The editor says that an officer from your district has informed them that Taylor is being held in connection with sexual offences.'

'Are they going to run with it?'

'As the informant was anonymous, she's prepared to hold back, although there will be a short "stop press" item to the effect that a local police inspector has been arrested in connection with unspecified charges', he said, adding ominously: 'What the hell's happening on your district, Mark?'

'One of my inspectors has been arrested on, as yet, unproven charges and someone has informed the press,' he replied calmly. 'I'm not clear how the leak is known to come from my district. Do you know, sir?' he asked logically.

'The point is', he said ignoring the question, 'that there is a problem on your district and it doesn't reflect well on you, Mark.'

'I'm sorry, sir', replied Faraday defensively, 'but if this was an operation on district that went wrong, I would accept responsibility for that. But the arrest of Inspector Taylor is incidental and, if anything, doesn't reflect well on the force.'

'The problem I have, Mark, is that you are a bright and imaginative, but unconventional officer, and I always feel uncomfortable with you. I'm never sure what you or your district are up to.'

'All our targets are met. Arrest figures are better than virtually all other districts. Sickness rates are continuously lower than most and our level of complaints from the public is astonishingly low'.

'That may be so, Mark, but the only complaint I'm interested in at the moment is the one concerning Taylor', replied the DCC. 'Meanwhile, contact with the press will only be through the Press Office via me'.

'I understand, sir'.

'Let's hope this doesn't get worse, Mark', he said abruptly and rang off.

But it would get worse. Mr Geoffrey Brittan was already in possession of a Section 44 Emergency Protection Order.

***

Colonel House-Layton found the Eucla Basin of the Nullarbor Plain an amazing sight, a panoramic aquamarine blue shimmering wilderness of eucalyptus and acacia trees, scarred and criss-crossed by light brown tracks, stretching into the parched distance where a crisp, pale blue horizon met a cloudless sky.

But the Great Victoria Desert was something else, thousands of square miles of stubbled nothingness, yet a landscape filled with many thousands of strange plants adapting to very specific conditions and most found nowhere else on earth. House-Layton's Australian liaison, Lieutenant-Colonel Doug Coulton, together with Reggie Tjamiwa, an Aboriginal nature reserve warden, had been splendid guides and tolerant companions, providing the overt exposure that House-Layton needed so as to confirm his apparent interest in crop diseases and pest control measures. Now a meeting with Dr. Noel Vindent, a plant molecular geneticist from RMIT University and consultant to the Plant Disease Diagnostic Unit, would put in place the final piece of the deception jig-saw.

They met at the Riverside Restaurant on the waterfront of the Yarra River, Melbourne. Colonel Coulton chose their table with care. It was his 'usual table', a table with a prime river view yet apparently secluded and discreet. But Coulton knew that their conversation could always be overheard by those seated the other side of the twin pillars and ornate trellis. He was confident that their conversation would be overheard today by the Russians – and it was.

Vindent was typically Australian. He spoke with directness and candour, with an accent as if the vowels had been flattened out. Highly intelligent but self-deprecating, it was not hard to maintain the illusion of showing keen interest in the doctor who made his specialist subject mysterious and fascinating.

'Jeez, the disease', he explained as they ate Salmon with Lobster Butter Sauce, 'is essentially caused by fungus-like plant pathogens that have the remarkable self-preservation ability to manipulate biochemical, physiological and morphological processes in their host plants with devastating results'. He paused as he pointed an empty fork towards House-Layton. 'The most obvious, I suppose, and a good historic example is the Irish Potato Famine of 1845, as a result of which over a million people died. You see, the fungus attacks the roots of plants that then die of thirst. It's as simple as that.   Once the disease takes hold you have an advancing wavefront of infestation'. The doctor replaced his knife and fork on his plate and, pushing the back of his hands away from his chest, demonstrated how the disease ravages all before it. 'This is why this disease is known as "DieBack".'

'DieBack?' asked House-Layton innocently.

'A good name, don't you think?' he asked rhetorically. 'You see, once the disease takes hold, it moves rapidly and is pretty difficult to control. It's a clever little bugger too, and capable of surviving for extended periods of time.   When the conditions become favourable, they germinate and start again, just like the salt water croc'.' He looked at them both with a huge grin, then winked as he learned forward. 'When you ain't expecting him, he bites you in the pants.'

'You say that this "DieBack" phenomenon is also connected with insects?'

"That's true. "DieBack" has three causes. One is the use of too much bloody fertiliser, but this need not concern us today. Another is the fungus and a third is insects. Insects, particularly bud, stem or root-boring beetles, can kill a sizable tree within weeks. Dutch Elm disease is a fine example. Of course', he said with a chuckle, 'they're little buggers. They bore away and that ain't too good for the tree, but the primary damage is the activity of a fungus discharged by the beetles in order to break down the wood. It's this fungus that allows the beetles to digest the wood. Then they flit from tree to tree and spread the disease. Bit of a pisser, wouldn't you say, with these little fellas munching away and spreading a disease at the same time.'

'Is this an unusual combination?' enquired House-Layton.

'Oh, Jeez, no. Humans are doing it every day. You only have to think of AIDS and HIV'.'

'I hadn't thought of it like that', remarked a slightly embarrassed House-Layton.

'No reason why you should', said Dr Vindent. 'It caught the Canadians by surprise too.'

'The Canadians?' asked House-Layton, pleased that the British Columbian dimension was neatly introduced into the conversation for the benefit of the Russians.

'Yep, the little Mountain Pine Beetle. This little fella is chomping its way through the British Colombian interior creating a dead sea of red trees covering an area of 17 million acres'. The doctor checked his watch, 'but, hey, we can discuss this further this evening over dinner. I need to get back to the office and you have some shopping for Mrs House-Layton before you fly home tomorrow.'

'No, not tomorrow', replied the English colonel. 'Doug has arranged a visit to Melbourne gaol tomorrow, then I fly up to Sydney the following day. Two full days with my cousins in Manly, then back home by 6am the 30th.'

'You'll like Manly', said Noel Vincent as they shook hands before he made his way back to his Swanston Street campus. The two colonels walked towards Melbourne's most opulent shopping area, the Block Arcade.

Chapter 20

Tuesday 25th September.

Melbourne, Australia and Bristol, England.

IN MODERN Melbourne, the three storey gaol doesn't seem as imposing, formidable and daunting as it had when it first opened in 1845. Back then it was Victoria's first purpose-built prison, constructed of local bluestone and modelled on London's Pentonville. It covered an entire city block between Latrobe Street and Franklin Street. Most of the inmates, men and women, were a mixed and sorry crowd, their crimes ranging from lunacy and illicit distilling to arson and murder.

The main gateway of the prison still stands today, as does the main cell block and a small part of the perimeter wall at Russell Street. New prisoners were lodged in the ground floor cells which measured about nine feet by five. They were kept in solitary confinement for twenty-three hours each day with a bath and church parade every Sunday. Each cell was provided with a Bible. The routine of daily work was governed by the ringing of a bell, a bell that told them to wake, to eat, to work, to pray and to sleep. The penalties for failing to comply with this regime were severe and included flogging. The guide, Mr Murchison, explained that when an official entered a cell the prisoner was required to stand in the centre of his cell, facing the door, hands at his sides and heels close together.

As they walked along the cool interior, the guide recounted knowingly the history of Melbourne Gaol, particularly emphasizing that the prison had been the scene of 136 executions by hanging. He pointed out some of the exhibits of death masks and old records describing the mad but beautiful Martha Needles of Adelaide who murdered one husband, two children and a brother-in-law and the tale of the flamboyant Frederick Deeming of Sydney who murdered two wives and four children. However, Mr Murchison considered that the most famous execution took place on the 11th November 1880. The condemned man was only 25 years of age. His name: Ned Kelly.

The three-storey cell wing was vaulted like a narrow cathedral nave. Colonel House-Layton walked along the landing of the first floor at the end of which was the place of execution, identified by a trap door. Above the trap door was a sturdy wooden beam, nine feet in length, fixed firmly into the masonry of the thick walls. From this beam would have been attached the noose. The guide positioned himself under the beam and, with accompanying dramatic hand gestures and facial expressions, described the grisly procedure, how the prisoner would stand on the trap door, the rope around his neck, the knot, as was the custom, placed under the jaw-bone on the left side. Mr Murchison explained, solemnly but objectively, that a successful execution was all a matter of weight and distance, the distance of the drop being such as to ensure that the rate of fall would break the condemned man's neck. If the drop were to be too short, then death would be by way of painful strangulation, the eyes would bulge and the tongue would swell, unconsciousness overcoming the victim within about four minutes and death about six minutes later.

***

The bell rang and the officers knocked on the door. There was no response. The bell rang a second time, but still there was no response. Both officers began to force the stout door until the lock gave way and the door flew back against the inside wall.

He was at attention facing them, hands at his side and heels together. An open Bible was on the floor. He seemed to move slightly, probably as a result of the swinging door. His eyes bulged in his head and his swollen tongue drooped sideways from his mouth. Inspector David Taylor was dead. He had hanged himself.

Chapter 21

Wednesday 26th September.

Bristol, England and Manly, Australia.

MARK FARADAY was already half-way along the corridor as Jane Hart called him back. 'You'll want to take this call', she said. Faraday knew that Jane Hart would not waste his time and returned immediately.

'Who is it?' he asked silently as he entered her office.

She closed the door to the corridor and mouthed 'Susan Tope.'

Faraday picked up the phone. 'Hi, Susan', he said to the crime scene manager, 'It's Mark. Do you have any news for me?'

Susan Tope was able to give Faraday some information, but she was in a difficult position. She had been given very strict parameters in which to work and her task was to report directly to the Investigating Officers, Jarrett and Cole, and not others, however genuine their interest. Nevertheless, Faraday quizzed her but carefully made limited requests of her. Her answers were specific when she was able, less so in respect of other issues. Nevertheless, she detailed her conclusions as a result of her examination of Inspector Taylor and his apartment, together with the findings of the post-mortem.

'So you see, Mark, there is very little doubt that Inspector Taylor committed suicide. There is not the slightest evidence of foul play or some other person's involvement in his death.'

'No evidence of someone else in the apartment?'

'Not really. There were, of course, the fingerprints of Taylor and his daughter and there were some other prints in the kitchen, dining room, bathroom and daughter's bedroom, but these were clearly of a young person, probably a friend of Emily. There was certainly no evidence of anyone wiping down surfaces of the doors or the computer or computer desk. There were no prints on the porno magazines and, whilst the front door lock and door jam were broken when the police broke in, there was no evidence of any previous attempts at a forced entry.'

'What about a cleaner?'

'Mark', she said patiently, 'there were no cleaners or delivery men. That won't be a fruitful avenue for you.' Susan Tope was going to say more, but couldn't. She hoped she had said enough. 'Look, I have to go. Just think about what I've said and ... and, if you come up with anything else, I'll have to act upon it', she offered and the line went dead.

Faraday realised, as he drove to Force Headquarters, that there would be no early closure. What he did not realise was how cruel and bloody that closure would be.

At headquarters, Faraday had spoken with the Assistant Staff Officer and had been asked to wait in the secretariat. He had been offered coffee which he had accepted and drank whilst looking out over the tranquil Gordano Valley. After only a few minutes, Detective Superintendent Jarrett and DCI Cole arrived, both carrying ominous-looking briefing files. They ignored Faraday as they were both quickly ushered into the Deputy Chief Constable's office.

Forty minutes later, Jarrett and Cole emerged, together with Wynne-Jones. 'Follow me, Faraday', said the latter as the trio exited the secretariat towards the chief superintendent's office. Obviously, thought Faraday, the DCC was distancing himself from the circumstances surrounding the death of the inspector.

By the time Faraday had collected up his cap and briefcase and returned the coffee cup to the side table, the three were already in the Welshman's office. Wynne-Jones, owl-like, had occupied his chair behind his desk with Jarrett and Cole seated in comfortable chairs to his right. Faraday was left to sit against a wall in a rather stiff-backed and uncomfortable chair so that he had the benefit of looking directly at Wynne-Thomas behind whom were three shelves filled with regimented rows of police caps from forces around the world. The shelves were clearly not part of the original fittings and would have looked more in-keeping with the stockroom of a theatrical costumers.

'I have had a long discussion with the DCC and I am grateful for the help I have received from Superintendent Jarrett and Chief Inspector Cole, as is the Deputy. This is a very sad business with a sad end. Fortunately for the force, Taylor's death means that we can draw a line under this affair. Mr Jarrett has spoken with Taylor's sister and his brother who lives in Saltash.'

'Torpoint, sir', corrected Superintendent Jarrett.

'Thank you', snapped Wynne-Jones, clearly irritated that the flow of his carefully prepared address had been interrupted. 'His brother, who *lives in Torpoint*, has agreed that the funeral will take place discreetly in Devon. The funeral will be a private affair and only attended by the brother. There will be no police representation.'

'No representation?' questioned Faraday.

'At the express request of the family', replied Wynne-Thomas with a thinly disguised smile, pleased that it had not been difficult to persuade the brother of the reasonableness of Jarrett's suggestion. 'Whilst I acknowledge your previous experience in handling the funeral arrangements for dead police officers', said the chief superintendent disdainfully with obvious reference to the murder twelve months before of Constable Karl Norris, a death that Wynne-Jones considered Faraday responsible, 'your expertise will not be required on this occasion. Nor will your input be required in respect of the only remaining matter, namely the question of the coroner's inquest. These papers will be prepared by Mr Jarrett.'

'And that's it?' asked Faraday.

'He was a flawed man, Faraday, a man with hidden and dark secrets', he said in a mournful tone. 'He's dead now and it is better for all concerned to ensure that his secrets remain very secret.'

'I understand that it will be better for the force, sir', replied Faraday realistically, 'but I feel uncomfortable. As far as I am aware, there has not been the slightest indication of Inspector Taylor's propensity for child pornography prior to the information received from London.'

'Faraday, there is no purpose in disturbing muddy waters now. We must think of his daughter', suggested Wynne-Jones reasonably. Faraday thought of Inspector Taylor's daughter and a mixture of sadness and anger assailed his thoughts, thoughts of a pretty young girl without a father or mother, a life stripped of the security offered by loving parents.

'Her name is Emily', he said, his anger barely concealed. 'It's Emily and Emily's life has been ruined already.'

'The police service didn't ruin her life, Faraday. We acted, properly, on information received. And I should not have to remind you, Faraday, that we did not take her into care. That was an entirely independent decision taken by Social Services as the result of anonymous calls to her headmistress.'

Maybe it was at this point that a doubt entered Wynne-Jones' mind as Faraday hung his head thinking of a vulnerable young girl being taken into the care of the local authority, the intimate physical examination and the personal questions that followed. He spoke again, for a moment, sympathy in his tone.

'Mark, it is best to leave this well alone'. Faraday remained silent and the sympathy was short lived as he continued more formally: 'The DCC's view is that, like many officers during their careers, Taylor was subject to a routine investigation which most of us are able to take in our stride. Unfortunately, Inspector Taylor, a hard-working officer who had, with hindsight, clearly not recovered from the death of his wife, took his own life.'

'And that will the official line?'

'That *is* the official line, Faraday, although we all know that there is little doubt as to his guilt.'

'Is there no doubt?' said Faraday quietly, knowing that none of these men would really listen.
'Taylor's sister is disgusted and ashamed which, I think, is very telling'. Faraday was about to comment that such a reaction would be reasonable and did not necessarily indicate guilt, but Wynne-Jones continued rapidly. 'There is, of course, the

irrefutable evidence of child pornography found on his computer and the obscene magazines discovered hidden under his bedside cabinet. I also firmly believe that a guilty conscious was well established by his use of a Biblical reference', concluded the chief superintendent.

'How?' questioned Faraday.

'The page at which the Bible was left open provides plenty of evidence of guilt', observed DCI Cole as he quickly opening a file and thumbed through some documents. 'For example, the Biblical references to "save me from all my transgressions" and "remove your scourge from me" and "you rebuke and discipline men for their sins"'.

'And which Psalm is that?' probed Faraday.

'39', replied Cole.

'But, as I understand it', replied Faraday without revealing the information he had been given by Susan Tope, 'the Bible was on the floor and open at two pages that contained Psalms 39, 40 and 41. There is no evidence that Inspector Taylor was drawing our attention to Psalm 39, was there?'

'I think that can be reasonably assumed', replied Cole defensively.

'Do you? I don't assume anything', replied Faraday sharply. 'Inspector Taylor could have been equally drawing our attention to Psalm 41 that talks about malicious enemies, people providing false evidence and people believing the worst.'

'I think your personal regard for Inspector Taylor has coloured your judgement', commented Jarratt.

Faraday realised that all three men had discussed not only Inspector Taylor but also his likely reaction and were of one mind. Common sense dictated that Faraday should accept the 'official' version of the events surrounding the suicide of the inspector but he opened his briefcase and removed a note pad.

'My judgement, if pressed, would be that Inspector Taylor may well have been drawing our attention to Psalm 41', he continued, 'particularly the references to enemies and false witnesses. If I am correct, I believe he was also saying something else. He was saying that the force had let him down. You only have to read the text about those in whom he placed his trust. This wasn't an admission of guilt, the text actually says: "I know that you are pleased with me ... In my integrity you uphold me and set me in your presence for ever".'

'How did we let him down?' demanded Wynne-Thomas indignantly. 'We acted in good faith.'

'We may have, initially, but Inspector Taylor was treated worse than if he had driven his car carelessly and accidentally killed a little child. He was deliberately isolated, denied any contact with his former friends and colleague. The force acted like a bunch of witch doctors.'

'What are you talking about?' Wynne-Jones' anger matching Faraday's.

Faraday was minded to explain the practice of some witch doctors who would cast their spells and destroy an individual in their community. Of course, it had nothing at all to do with the witch doctor's professed magical powers, it was all to do with isolating completely the victim who, denied contact with others, having no where to go and knowing that he was finished, would just give up and die.

'Nothing, sir', replied Faraday. 'A silly comment to make. I should have taken some leave in June. Maybe I should take a few days off.'

Wynne-Jones was always wary of crossing swords with Faraday and so was relieved that there was an opportunity for the meeting to finish on a positive note.

'You *are* looking tired, Faraday. You should take a few days off', he said enthusiastically.

'If you don't mind, sir, I think I will.'

***

As a sailor approaches Sydney Harbour, he will see to port the craggy outline of South Head and to the starboard the wooded North Head with the old quarantine station, beyond which is the suburb of Manly. The harbour of Sydney has a shoreline that extends for more than 150 miles and consists of dozens of back bays and hidden coves. An efficient passenger ferry service connects all the coves, inlets and landing stages with the main ferry terminus at Circular Quay in the heart of Sydney just below her great harbour bridge. Every twenty minutes or so, a ferry will dock alongside the jetty at Manly Cove. Passengers will disembark and walk up the slight rise and, along The Corso with its shops and cafes, to cross this isthmus of land to Manly Beach and the Tasman Sea.

Manly Beach is a magnificent mile-long, palm-lined beach of pure white sand. At the southern end of the beach is a pleasant coastal path leading towards the small and sheltered Shelley Beach. At a point where this coastal path changes direction and the traveller turns his back on Manly, there is a wooden bench providing a perfect view of the beach. On the bench is fixed a neat brass plate engraved with the phrase: *'Another Day in Paradise'*. Colonel House-Layton thought that the phrase described perfectly the view, as he sat there with his cousins, Rachel and Paul, and the evening sun began to loose its brilliance. But a telephone call interprupted his moment in paradise and brought the colonel sharply back to reality. He stood up and pulled his mobile from his pocket.

'Yes?'

'It's Andy, sir. We have a problem.'

'Go on', he said, smiling and raising his eyebrows to his cousins.

'A police inspector has hanged himself and the press have got hold of the story.'

'No doubt the press would', he replied without committal, always conscious that the conversation could be monitored or even recorded by Chappell himself.

'It's headlines. Over the front page', said Chappell, his voice laced with anxiety.

'Do the newspapers speculate as to the reason for this man's foolish behaviour?' asked House-Layton reasonably.

'No.'

'Which newspapers carry the story?'

'Local and national.'

'Headlines in both?' he asked calmly.

'Headlines in the local paper.'

'And the nationals?'

'Yes.'

'To what extent?' asked the colonel, exasperation mounting as he had to extract the most obvious details from the captain.

'Five or six lines on the third page of *The Independent* and on the fifth page of *The Telegraph.*'

'You said that there was a problem, Andrew. There is only a problem if *you* make it so. Very tragic, of course, but as far as I am concerned, this has nothing to do with our enterprise. We can meet up in two days', he said, finishing the conversation abruptly by closing his mobile.

As occurs in the southern hemisphere, sunset came rapidly at Manly Beach and, for Colonel House-Layton, this moment of paradise was lost forever.

Chapter 22

Monday 1ˢᵗ October.

Bristol, England and Venice, Italy.

JANE HART had driven Faraday, in her neat yellow and silver coloured Smart car, to Bristol International Airport at Lusgate Hill, eight miles south of the city. It was easy for him to always enjoy her company. She was pretty, bright and optimistic. Her conversation was light, but she was also knowledgeable and widely read, consequently, there was much that they would talk about.

On Faraday's *Application for Leave* form, he had endorsed the destination of his holiday as 'touring Italy', although Jane, and Jane alone, knew the details of his Venetian hotel. But, whilst he felt relived to be taking a short holiday, he felt uncomfortable taking leave at this time, although he knew it would be, in part, a working holiday.

'Don't feel guilty about taking some leave', she said as they approached the airport. 'You were on duty all over Christmas and the New Year. And you didn't take your leave in June, just those few days in April. Anyway, you might find out something about Barry Atkins in Venice.'

'Let's hope so', he replied, slight depression evident in his voice. 'There's not much more to go on, which reminds me, can you remind Kay about those tyres. We know they were an MOD order, but we need to know the unit allocated. Can you do that? I know she was being stone-walled'.

Jane Hart took her hand off the gear stick and touched his knee reassuringly. 'Kay was waiting for a contact in the MOD police to get back to her, but I'll remind her', she said, 'Don't worry.'

'This is a frustrating business', he said as they pulled into the kerb in front of the terminal. 'I don't mind the operational stuff, but HQ seem to be more concerned with the bureaucracy and playing politics. Politics are necessary, I suppose, but there always seems so much to do, one futile meeting after another and more and more reports to read or write, all with unnecessary, ever diminishing, deadlines', he replied as she switched off the engine. 'It's a bloody good job that you are there to support me, Jane. I would be a complete mess without you.' He squeezed her hand gently.

'Yes you would, wouldn't you', she said with an Audrey Hepburn smile as they got out of her car. He slammed the passenger door and picked up his bags but stood in the road as she stood on the kerb so as to make up for the difference in their heights.

'You know how much I rely upon you', he said, a statement not a question. Jane Hart didn't reply as they kissed each other on the cheek. It was a small gesture, full of mutual affection that did not go unnoticed by the two men, both leaning on the first floor railings of the terminal building, overlooking the arrival of passengers and the check-in desks.

***

Four hours later, Faraday at last began to relax. He smiled at vivid thoughts of indistinct origin as his *vaporetti*, a water bus of Venice, pulled away from the jetty and made way, gradually increasing its speed.

The ride of the water bus was smooth but cumbersome in comparison with the craft he passed, their pilots so typically Italian thought Faraday, glossy black hair, dark glasses, confident tans and wide grins, who manoeuvred their sleek speedboats of black hulls and varnished wooden decks with disarming skill, effortlessly responding to their deft touches on helm or chrome throttle. These fast boats seemed to be able to pirouette to a halt or gain speed with elegant ease as the waterborne traffic made its way back and forth between the straight corridor of massive wooden stakes, each a pointed cluster of three bound at the top with a thick iron hoop, a watery highway Faraday had seen from his Easyjet Boeing 737 as it made its final approach across the *laguna* to Marco Polo airport.

It was a beautiful, sunny, afternoon and the water was otherwise so still, disturbed only by the fluorescent wake of the speedboats or more portentous launches. He travelled light, one small suitcase and one piece of hand luggage – he only required toiletries and a change of underwear, socks and shirts. He told himself that he was on holiday. The visit to Venice, once described by Nicetas Chroniares as the 'eye of all cities' was unofficial although he had spoken with the International Police Association in Nottingham. The IPA had provided, as they would for all police officers holidaying abroad, the contact details of a fellow IPA member in Venice.

Whilst at Bramshill, the police staff college in Hampshire, Faraday had met police officers from Rome and Naples as well as members of the Carabiniere whom he thought wore the finest police caps in the world. He knew that the police structure in Italy was quite complex with state and penitentiary police in addition to the Carabiniere. And then there was the more local police, the Polizia Provinciale and Polizia Municipale, but there was another important arm of law enforcement, the Guardia di Finanza who dealt with fraud, money laundering and tax evasion. Faraday's IPA contact in Venice would be Ispettori Vincenzo Molino of the Guardia di Finanza.

As the *vaporetti* passed to the left of the Island of Murano, famous for its glass making, glimpses of the *Loggetta*, the clock tower of St Mark's Square, could be seen beyond. Within a few minutes the *vaporetti* approached the Lido where the waters of the Lagoon of Venice met those of the Adriatic and resulted in a gentle, but discernible swell. Mark Faraday's hotel was situated on the Lido itself, one of a series of long, narrow islands that protect the *laguna* from the harshness of the Adriatic Sea. The boat berthed, exactly on time, at the Piazzale Santa Maria Elisabetta and, with others, Mark disembarked to walk the short distance along the road of the same name.

The hotel was a 1930's version of a Venetian *palazzo* and abutted onto the main road. It was quiet and modest, a four storey building with a small reception area off of which was a dining room that served only breakfast. The receptionist was welcoming and spoke excellent English. Forms were endorsed and identification exchanged for brass keys – no swipe cards here. The staircase and the hallways were shaded and cool, Mark's bedroom clean with an en-suite. The second floor bedroom itself had three tall windows overlooking the main road, the middle of which were French windows leading out onto a narrow balcony, deep enough to stand and admire the view up and down the road. On each side of the road were inviting pavement restaurants, the proprietors of which were bustling about preparing for the evening trade. Faraday checked his watch and returned to the bedroom.

He unpacked his small bag and took a refreshing shower before strolling down the Gran Viale Santa Maria Elisabetta, stopping to window shop for shoes and shirts. Near the Via Scutari he was attracted to Casamia's. Maybe it was the bright awning, the red and white chequered table cloths or the urns with their neat shrubs that attracted Faraday, although it was probably an unconscious decision, a natural choice of venue that provided a clear view of the road junction and pedestrians walking up from the jetty or down from the Piazzale Bucintoro.

Faraday settled into a comfortable wooden and canvas seat at a table set for two. The waiter approached without fuss and enquired in English if Faraday would be dining alone. Faraday reflected that he must have appeared very English as he explained that he would be alone. The waiter cleared one place setting at the same time apologising that Faraday was alone but assured his diner that the cuisine of Casamia's would be something to be remembered. And it was. Faraday chose *Funghi al Olio*, mushrooms marinated in garlic and lemon, as his starter, followed by *Pollo alla Diavolo* as his main course. He drank still water and sat quietly, avoiding the temptations of the sweet trolley but finishing with a coffee.

An Italian family nearby pulled on cardigans but Faraday did not recognise the slight chill in the air and welcomed the opportunity to relax in an evening without interruption from pager or telephone, surrounded by care-free people at ease with their world. But he was suddenly alert again. He stiffened in his chair and studied one of the assistant chefs just beyond the marble step that led up to the wide entrance of the inner restaurant.

The attentive waiter had noticed Faraday's interest and came across to his table. He enquired if Faraday had changed his mind and wanted, after all, to choose a dish from the sweet trolley. But Faraday declined asking instead for a second *latte* and the bill. The waiter returned to the building and, as he mounted the single marble step, turned towards Faraday and gestured with both hands towards the sweets then shrugged with mocked sadness before he disappeared into the gloom.

The sweet trolley was a large, three-tiered affair with peaches in Chianti wine, milk and caramel puddings and crepes with Mascarpole cream. There were *Zabaglione* cakes as well as a glass bowl of fruit salad and a coffee and cheese cake trifle. But it was the *Tiramisu ai fruitti di Bosco* on the lower tier that had attracted him or, more accurately, the way in which the assistant chef had knelt down and placed this sweet on the shelf alongside a huge whipped cream trifle. He had worn latex gloves. Susan Tope had said that no fingerprints had been found on the pornographic magazines hidden in Inspector Taylor's apartment and had she not encouraged him to 'just think about what I've said'.

Faraday closed his eyes. He recalled Susan being very positive about Faraday not bothering to pursue enquiries regarding cleaners or delivery men. She had made it clear that she had been denied her usual freedom to operate unhindered and was acting within unusually strict operational parameters under the direct control of Jarrett and Cole. But, reflected Faraday further, had she not said something about 'if you come up with anything, I'll have to act'? Was she really encouraging Faraday to think the unthinkable? He was thinking now and a picture rapidly formed in his mind, a picture which panned Inspector David Taylor's bedroom. His heart rate and anger increased as he imagined an intruder, wearing latex gloves, kneeling down in front of the bedside chest of drawers, removing the bottom drawer and placing the pornographic magazines in the space below.

As he continued to think, Faraday relaxed a little. In one sense he was relieved. Originally, he had intended to take a long overdue break and make some speculatively and unofficial enquiries at the Palazzo Vendramin-Calergia casino. Even so, he had felt he should have been back in Bristol, at least close to the case, even if he could not be officially part of the enquiry. Now he felt more comfortable as he thought about the magazines. At a time when most magazines were produced by computers and packaged by machines, the possibility that no fingerprints at all had been detected on the pornographic magazines was extremely unlikely and disturbing. The thoughts of a possible intruder with latex gloves refocused his mind. He was not scheduled to meet with Ispecttori Molino until 3pm the following day and so he would easily occupy his time sight-seeing as planned. Meanwhile, at least he could consider what he already knew – and what he didn't know.

He reached his hotel at a little after eleven, but his sleep was restless, not helped by an unfamiliar bed and the slight, but continuous, rattle of the ornate ceiling fan.

Chapter 23

Tuesday 2nd October.

Venice, Italy.

IT WAS already a pleasant 22 degrees as Faraday sat in the hotel dinning room for a light breakfast of a few bread rolls and coffee at a small table overlooking the street. The aroma of freshly baked bread was quite different from the bread back home, bread he always thought had the texture of putty. The street outside was busy, a constant procession of pedestrians purposefully making their way to work but still seeming to have the time to stop and speak to friends and acquaintances. He studied their body language, their stances, their gestures and facial expressions and wondered what it all meant in this the city of the *masques*, the masked pageants of Venice, outwardly festive but so often linked to political events and a complex web of personal intrigues.

After breakfast, Faraday quickly returned to his bedroom then strolled the half mile to the Piazzale Santa Maria Elisabetta where he purchased a three day ticket. His wait at the quay side was short, the *vaporette* on time, the crews with well practiced flicks of their wrists, coiling their ropes around cleats to secure their vessel. Faraday had consulted the ferry notice board. The *vaporette* seemed as good a way to tour Venice as any other. The number one crossed to the Parco delle Rimembranze, from there to the Arsenale and then onwards through to the Grand Canal itself.

On board there appeared to be no rush. Regular passengers knew that impatience was a futile pursuit. Whatever their inner anxieties, their journeys would be dictated by the reliable timetables. As they entered the Canale di San Marco, Faraday imagined that Venice probably looked very much as it did in the 13th century, a city of eighteen islands connected by over 350 bridges spanning 160 waterways. The longest and widest of these waterways was the Canal Grande that divided the city in two, although each part was connected by three bridges: the Accademia, the Scalzi and, of course, the famous Rialto.

They passed the Palace of the Doges on their right. To their left loomed the Punta della Dogana, the 15th century customs house, behind which was the magnificent Baroque church of Santa Maria della Salute, reminding Faraday that the Venetian Empire was primarily a trading empire that had lasted for 600 years, longer than any other European empire with the exception of Rome.

Maybe the city's title of *La Serenissima*, 'The Most Serene Republic', told Faraday something about its ladies too. They seemed to possess an elegance, something the French would probably describe as *hautre*, although certainly not an arrogance, more a confidence born of the knowledge of their remarkable place in the history of Italy and the world.

Faraday was completely absorbed with the architecture they passed, whether the imposing Renaissance elegance of Ca' Granda and the seat of the Prefecture or the majestic Ca' Persaro, the home of the Museum of Modern Art. Many of these beautiful buildings were now graceful hotels or imposing banks or, like the Palazzo Grimani, the venue for the Court of Appeal. Even the neo-Gothic utility of the Pescaria, headquarters of the fish market, and the imposing 16th century Fondaco dei Tedeschi, once a warehouse, did not fail to bring a smile of admiration to Faraday's face. But the building that brought his thoughts back to the disappearance, and probable murder, of Barry Atkins was the Lambardesque-styled Palazzo Vendramin-Calergi, one of the city's finest Renaissance buildings and now the Casino Municipale. As they sailed on, Faraday looked back at the cluster of gondolas that had gathered around white and blue poles in front of the canopied arch of the water entrance to the casino. As they progressed further, other gondolas proceeded languidly in the wake of the water bus, ribbons fluttering from the straw hats of their straining gondoliers.

Faraday disembarked at the Campo San Marcuola and walked through the Callel del Cristo to the Callel Colonna. It was easy to find. Salvatores was not only a photographic studio but the interior a bright shop that also sold the most remarkable framed photographs of Venice. Faraday entered. There was one in particular that caught his eye, taken from a boat on the Grand Canal looking towards the *palazzos* of Contarini di Figure and Mocenigo, the facades of which looked golden in the sun, soft shadows caste by the delicate stone tracery, harsher shadows by arched doorways and balconies, in front of which was a festive collection of poles, some red and white, others blue and white, the water disturbed only by an approaching gondolas, the surface of which had a dancing, prismatic quality.

'The picture is beautiful, would you say?' asked the proprietor in a charming accented English.

Before he answered, Faraday reasoned that he must have a very serious issue with his choice of clothing which was plainly far too English.

'*Buon giorno*', replied Faraday, completely exhausting his knowledge of Italian. 'I like it very much. Could you tell me the size?'

'Of course', he replied, smiling. 'It is 900 by 810'.

The picture was very captivating, capable of taking your imagination through the centuries. Faraday gaze explored the painting, his eyes darting from balcony to balcony and archway to archway; from the dark *calle* between the buildings to the even darker figures seated in the gondola. He had decided and he knew precisely where it should hang. But he hesitated. He needed to know more.

'Is the photographer local?'

'It is I', he replied modestly, delighted to share his work with others.

'It's beautiful.'

'Thank you, but it is not difficult to make a photograph when you are, all the days, surrounded by beauty.'

'And the young ladies, too', observed Faraday, gesturing towards a screen hung with portraits and, before Salvatore could respond, Faraday pointed towards one particular photograph. 'She too is beautiful and a favourite?' he enquired.

'Her name is Anna, and yes', he said, his right hand flowing in an arch towards another group of photographs, 'I take many photographs of her. It is her eyes that are so remarkable, would you not agree?'

'And is she local?'

'Yes, a daughter of Venice'.

Faraday returned to the picture he was determined to purchase and stood for a moment looking at the indistinct, sinister figures huddled in the gondola. He noted the unframed price: 170 euros. 'I will take one. Would you care to sign it for me?' he asked, unnecessarily making a gesture of writing.

'Of course', he said will a slight bow.

Salvatore disappeared through a rear door, only to emerge cradling a print gently in his arms. He laid the print down and spread it almost reverently upon the glass counter top. He placed a blotter between the print and the glass, extracted a Mont Blanc pen from his pocket and carefully, but with a rapid flourish, wrote his name. Equally carefully he rolled the print and inserted it into a cardboard tube, sealing the plastic caps at each end with a gold coloured sticky seal of Salvatores of Venice.

They shook hands and Faraday left the shop and walked towards the Rio Tera San Leonardo. Exactly on schedule, the number 52 arrived. The journey on this water bus was less romantic, travelling along the Canal di Cannaregio and into the *laguna* itself, skirting the main island and passing the island cemetery of San Michele, taking an intriguing professional interest in the water ambulances attending at the Ospedale Civile, before the Grand Arsenal came into view, the ship building yard that down the centuries had built the galleys whose flashing oars had propelled them ruthlessly along the trade routes of their empire.

Faraday stepped on to the quayside at San Zaccaria and walked the short distance to tread the grey trachite stones of St Mark's Square. He took a seat at a vacant table of the Caffe Quadri and ordered sandwiches and tea. As hoped, he was not disturbed by others wanted to share his table. Seated there in the sun was a strange experience. Faraday was surrounded by movement, whether the quiet efficiency of the waiters, the milling multitudes, the ever-present pigeons or the gentle breeze that kissed the linen blinds of the arcades that surrounded the *piazza*, yet, there was no intrusion into private thoughts and no disruption of personal tranquillity.

At ten minutes to three, Faraday walked towards the Clock Tower. The 15th century clock depicts the passing of the seasons, the phases of the moon and the movement of the sun through the signs of the zodiac. He looked up at the clock face, above which could be seen the Lion of St Mark and the bell. As the two mechanical figures struck the hour, the Italian spoke.

'Marco Farrada?' asked Ispettori Molino.

Faraday turned to see a tall, handsome man, tanned and smiling, a little over thirty. 'You must be Vincenzo Molino?' asked Faraday unnecessarily as the policeman was wearing the smart grey uniform of the Guardia di Finanza. He threw up a perfectly executed and slightly exaggerated salute.

'It is good to meet a companion from England', he replied in excellent English. 'You told that you only have a little moment and suggested we have enough for tea or, maybe, coffee.'

'Coffee would be fine, thank you'.

'Let us sit a little here', he suggested as he walked towards the Caffe Florian, its orchestras competing gently with that of the Caffe Quadri.

As if expecting their arrival, Ispettori Molino and Mark Faraday were immediately shown to a table. The table was situated in a prime position, near the orchestra and with a fine view of the square, although set apart from the others. There were only two chairs at their table, whereas the remaining tables were set for four. They ordered coffee and cakes as the orchestra began to play. Smiles were exchanged between the conductor and Molino. As they sipped their coffees, they spoke of their respective homes and their forces. During their conversation, Faraday produced a small box, about 8" by 4", and passed it to the Italian who eagerly opened it and admired the coat of arms of the Severnside Police. For his part, Ispettori Molino presented Faraday with a cap badge mounted on a grey marble base with a description, in English, of the history of his force, founded in 1774 by the King of Sardinia.

'You send me a photograph of a lady, the most beautiful', smiled the Italian. He brushed a few crumbs from his immaculate uniform before he continued. 'I know of this lady, but we know nothing, if you please to understand.'

'You mean that you can not give me any information. I understand that. My visit to your city is quite unofficial', said Faraday, slightly embarrassed.

'No, no. I have explained poorly', he said apologetically. 'Forgive me. I know who the young lady is but she has never, how you say in English, be in trouble with the police, eh?'

'I understand.'

'You say in the e-mail that your enquiry is concerning a person missing?'

'That is right.'

'Please, to be excused', said Molino. He learnt forward and for a moment the smile left his charming face. 'How must it be that a *sovrintendenti* should concern himself with one who is missing only, please?'

Faraday spoke in short sentences. 'This man is a lorry driver', he explained. 'He owns his own lorry. He has a good business. Small', he said, making a gesture of size with his thumb and forefinger, 'but comfortable. Yet he is able to have expensive holidays and visits Venice often. I know that he gambles in England. I believe he gambles here.'

'Is he a large gambler?'

'No, I don't think so.'

'And the reason for your enquiry?'

'My superiors consider him simply to be a missing person, but I think he may be dead.'

'And the lady?' he asked with the slightest of smiles.

'I think the lady's name is Anna, that she is a croupier and that he would visit Anna.'

He raised an eyebrow. 'And they were lovers, yes?'

'I'm not sure, but Anna may be able to give me some information. The truth is that all my other enquiries have been negative.'

Vincenzo Molino relaxed into his chair. 'The lady is Anna, Anna Manin, my friend', he said, pleased to demonstrate the efficiency of the Italian authorities. 'She is a croupier at the Palazzo Vendramin-Catergi. It is most expensive, many more money than a driver would be affording. I have made my enquiries. Barry

Atkins was the regular visitor to the casino. He describe himself as the man of business'. The Italian policeman pulled the e-mail from his tunic pocket and laid it on the table. 'This picture was not taken in the casino.'

'How do you know?'

'Patrons must wear the bow tie', then added with the assured knowledge of a Venetian, 'I am most certain that this photograph was made in April at the festival of St Mark'.

'Because of the rose?'

'The *boccola*', he said with the distraction of one thinking of forgotten lovers.

'It is probably not important', probed Faraday, 'but would the casino not have been a better place to be photographed with a beautiful lady.'

'That is most true, but the casino is opening only during the winter times.'

'Only the winter?' asked a surprised Faraday. 'What about the remainder of the year. Is it closed?'

'No. The Palazzo Vendramin-Calergi, it is much use for grand receptions, important conferences, the corporate promotions.'

'And Anna Manin?'

'When not a croupier, the lady employs as the receptionist and the hostess.'

'Would it be possible to speak to her?'

'Of course.   It has been arranged', he replied as if the arrangements were of no consequence at all. 'She will be in her apartment at the Campo Santa Margherita at eleven in the morning. I will see you there'.

'It has been arranged?'

'This is Italy, Marco. No one wishes the enemy of the Guardia di Finanza. We tell them and they will do. Not like England.'

Chapter 24

Wednesday 4th October.

Venice, Italy.

MARK FARADAY made his way to the Campo Santa Margherita, through the maze of narrow alleyways with unsuspected turns, of flaking plaster and exposed ochre-coloured bricks. Ispettoris Vincenzo Molino had originally arranged for him to visit Anna Manin at her modest apartment in a house of steep stairs and tiny kitchens, but Faraday preferred not to meet alone with a woman, particularly one as beautiful as Anna, conscious that all manner of allegations could be made, allegations often hard to prove but, inevitably, harder to disprove.

Both men had been seated at the tables of the Antico Capon restaurant – a restaurant highly recommended by Vincenzo Molino. Both stood as Anna approached. She was probably 26 or 27 years of age, thought Faraday, certainly beautiful with jet black hair cut short in the style of the *femme fatale*, with a beautiful smile and perfect teeth. Her strides were measured and full of poise, the white pleated skirt she wore floating around her long, slender legs as she walked. But it was her eyes, an intense crystal blue, so un-Italian, that captivated.

Initially, Ispettoris Molino spoke in Italian as he introduced Faraday. 'You will hear, Sovrintendenti, that Anna speaks the English well. She will answer your questions for you'.

Faraday thanked her for agreeing to meet him and Lattes were ordered. He showed Anna the photograph of Atkins with the rose, explaining that Atkins had been missing from the beginning of September and that he was concerned as to his safety.

'Have you seen this man recently?'

'No', she answered innocently.

'How often did he visit Venice?'

'Four, maybe five years. Now, only one. Last year and now, three times'.

'Three times?' asked Faraday having difficulty following Anna's explanation.

'Yes. In the early year, not the summer time'.

'Not during the summer months?' clarified Faraday, keen not to imply that Anna's English was a little confusing and so as not to interrupt her willingness to help him.

'No. In the April, then one time or two time in the winter'.

Faraday realised the significance but nevertheless asked: 'The winter?'

'When the casino, it is opened'.

DI Yin had only found one card from Italy in Atkin's apartment, the sender unknown, although one drawer had contained a strip of blue Air Mail stickers, and so Faraday asked: 'You wrote him cards and he wrote to you. When he visited Venice you must have talked a great deal. What do you know about Barry?'

'At first he tell me that he had big business with many trucks'.

'You did not believe him?'

'No', she replied with a smile.

'Why not?'

'His hands they tell me'. Faraday said nothing and waited for Anna to continue. 'When I stand at the table I see only the cards and the hands. His hands were the hands of hard working'.

'How were you able to talk with him?'

'He come here as you come here to this restaurant and seat. One morning he see me and we talk'.

'Why with him?'

'I like my work. It permit me to be in big house with the fine things. I eat the food of the guests, not in the dinning room but in next to the kitchen'. She stopped speaking and looked towards the Italian policeman and directed her next remark at him. 'We are permit to eat the food, you understand. They give us the good clothes and the casino, the presentations commercial, are exciting but, the men, they look down you or stall you'.

'Stall you?' queried Faraday.

Ispettori Molino suggested: 'I think Anna means the stalk'.

'*Mi dispiace*', she said, slightly flustered. 'It is difficult for me. I mean that they stalk you with their eyes'.

'I understand', nodded Faraday with a smile. 'And Barry?'

'He only wishes to be with the beau … the ladies'.

'Where there other ladies?' he asked.

'No', she replied positively.

'You are beautiful of course, Anna, but why you?'

'I not know'.

'You must?' he questioned with a knowing look.

'I did not mind being in the companies of the truck driver'.
'I can understand why Barry would be pleased to be with you, but why were you pleased to be with Barry?' he persisted.

'I come from my poor home in the Eugaean Hills but, from these table, Sovrintendenti, I was travelling your country'.

'How do you mean?'

'Barry, he would speak of London, the district of the lakes and the mountains of the Wales people'. A sadness came over Anna Manin for a moment as she realised that these pleasant conversations with Barry Atkins were very unlikely to occur again. She shrugged. 'And my English, it improve also'.

Faraday changed tack. 'You wrote to him?'

'Small times'.

'And he wrote to you?'

'He tell me when he would come to Venice'.

'When was he going to visit Venice again?'

'The next month. The October'.

'In his letters to you, did he ever say that he was frightened or worried?'

'No letter, the little card with the picture'.

'I see. Did he ever write or speak to you about being frightened or worried?'

No', she replied immediately, then her face creased with a mischievous smile.

'Why do you smile, Anna?' he asked.

'When the Guardia di Finanza come to the casino, many have that frightened look, but Barry, no'.

'He only had eyes for you'.

'Maybe', she replied lowering those intense eyes and fiddling with her cup in the saucer.

'It would be natural for any man to wish to impress such a beautiful woman as you, Anna. How did he explain that a truck driver could afford the casino?'

'He tell me that he is much careful with money and take the investment'.

'Did he ever visit the casino with other men?'

'No'.

'But you must have seen him with other men?'

'No'.

'One last question, Anna. If you had to describe Barry, what would you say?'

'You mean him, not what he look?'

'Yes, him as a person'.

'He had sadness', she replied, then added: 'It was important for his self that he come to Venice'.

Faraday turned to Ispettori Molino. 'I have nothing further'.

'That is good', said the Italian with a smile. 'Thank you, Anna'.

Both men stood and Faraday shook Anna Manin by the hand, saying: 'Anna, it has been a delight to meet you. Thank you for talking with me. I can assure you that you have done nothing wrong and no reports will be sent to the casino. You have been very helpful. What you have told me confirms my thoughts that Barry Atkins was a good man'.

'*Arrivederci*', she said to Faraday who had not the slightest difficulty in understanding why Barry Atkins found Anna Manin's company so enchanting.

As they watched Anna Manin returned to her home, the Italian policeman asked a question.

'You said that this Barry Atkins "was" a good man. You believe him dead?'

'I think he probably is'.

'Was he a good man?'

'I think he was a good man. If I find him alive, I will arrest him for theft, but that doesn't mean that he was a wicked man'.

'That is good', said the Italian nodding. 'Now, a police launch is waiting to take me to the office. You will please to be my guest'.

At the Campo San Marcuola landing stage, a grey police launch waited. As they slowly moved off down the Grand Canal, Vincenzo Molino spoke affectionately of Venice whilst the pilot and the other uniformed member of the crew sat woodenly at attention, seemingly eyes fixed directly to their front, confident that none would cross their path or impede their passage. But policemen of any nation are rarely oblivious to their surroundings.

Faraday had received a text message from Jane Hart, but was having difficulty in replying and so at the Procuratie Nuove in St Mark's Square, Faraday was able to use the telephone privately. He dialled Jane Hart's office.

'Jane, how is everything?'

'Did you get my text message?' she asked.

'Yes, I did, but I'm not certain what it means?'

'You asked DI Yin to check with the alarm company?'

'Yes, that's right'.

'The alarm company confirm that Inspector Taylor's alarm system was turned off for a few minutes on the 20th September using the engineer's code but, they have checked their records and none of their engineers attended at Mr Taylor's home. In fact, the last time they attended was in February because of a fault in the system'.

'Any up-date on the tyres?'

'Yes. The tyres where shipped to three completely different military depots'.

'Oh! Any clue why different depots?'

'No. The tyre people thought it strange because, as far as they were aware, the British Army didn't use Mercedes-Benz trucks, although they did say that the tyres would be suitable for the sort of terrain encountered in Africa. Places like that'.

Faraday's mind raced as he tried to make sense of what he had just been told. 'You mentioned the tyres being "shipped". That's just given me a thought. David said that those guys at Avonmouth mentioned that the tankers were intended for a company in Portsmouth. Ask Kay to check outward-bound shipping from Portsmouth for the next six weeks. Ask her to also check Avonmouth and the Royal Portbury Dock for any listings of three Mercedes-Benz tankers'.

'Of course. Any success?'

'Not really. Only confirms what we already know. Barry Atkins wasn't a bad guy. He liked the ladies and no doubt had a little racket on the side, but I think he got out of his league'.

'Nothing else I can do?'

'No, other than not to forget to pick me up tomorrow. The flight gets in at 10:44'.

'I know, I've checked'.

Three doors down the corridor from the office where Faraday had made his call, Ispettori Molino replaced the receiver. When Faraday left the Italian police headquarters, Molino returned to his office and shut the door. He sat behind his computer terminal and punched in his personal code. As he waited, he glanced at the shield of the Severnside Police now mounted on his wall and thought of his own police unit. He punched in a second, more confidential code. He reminded himself that whilst the Guardi di Finanza came under the jurisdiction of the Ministry of Economy and Finance, it was, first and foremost, a military corps and an integral part of the Italian armed forces, not only responsible for the investigation of fraud, money laundering and tax evasion, but also responsible for customs control and border security.

Ispettori Molino had overheard Faraday's conversation. He had heard mention of the British Ministry of Defence and military units, of Mercedes-Benz trucks and tankers at Avonmouth. He could vaguely remember an alert notice regarding three Mercedes-Benz tanker trucks carrying highly toxic chemicals, travelling from the UK to Turkey via the Italian port of Palermo. He read the details again as they appeared on his screen. The ship was the *Santo Stefano* and the orders were clear: the chemicals carried by the Mercedes-Benz tankers were extremely hazardous

but safe and that, as a result, the vehicles and their cargo need not
be inspected.

What he had overheard could be of no importance, of course, but
Ispettori Milino knew his duty. He reached for the phone and
called the Comandi Regionali.

Chapter 25

Friday 5th October.

Bristol, England.

SUPERINTENDENT FARADAY was tired. His leave finished at midnight on Thursday and by 02:27 was woken by a call and had attended the firearm's incident in Richmond Road involving an estranged husband, armed with a shotgun, who had barricaded himself in a bedroom with his four year old son. These situation, Faraday knew, were never easy to resolve, particularly as the man's demands were so unclear and rambling and a clumsily word spoken in haste by the police, the unexpected reaction of the child or simply fear could all play their part in a disastrous outcome. Homes in the immediate area had been cleared, access and egress routes secured and roads sealed. Neighbours were interviewed. Some were disinterested or critical of the father. Most were helpful. Technical Support and snipers were deployed, but Faraday had been prepared to rely upon the senior negotiator, Inspector Bob Porch. Faraday always found Porch an irritating and ponderous fellow but, for this task, he performed his role to perfection and bored the gunman into surrendering. By 11am, Faraday was in his office.

Chief Inspectors Alan Moore and Geoff Fowler briefed their superintendent on events on the district during the previous four days, the arrangements now in place to cover Inspector Taylor's absence and the inquest at 2pm.

As the two men left his office, the DCI winked at Faraday: 'I think DI Yin wishes to speak with you, sir'.

Once the detective inspector was in his office, Faraday asked: 'Do you have a plan?'

'Of course', she replied with a conspiratorial smile.

'Involving DC Pau?'

'Absolutely'.

'Then you had better implement your plan', he said almost casually but, as she reached the door, he spoke again in a much more serious tone: 'Kay'.

She turned and spoke before he could say anything more. 'It's OK. Like you, I sense there's danger, but I spent my early career in the backstreets of the Sheung Wan District. It was a tough school. I'll be fine'.

Shortly after the meeting, Jane Hart brought an early sandwich lunch into Faraday's office. This should have allowed him enough time to walk across the City Centre, along Rupert Street and through The Haymarket to the Coroner's Court but, wearing full uniformed meant that he was stopped more times than usual by members of the public.

The Coroner's Court was housed in a chapel-like building surrounded by a plain, tarmac car park enclosed by Gothic-styled black railings, overlooking the front entrance of a tyre fitting depot and the back entrance to an old public house. He entered the building and climbed the spiral stone staircase to the first floor, tucking his uniform silver braided cap under his left arm as he went. At the double doors he peered through a little window. He could see Chief Superintendent Wynne-Thomas and Superintendent Jarrett in the wooden pews, each side of a man whom Faraday assumed to be David Taylor's brother. Only a few people occupied the remaining pews: Craddock from the local Bristol Evening Post and Western Daily Press, the pathologist and the two officers who had been the first on the scene and broke down the door. There were a few others, another reporter whose name Faraday couldn't remember, a man scribbling on the crossword page of his newspaper and the usual collection of old cronies who spent the evening of their lives as interested speculators in the warmth of the court building.

The superintendent eased open the door. Her Majesty's Coroner glanced up. Discreet smiles were exchanged as Faraday slid onto the back seat. Wynne-Thomas turned around, his smile much less warm.

The inquest was a mechanical affair, like a funeral, a necessary ritual seriously undertaken, in the case of any violent or unnatural death, to establish who the deceased was and how, where and when he came to his death, in strict accordance with Section 8(1) of the Coroners Act, 1988.

The first officers on the scene gave their evidence as did the pathologist who confirmed that death was as a result of strangulation and that the injuries were entirely consistent with suicide. Chief Superintendent Wynne-Thomas told the court that no suicide note was found, a fact he explained away by saying that Inspector Taylor was essentially a private person. This outwardly plausible, but nonsensical, explanation was not questioned by the court. The chief superintendent dismissed the question of the inspector's suspension as a routine precautionary measure normally associated with any disciplinary investigation, saying that he himself had once been suspended from duty for two weeks some years before. He made no reference to the pornographic material or the opened Bible at the scene, instead saying that

Inspector Taylor had been hard working and had commendably undertaken the responsibility of raising his daughter after the very sad death of her mother. In particular, he stated that a thorough forensic examination of the late inspector's apartment had established that there was no evidence at all to suggest that other persons were associated with the unfortunate death. Inspector Taylor's brother told the court that David Taylor was often a solitary individual who tended not to share his worries and concerns with others. Finally, David's doctor was called and testified that Inspector Taylor had shown signs of depression ever since the death of his wife and medication had been prescribed accordingly.

The verdict that Inspector David Taylor had committed suicide was the inevitable conclusion. The coroner endorsed his papers and the matter surrounding the untimely death of David Taylor legally came to a close.

Faraday left the court room first and waited in the car park outside. Chief Superintendent Wynne-Thomas appeared with David Taylor's brother whom he seemed to quickly usher away whilst Superintendent Jarrett approached, or more accurately intercepted, Faraday.

'Glad that's all over, Mark', he said in the friendliest of ways. 'Unfortunate business all round'.

'May I ask a question of Phil?' said Faraday and, without waiting for a response continued: 'The only pornographic material found on David Taylor's computer relates to the 20th September?'

'Yes'.

'And the only hardcopy pornographic literature was found in David's bedroom?'

'Yes'.

'And David's fingerprints were not found on these magazines?'

'They were found under his bedside chest of drawers', he replied, avoiding the question.

'I know that not a single print was found on the magazines', persisted Faraday. 'Don't you think that curious?'

'No'.

'How many magazines were found?'

'We were only able to find six', he replied, implying that there were probably many more previously disposed of.

'What, maybe of 30 or more pages each?'

'Probably. I couldn't say with any degree of accuracy off hand. Not my usual weekend reading material'.

'And no fingerprints were found on any page?'

'He must have worn gloves'.

'How is it that the alarm was by-passed on the 20th September by an engineer's code, yet I know that no engineer attended on that date?'

'The engineer's code is often known by the householder'.

'But we know from Taylor's duty sheets and operational log that he could not have returned to his home at that time'.

'It could have been another'.

'What do you mean "another"?'

'It could have been another paedophile. A lover, maybe'.

'Oh for God's sake. Is that really the best we can do?'

'Mark, you and I have known each other for years. When you were a PC and I was your inspector, I recommended you for promotion. We don't have to fall out over this. You know that Taylor was a fine officer, but his life started to go down hill when his wife died. If my wife died, I don't know how I would cope and I don't know what was in Taylor's mind either. What we do know is that pornography of the most obscene kind was found on his computer and in his bedroom. There are a few inconsistencies in this case, I know that, but my brief is to protect the force and Emily Taylor. I'm not being smug, but I know you Mark. You will want to protect Emily as much as I do. So, let this matter die with David'.

Chapter 26

Saturday 6th October.

Bristol, England.

DURHAM DOWNS is 442 acres of municipal parkland in the heart of Bristol – more extensive than London's Hyde Park. In its northern quarter is a small collection of trees known locally as the 'Five Sisters'. Near these trees is a solitary park bench. It was here that Colonel House-Layton sat with Captain Chappell, the former approaching from Upper Belgrave Road, the latter from Parrys Lane.

'Unfortunately, Andrew, your work is incomplete', continued the colonel casually as he looked out across the park.

'I'm sure everything is done, sir', said a bemused captain, adding with apparent confidence: 'And no adverse press after the inquest either'.

'Yes, that may be so. But that is in the past, Andrew', he replied as if of no consequence. 'But what concerns me now is the present and the future. I have been informed by our military colleagues in Italy that a police superintendent from Bristol has been snooping around in Venice. This superintendent knows about your lorries and he knows that they are military lorries. I think we can assume that he also knows their date of embarkation and sailing and even their destination'. He stood up and towered over Chappell as he continued: 'No question about it, Andrew, he has to be stopped', adding reasonably: 'Get your mates on to it. Can I leave this, this final task to you, Andrew?'

'Christ, sir. It nearly went wrong last time'.

'No, not at all. It went splendidly. A meddling copper is out of the way and the coroner's inquest went very smoothly indeed'.

'Sir, I needn't remind you that I would do anything it takes, but this bloke is a superintendent. He won't be got rid of so easily'.

The colonel rounded on the captain. 'And I don't need to remind you that four of our soldiers were killed in Afghanistan last week', adding more gently: 'Now, I don't want your chums to get rid of him, I just want him off the case until your lorries are in international waters. Get this superintendent involved in a nasty fight, when off duty, of course. Or he must be shagging someone', he suggested reasonably. 'Get him caught on camera with his trousers down', he added with a smile, concluded firmly. 'I will leave it to your imagination'.

As the colonel looked at his watch and took a step sideways, Chappell stood up. 'I'll see what I can do'.

'No, Andrew. This is a *must* do', said the colonel, his cold eyes boring into the captain. 'Don't for heaven's sake fall at the last fence and allow your promotion to slip from your grasp after all your excellent work'.

Chapter 27

Monday 8th October.

Bristol, England.

DETECTIVE CONSTABLE Samuel Pau peered around DI Yin's office door. 'You wanted to see me, ma'am?'

'Come in', she said easily. 'Shut the door and take a seat'.

DC Pau of the Vice Squad sat down, unclear as to the reason for being asked to see the CID Inspector.

'It's Samuel isn't it?'

'Yes, ma'am', but everyone calls me Sam'.

'Do you like to be called Sam?'

'It's what my family have always called me'.

DI Yin thumbed through the personnel file on her desk. 'Your father is English and was gazetted into the RHKP, then returned to the UK and joined the West Yorkshire Police?'

'Yes, ma'am'.

'And your mother is Chinese?'

'Yes, ma'am'.

'You were born in Hong Kong and must now be 27 years old?'

'Yes, ma'am'.

'Before I explain the operation, show me your finger nails, please'. DC Pau extended both hands for inspection at a complete loss as to the reason for the request. Apparently satisfied, DI Yin spoke again.

'Your girl friend, Debbie, does she call you Sam?'

'Yes, ma'am'.

'Right, two observations', she said leaning forward over her desk. 'Firstly, on this operation I will always call you Sam and you must only call me Kay. If you call me ma'am, you will be back wearing a funny pointed hat. Secondly, your hands and nails are too clean. Dirty them up'.

'OK …', he replied hesitantly, resisting the impulse to call her ma'am.

'This operation will involve only you and I', she said. 'The District Commander is completely in the picture, of course, but you will discuss it with no one. You will commence your new duties tomorrow by collecting me in your car from my home at 0630'. She scribbled her Redland address on a slip of paper and passed it to the DC as she continued to speak.

'You drink coffee, Sam?'

'Yes, ma'am'.

'Milk and sugar?'

'Yes, ma'am'.

'Good. I will bring the coffee and bottled water. You will dress as if you are a labourer, a cleaner. Wear an old sweat shirt, jeans and trainers, but I don't want you to look like David Beckham going for a stroll in the park with his kids. Any questions, Sam?'

'Can you tell me what the job will entail?'

'I will brief you when you collect me from my home. For the moment I need only tell you that Mr Faraday and I will rely upon you.

'OK', he said with a huge grin and stood up, hesitated again then asked: 'Can I ask how I'm qualified for this operation?'

'It's very simple, Sam', she replied, 'You are known to be discreet, you're Chinese and your car is crap'.

***

'I've been waiting all bloody day', said Captain Chappell angrily into his mobile phone as he paced his Shirehampton apartment. 'What's happening? Have you got anything for me yet?

'Yes, I've got a lot for you, a lot of nothing at the moment', replied the ex-14 Company man irritably. 'He drives a flashy Volvo convertible. We know where he lives. .He lives alone and we think he's got a girl somewhere in the Redland area – still working on that. He's in his office now and we are on the case. As soon as we have something you can use, we'll get back to you'.

Chapter 28

Tuesday 9th October.

Bristol, England.

THE TWO Chinese cleaners sat in the window of Ma Brown's café. They only attracted mild attention from the other diners as they quietly gabbled in Cantonese. The male had abandoned his contact lenses and was wearing a pair of glasses repaired with black insulating tape. He had deliberately worn a sweat band around his head before going to bed the night before and the result was that his hair now stood up on his head, as intended. DC Pau's hair style did not look unlike that of a coconut. DI Yin wore no make-up at all and her hair had been pulled into two bunches, one on each side of her head. They sat opposite each other in a window seat, the DC facing in the direction of the blue roller doors, the DI facing towards the main road and all incoming and out going traffic. For appearance sake they read the job vacancy pages of the local paper, making a point of circling a number of items and scribbling Chinese notations in the margins as the ate their breakfast, both adopting the Chinese manner of eating, using both knife and fork to take food to their mouth.

At 9.20am, later than anticipated, a Ford Mondeo saloon approached and pulled up at one of the blue roller doors. Both occupants entered the building and activated the roller door mechanism. The door trundled up and remained open. DC Pau made an evidential note in the margin of their newspaper.

During the next forty minutes the two males would emerge from time to time to dump paint tin, sacking and sheets into a large waste bin on the haulage way for apparent collection. DI Yin's attention was elsewhere, however. Ma Brown's provided a useful but only a preliminary observation point. Whilst the café, situated on the bend in the road, gave an excellent line of sight towards the four blue roller doors, the officers could not remain there for much longer. To do so would either draw attention to their presence or irritate the café owner. Fortunately, Faraday had drafted the operational order so as to provide for a fluid and ever-changing operation which would allow DI Yin to respond to the unpredictable, but within the authority granted by a superintendent in compliance with the Regulation of Investigatory Powers Act. She had seen enough.

In case of the need to leave the café promptly, the Chinese officers had paid for their food when they ordered, an eagerness to pay that was greeted by an 'if you like' shrug from the proprietor. Once they had finished their teas, they left the café unhurriedly and walked to the DC's rusty and 19 year old Morris Marina TC parked nearby. At the DI's direction, they drove to the side of Gray, Wedge and Hodge Ltd, Coffin Makers, situated on the opposite side of the road from Ma Brown's, but further back towards the main road, and parked in the bay reserved and signed for the exclusive use of a Mr Hodge.

They both remained in the parking bay, but knew that the wait would be a short one. Inevitable some one would question their presence and, although DI Yin had anticipated that they would be approached by a member of staff, it was to be Mr Hodge himself. He drove his Jaguar into the visitor's bay and approached the passenger door of the Marina. He was probably nearing 70 years of age, tall, greying hair and well dressed, charming, although clearly annoyed that his parking bay was occupied.

'Good morning. My name is Hodge. Can we help you at all?'

'Mr Hodge, I am Detective Inspector Yin and this is my colleague, Detective Constable Pau', she replied, holding her warrant card in her lap. 'I do need your help, sir', she said, the sophistication of her speech giving credence to her story. 'For appearance sake, let us exchange parking bays. If you would care to go to your office and explain to your staff that we are new cleaners on trial whom you wish to speak with. We will follow you in with our cleaning materials. But, when we enter your office, please remain seated at your desk.'

'Of course', he said smiling, intrigued as well as conscious of her allure.

'Don't smile, sir', she said crisply. 'You are still slightly annoyed that cleaners have occupied your bay'. She winked, her smile exposing her beautiful teeth.

'Absolutely', he said, his expression changing to one of mock annoyance.

Shortly, the officers entered the managing director's office which was surprisingly modern for such a long established business. Mr Hodge was at his desk, his office window to his left, as both Chinese officers stood before him. They remained standing as Kay Yin spoke.

'Thank you for your help, sir', she said. 'Let me explain why my colleague and I are here. Please don't look out of your window,' she continued, fixing his eyes with her stare. When she had Mr Hodge's absolute attention, she continued. 'I need to know what is going on across the road and I would like to use your premises today and probably for another two days. Is that OK?'

'Well, yes,' he replied slightly confused, 'but I'm not sure how I can be of practical help to you'.

'You see, I think you can, sir', said the DI. 'There appears to be a room on this floor which is not occupied?'

'No, all the rooms are in use', he replied with a furrowed brow. 'We have been keeping observations on the building opposite but I noticed that the room, it must be the next one along from your office, has the blinds closed'.

'The old stock room', he said, grasping the significance. 'I see. You're right, of course. It contains all our hard copy records, brochures, that sort of thing. No one is in there, as such'.

DI Yin looked at DC Pau and nodded. 'Well, that better than we could have hoped. Could we have a look in there please?'

'Of course'.

'You lead the way Mr Hodge. Don't allow me to go first', she said, anticipating that this gentleman would stand aside for her to pass. 'Let us cleaners trail behind you'.

Mr Hodge led the way out of his office but, as they approached the old stock room door, DI Yin touched him firmly on the arm. 'Do *not* switch on the lights, sir'.

'Right', replied Hodge with slight excitement in his voice, pleased to be party to the officers' plans.

The room was perfect. A number of large, floor-to-ceiling cabinets provided obstructions behind which observers could be concealed away from the window and by slightly adjusting the blinds a clear view of all four blue roller doors opposite and to the left was gained.

'Your staff, do they leave the premises during the day?' asked DI Yin.

'Only for deliveries to undertakers'.

'What about lunch time?'

'No, I'm sure they don't. Most bring their own sandwiches or, oh, well yes, they might leave for a few minutes to collect sandwiches and pastries from a van that calls ever day'.

'Latimer's?' checked DI Yin, recalling the van that she had seen making its rounds at a little after ten.

'Yes, they're good people. Have a place in Blackboy Hill. Everything is fresh and of good quality. In fact, my secretary collects my lunch from them'.

'That's OK, Mr Hodge', concluded DI Yin. 'I'm merely trying to minimise the possibility of anyone in this building being involved in a conversation with the men who are working across the way behind those blue roller doors'.

'There wouldn't be any reason for that, I shouldn't think'.

'Why would that be, sir?' asked the inspector, grasping the opportunity to glean as much intelligence as possible.

'The premises were empty for months, then some men turned up, in early September I think. Vehicle maintenance or repairs, I suppose. On a couple of occasions vans have turned up, I assumed with spare parts, but other than that we hardly see them at all. Certainly not to speak to'.

Detective Inspector Yin thought for a few moments, then made her decision. 'OK. This seems ideal, Mr Hodge. In this gloom and with the tall cabinets, no one will see us here and we have ease of access. If you agree, tomorrow, my colleague and I will come here, either as cleaners or as representatives from your suppliers. It will all depend on how our observations progress today. We may have to leave quickly, of course. Meanwhile, we will be self-sufficient. We have flasks in the car. We merely need to know where your toilets are'.

'What should I say to my staff if they need access to the stock room?'

'Put a notice on the door', she suggested. '"*Defective wiring. Access only via Mr Hodge or secretary*", something like that, maybe?'

Hodge nodded and smiled but Kay Yin noticed the slightest trace of anxiety in his eyes.

'You have a question, Mr Hodge. Something is on your mind?'

'You hear so much nowadays', he said, slightly embarrassed to show any sign of anxiety, adding: 'You know?'

'I can't tell you the nature of my interest in these men, but what I can tell you is that you are being of great help to me', replied the DI with her most genuine of smiles. 'I can also tell you that these men are *not* terrorists, they are *not* making bombs or anything like that at all, sir'.

Reassured, Mr Hodge returned to his office and sat at his desk for a while. He thought of years gone by and his military service in Korea. His memories returned much stronger than he would have imagined as he thought of Kay Yin's smile, a smile he had found difficult to resist.

During the next hours, another bin containing metal scrap was wheeled out of the building across from Gray, Wedge and Hodge and larger pieces of metal were placed neatly on the concrete haulage way and around the bins by the two men. The removal of scrap and rubbish apparently finished, one of the men drove the Ford undercover behind a closing blue roller door.

At about 1.20pm., a refuse truck arrived and took away some of the waste bins, followed shortly afterwards by a flat-bed lorry owned by a local scrap metal dealer who struggled to pull and heave these treasures onto his vehicle. Photographs were taken and the details of each vehicle were logged, although DI Yin realised that their contract would undoubtedly be with the mysterious International Bodyworks of Swindon. Nevertheless, DI Yin called the duty manager of the council's recycling centre at Kings Weston Lane in order to have the waste bins discretely intercepted for later inspection.

At 3.22pm, the blue door on the extreme left rolled upwards and the Ford Mondeo edged forward to stop on the slopping concrete haulage way. The second man then emerged as the door began to roll down and got into the passenger seat. The police camera clicked as more photographs were taken, then DI Yin and DC Pau rapidly collected their cleaning kit into which they thrust the bulky camera, log book and coffee flask and made their way down the stairs to the DC's battered old Morris Marina.

The Ford was driven quickly, turning right on St Andrew Road, then north-ward on the A403 towards the Severn Bridge.

'This will be tricky', said DI Yin as DC Pau gunned the Marina TC. 'With little traffic on the road, Sam, we need to keep back as far as we can without loosing contact'.

'Yes, ma'am', he replied without resentment, acknowledging her greater experience.

The officers sped on, but, as the road curved, visual contact would inevitably be lost, anxious moments constantly repeated.
'We've lost him again', he said.

'Don't worry, Sam', said DI Yin looking up from her laptop. 'There's a dual-carriageway coming up soon, we will gain on him then'.

As they reached the dual carriageway, DC Paul gunned the Marina's 1.8TC engine to speed past the few vehicles on the road, the old car responded well to the punishment.

'There he is, ma'am', said DC Pau as they made up time.

'Well done, Sam. We are just in time. He's taking a left on the B4055 … which is towards north Bristol. We have no choice but to get in lane immediately behind him'.

The Marina was brought to a halt behind the Ford at the red signals as DI Yin leant over towards DC Pau, her head resting on his left shoulder. 'I think I know where they are going, Sam, unless they have clocked us and this is a counter surveillance move by them', she considered, talking almost to herself as much as her companion. The traffic lights began to change their sequence to green and the Ford moved purposely forward. 'We will see where they go, Sam. But no tailgating'.

The B4055 is full of bends, a rolling road with a deep drainage ditch alongside for virtually all of its length, a death-trap at night for the unwary. They had been travelling for less than three miles when the Ford suddenly lurched to the left and shot down a narrow, hedge-lined road.

'Straight ahead, keep going', said DI Yin sternly.

The officers drove on over the crooked bridge that crossed the rail track, beyond which to the left was a rough area of land to the side of the road.

'Pull in here, Sam, and reverse as quickly as you can behind that mountain of gravel and switch off'. His response was immediate. Both officers said nothing as they waited.

After a few minutes, DC Pau spoke. 'They could have driven back to Avonmouth, ma'am?'

'Always a possibility, Sam. But I think they have packed up for the night. We will wait another five minutes or so', she said, tapping the keys to her laptop.

'That's the latest, isn't it?' he asked, peering at the screen.

'Yes, it is, Sam', she replied with a mischievous grin. 'I borrowed it from Special Branch. It's a laptop plus internet, GSP, vehicle tracking, plus all the connections we need with DVLC, PNC and force HQ systems. I'm just checking back on a report', she said, not referring to the author as Inspector David Taylor. 'There are a number of houses and bungalows down that lane. The taxation people list two of the houses as small working farms and the Local Authority's Planning Department list the use of the third as short-term lets. We will drive on, Sam, I think'.

'You don't think we should have a look?' he suggested. 'I could probably cut across the fields at the back?'

'Sam', she asked incredulously. 'When was the last time you saw a Chinaman creeping along in a field behind a farm?'

'Good point, ma'am'.

'I think we can assume that those guys will be back at Avonmouth tomorrow. We can't realistically do any more at the moment', she reasoned. 'If you drive straight ahead, it will take us back to Junction 16. You can take me home so that I can clean up before I go back to HQ, but you have an early night yourself. Tomorrow, you will wear smart-casual, collect me from my home but use a pool Astra. I will make sure there is one for you. The keys will be with the front office'.

'You are going back to the station, ma'am?'

'Yes. I need to see the superintendent'.

***

The budget meeting had finished at 5.15 and Faraday helped Jane Hart clear away the cups and saucers and empty biscuit plate, the clatter interrupted by DI Yin.

Faraday had forgotten about the small raid scheduled for Thursday morning. They hoped to recover stolen tins of food which were being systematically stolen by staff from a supermarket. The raid would consist of a couple of DCs with some uniform support and a large police van and the DI needed the superintendent's signature for the finalised operational order. He sat at his desk and signed the paper with a careful flourish.

'We need to get to our homes', he said as Jane Hart brought into his office one last file for his signature. She opened the file and turned it towards him as she placed it on his desk in front of him. She pointed an exquisite finger at a dotted line on the last page of the thick document and he signed the file unquestioningly.

'It's time to go, Jane', he said. 'And I will walk both you ladies to your cars'.

As they walked along the corridor they burst into barely restrained laughter in response to one of Jane Hart's spontaneous little jokes. They made a light-hearted trio. In a short time they had become a team, at ease with each other, an ease cemented by mutual trust, a trust impossible to share with Inspector Trench whom they passed on the stairs.

The car park at the District HQ was on the left-hand side of the ground floor of the building, the outside walls of which were either a Cotswold stone or granite, above which was the first floor accommodating offices for the CID and operations and the second floor containing the offices of the District and Deputy District Commanders and administration. The first six foot of the lower part of the ground floor which faced onto the main road to the front, the side facing the municipal car park to the left and the rear wall facing the harbour itself, consisted of honey-coloured stone, immediately above which was a thin course of grey granite, followed by three rows of perfectly square Cotswold stone interspersed by identical empty gaps. A thin course of granite was immediately above this chequered pattern which was topped off by another six foot of Cotswold stone. The architects had been rather pleased with this arrangement which replicated the police chequered cap band whilst also allowing for ample through-ventilation for the large, police car park. Mark Faraday's vehicle was parked near both the staircase and the secure car park entrance. No one noticed the small remote microphone placed in one of the ventilation gaps directly opposite Faraday's car. Nor did anyone pay any attention to the two men seated in the crowded municipal car park as they drove out into The Grove and the already dense evening traffic.

***

'Yes?' snapped Captain Andy Chappel.

'We picked up a comment by the target as he left his office. He's meeting up with his girl friend tonight at eight. We know where her apartment is. Do you want her details?'

'Hey, I don't want details, I want you to do the job'.

'Some jobs we do but this one is too hot', he said with a guffaw. 'You weren't completely open with us, where you?'

'What do you mean?'

'My information is that you're already compromised and you didn't tell us that. You'll have to get someone else. Do you want the details or not?'

'Who can I get at this short notice?' he protested.

'I don't know. Get that nutter you've used before. But we aren't doing it. Now', the voice repeated. 'Do you want the details or not?'

'Of course I do'.

'Then that will be two Ks'.

***

What was scary about Mad Mike Mason was that he didn't look the slightest bit insane. In the darkened streets of Redland, he walked by unnoticed. He was neither tall nor short, old nor young, fat nor thin. He was a nobody, yet, he was everybody. He had no outstanding features at all nor any mannerism that were noticeable, other than the fact that he was always picking his nose with his index finger. For this delicate task he had allowed his nails on each index finger to be longer and, consequently, grimier that the others.

Mad Mike found the address easily enough and the parking bay allocated to number four was empty. That was good.

The front door to number four was straight-forward to open and he found himself in the darkened hallway without difficulty. This would be easy money, he thought. He went first into the kitchen at the far end of the hall, then entered the lounge, the large bay window of which gave a pleasant view of the city glittering in the street lights below. He checked the bathroom with a sniff and picked his nose again, rubbing the contents between forefinger and thumb and returned to the hall. As he did so, he heard a key turn in the front door lock and darted into the smaller of two bedrooms containing an open wardrobe lined with clothes, some outdoor coats and two ball gowns. He hid behind the clothes, inhaling the scent of her perfume through his nostrils as she entered.

Even when she turned on the bedroom light, she did not notice him. As she pulled aside some of her clothes to make a space for her car coat, he struck. His index finger jabbed violently forward and burst her beautiful eyeball before penetrating her brain. Death was instantaneous. She seemed to float down to the carpeted floor, the only sound a slurping noise as his finger broke free from the suction. He stepped over the crumpled body and, as he walked to the front door, seemingly totally unaffected by her death, there was another slurping sound as he sucked his bloody index finger.

Chapter 29

Wednesday 10th October.

Bristol, England.

THE EARLY morning was uneventful. It was not until twenty past nine when the Ford Mondeo came into view that there was some activity opposite the premises of Gray, Wedge and Hodge. The Ford drove up onto the haulage way in front of the blue roller doors and the passenger got out. DC Pau's adjusted the focus, the camera's motor whirled and potential evidence was captured on film as the man entered the reception area. Within moments, the blue door immediately in front of the Ford rolled open and the Ford drove into the building and was lost to view as the door laboriously trundled shut for the next six hours.

At a little past one o'clock, the mobile phone rang. She held it to her ear. As Faraday spoke it was as if a huge weight was crushing down upon her. Her shoulders sagged and her lungs seemed to deflate as her eyes filled with tears. She clenched her teeth together as she listened but she was unable to prevent her bottom lip and jaw trembling. She pressed her left hand to her forehead, trying to drive out the words and images but tears tumbled down over her cheeks.

'Ma'am?' asked a startled DC Pau.

DI Yin listened intently as Faraday spoke, her thoughts of those beautiful eyes and her smile crashing into the logical reasoning of a detective.

Faraday spoke for a few more minutes, his speech desperately strained and sometimes completely broken as he described as much as he knew. As he spoke of his interview at the hands of a haughty Chief Superintendent Wynne-Thomas, there was anger mixed equally with desperate sadness.

'Do you want me to close down here?' she asked.

DC Pau looked on, realising that something personal and dreadful had overtaken them.

She nodded. 'I understand, sir', she said, and slowly lowered her arm and closed her mobile phone shut.

'Ma'am?'

Kay Yin didn't answer, but sniffled and began wiping the tears from her face.

'Ma'am', said Sam Pau gently, 'I don't know what to say to help?' She dabbed her eyes with her handkerchief and cleared her throat, breathing in deeply before she spoke.

'Some complete shit has murdered Jane Hart', she said as the tears tumbled down her cheeks again.

DC Paul moved towards her and hugged her, tentatively at first and then more strongly. She didn't resist.

After a few moments she said without harshness: 'Enough of this', and pushed him away. She wiped her eyes again. 'Thank you, Sam, but we have a job to do'.

'Are we closing down, ma'am? What did Mr Faraday say?

'He said that we must go on, Sam', she said, thinking of his words and, looking directly at her younger colleague, she added in a tone that brooked no argument. 'And he's right, Sam. We keep going'. For the next two hours there appeared to be no activity in or across the road. In the little stock room of Gray, Wedge and Hodge, Coffin Makers, the time passed slowly and in silence for DI Yin and DC Pau, a silence they could almost hear.

At 3.35pm, the phantom black Audi pulled onto the haulage way in front of the fourth blue roller door, reversed and turned so as to face the way it had been driven. The Audi stopped, engine running, whilst the driver remained in his seat. DC Pau rested on the filing cabinet and adjusted his camera again to focus, pin sharp, upon the driver's head, held his breath and pressed the shutter button. As he did so, two of the blue doors to his right rolled up in unison. DC Pau refocused so as to record the registration letters and numbers of the red-on-white trade plates fixed to the front of the two Mercedes-Benz lorries. As if in response to a silent signal, their V8 539hp engines burst into life, dark grey exhaust smoke following them as they edged forward into the outside world. They were impressive, powerful-looking, eager units, their engines' seemingly grumbling as they were made to wait on the haulage way as their drivers step down from their cabs to walk back and finally lower down the roller doors which had imprisoned them. Both drivers returned to their cabs and mounted in unison as if on parade, then they moved off, followed by the Audi.

'OK, Sam. Let's go'.

'Yes, ma'am', said Pau, pleased to be active.

As anticipated, they caught up with the two Mercedes-Benz about 400 yards from the junction of St Andrew's Road with Crowley

Way. The target vehicles turned left onto the eight-lane M5 motorway south-bound at Junction 18 and across the Avonmouth Bridge that spanned the Avon River. At Junction 19, the two Mercedes-Benz and the Audi left the motorway and entered the Royal Portbury Dock Road. This group of vehicles then approached a second roundabout and the Mercedes-Benz lorries and the Audi exited at 12 o'clock, continuing toward the dock gates. The police officers did not follow.

'3 o'clock … carefully', ordered DI Yin and DC Pau responded, driving unhurriedly into Gordano Way and then left into Marsh Lane. 'Carry straight on', she said, tapping the keys of her small lap-top. 'This road will narrow and then finish at a dead-end, so just keep going for a while'.

After about a half mile the road began to narrow, bushes and brambles appearing each side as they left the industrial units behind.

'We can do without all this vegetation, ma'am'.

'I'm hoping that when we get closer to the quays, this will clear'.

They drove on and, as the lane curved to the right, they could see, further on to the left, the tall red oxide-painted metal fence that protected the docks from trespassers. DI Yin pointed to a gap in the bushes and DC Pau pulled the Vauxhall Astra to a stop. Through the bars they could both clearly see the roll-on, roll-off ships, bulk carriers and tugs. Vehicles awaiting loading onto the ferries had already been or were being marshalled in preparation for embarkation. The officers waited in silence. Within less than ten minutes the Mercedes-Benz lorries pulled into view to be shepherded into elongated parking bays by arm waving, yellow-jacketed officials.

DC Pau stretched over the seats and pulled the camera from the cleaning bag. He adjusted the lens, satisfied he leant forward across DI Yin to peer towards the ships docked in the port. As he did so, their cheeks touched.

'Sam', she said with a warning glare. He backed off.

'Sorry, ma'am'.

'Let me do it', she said patiently, taking the 300mm camera and adjusting the depth of field before taking the pictures of the Mercedes vehicles manoeuvring into bays and, a few minutes later, both drivers talking to the driver of the Audi.

'OK, Sam', said DI Yin. 'There's no need to follow. I am sure that the Audi will take the two drivers back to their Mondeo. If we drive to that open-air car sales lot in St Andrews Road and tuck ourselves away, we should see them return. You happy with that?' 'And who do we follow after that?'

'Only two choices, Sam, but I think it should be the Audi. We don't know anything about this player and I'm interested to know what he's up to'.

DC Pau started the car and drove back across the River Avon as the DI continued to consider her limited options. She checked her watch.

'It's nearly quarter to five and rush-hour traffic will be building up so I doubt if those two drivers will move the remaining Mercedes-Benz until tomorrow. If that is the case, then there is a good chance that chummy in the Audi won't be needed to act as an escort or chauffeur and we won't be seeing him again', she reasoned. DI Yin hesitated for a few moments and then made her decision. 'Tomorrow, we'll use my car as well as yours, just in case he makes another guest appearance. Meanwhile, we'll lay-up in the car sales lot and wait'.

At twenty-five past five, they both spotted the black Audi approaching along St Andrew Road, the Astra anonymous amongst a collection of second-hand vehicles. The Audi turned to its right towards the commercial units and was lost to sight. DC Pau endorsed the evidential log again as they waited anxiously. At about 5.32pm, the Ford Mondeo appeared at the junction and turned to its right, followed immediately by the Audi which turned to its left and drove back towards the motorway.

'Wait', cautioned DI Yin as DC Pau leant forward to start his car. When the Audi had travelled for about 100 yards, DI Yin spoke again: 'OK, now start her up'.

The DI's eyes were fixed upon the column of heavy vehicles approaching from the right that would provide a good screen when they needed to cross the road. As the heavy vehicles came closer, she looked to her left and ordered him forward. 'Go, go', she said and the Astra shot neatly across the road in front of the heavy vehicles to join the flow of traffic four cars behind the Audi.
'I don't think that the driver of the Audi is an amateur, so, no weaving from side to side, Sam', she said. 'Just leave me to keep him in view. Ensure that no vehicle gets between us and the vehicle in front and see if we can remain at least one car behind him'.

As the Audi approached the roundabout at the junction with the Avonmouth Relief Road, DI Yin advised DC Pau again.

'You will have to be nibble at roundabouts and junctions, Sam, or we will be left behind, but, do not draw attention to ourselves.

Remember, we are not *following* the Audi, we are *imposing surveillance on a target.*

'OK, ma'am', he replied approvingly, conscious that he was benefiting from real on-the-job training.

At the third roundabout, the Audi exited along Avonmouth Road, however, within moments the vehicle in front of the two officers turned left into Atlantic Road. They were now immediately behind the Audi.

'Everything is slowing down for the pedestrian crossing up front. You need to slow it a little more'. She learnt over towards him as if they were lovers, resting her head on his shoulder again but looking directly ahead, constantly alert for an opportunity. 'Check the next junction on the left, Sam. The boy-racer in the supped-up Citroen. Let him out, but *do not* flash your headlights'.

The little Citroen's front tyres squealed as it tucked itself between the Audi and the police Vauxhall, only to break sharply as they approached the traffic lights at the junction of Kings Weston Avenue. The lights showed green, but the officers were tense as the traffic moved slowly towards the junction. Just as the Citroen reached the stop line, the lights changed to amber, but the Citroen lurched forward, tail-gating the Audi. DC Pau drove quickly forward to cross the junction. As he did so, the Citroen moved to the right and raced up Lower High Street, over-oiling and noisy, for about 30 yards only to break sharply again as he joined the line of more patient commuters. DI Yin resumed her position, resting her head on DC Pau's shoulder.

Two junctions on the left later, the driver of the Audi indicated and turned left, then sharp right, into the gated entrance of Penpole

Court, a three-storey block of new apartments opposite a Texaco petrol station.

'Steady, Sam', she ordered. 'Take a right. Don't rush. Then right again into the filling station'.

DC Paul executed the manoeuvre perfectly and without fuss, pulling up alongside one of the pumps facing towards the apartments.

'Sam', she said. 'Fill her up but don't on any account look towards the apartments. Leave that to me'.

DC Pau nodded, got out of his car and began filling the tank with fuel.

***

They sat drinking coffee. Mark Faraday told Kay Yin as much as he knew of the murder of Jane Hart. He said that he had not visited the horrible scene but he knew how she had died. He spoke of the silver-haired Detective Chief Superintendent Arthur Thorpe who was in charge of the investigation and how Thorpe and the ACC had been present at Force HQ when Faraday had been interviewed by Chief Superintendent Wynne-Thomas, the ACC a mute finger in the background distinguished only by his shining bald head.

Faraday spoke to her of how he had been collected by a staff car from his District HQ and taken to Force HQ with Superintendent Jarratt. Both superintendents had sat in the rear of the car but on their journey there had been no communication at all, only the fleeting glances of the grim faced driver in the rear-view mirror. At least that ritual had forewarned Faraday of the seriousness of his situation and he had been able to prepare himself.

Faraday recounted how, at first, the questions had been posed by the detective chief superintendent regarding his whereabouts the previous evening. He had been able to reply that he had left his office at about 5.30pm, returning to his apartment at a little after 6pm. He recalled the interview.

'I don't wish to be obstructive, sir, but I have been brought here without explanation. Clearly you are investigating a serious matter. Would you care to tell me what this is all about?' Faraday had asked.

'All in good time, Faraday', said Wynne-Thomas.

The detective chief superintendent ignored Wynne-Thomas' interruption as he continued. 'This shouldn't take a few moments more, Mark', he said kindly, like a friendly uncle. 'You know what enquiries are often like. We need to eliminate a huge range of people from our enquiries quickly, particularly those who might be able to provide really useful background information so that our enquiries can move on. Now', he had said, trying to keep a grip on the interview, 'you said that last evening you left the station with Miss Hart, is that right?'

'That's correct'.

'Now', interupted Thorpe. 'Miss Hart's travel arrangements. Have you ever taken her home?'

'Yes, I've taken her home many times'.

'I suppose that on those occasions you have actually been inside her home?'

'Oh, yes. Of course', he replied.

'Could you tell me something about her home, her friends?'

The questions seemed intrusive and he attempted to avoid discussing Jane Hart's private life. 'It was a very neat and tidy home. Dainty. Very feminine, what I would have expected of such a person as Jane'.

'Very feminine, you say', interjected Wynne-Thomas. 'Miss Hart had been your secretary for nearly a year now. You must have known her well?' he asked.

'You never know a person entirely', replied Faraday, alarmed and uncertain as to the reasons for the question.

'If you were simply taking Miss Hart home, why was it necessary to enter her home?' asked Wynne-Thomas clumsily.

'To have coffee, usually'.

'Could you give us details of these visits?' probed Wynne-Thomas gesturing towards Detective Chief Superintendent Thorpe and a passive ACC, as if by indicating his senior colleagues gave him added authority.

'There are no details to give', replied Faraday calmly. 'If I took Miss Hart home, I would often stay and have a coffee with her'.

'Like *Breakfast at Tiffany's*?' snarled Wynne-Thomas, looking towards his colleagues triumphantly as if he had just played his master card.

'No', replied Faraday calmly. 'That expression was strictly reserved for coffees together whilst at work'.

'Do you really think', sneered Wynne-Thomas, 'that having *"Breakfast at Tiffany's"* with a secretary was appropriate?'

'It is entirely appropriate', replied Faraday keeping his tone completely level. 'Whether you like it or not, during these coffee breaks, work was the principle topic of conversation', replied Faraday.

'Mr Faraday', asked Chief Superintendent Thorpe, attempting to gain some control over the direction of the interview. 'You say "principle" topic. Out of interest, what were the secondary topics?'

'It could be many things. Her holidays or hobbies; her studies or weekends'.

'Her hobbies? Her weekends?' interrupted Wynne-Thomas. 'Is that what you used to do? Do you really consider that senior officers should spend their time discussing hobbies with their secretaries?'

Thorpe sighed visibly at the interruption as Faraday answered: 'Well I don't know what you discuss with your secretary', replied Faraday, anxiety mixing with anger at the constant sneering of the Welshman. 'I get the impression that you don't have time to discuss or take an interest in anyone, other than yourself, of course'.

'How dare you talk to me like that, *superintendent*'.

'Jane Hart is a very bright and lively girl', continued Faraday as he began to grapple and make sense of his worries. 'She takes interesting annual holidays and is studying psychology with the

Open University. We often talk about her OU studies or her visits abroad. In fact, she is off to New Zealand next year'.

'How would describe your relationship with Miss Hart', asked Thorpe, hoping to bring the interview quickly back on course. But his intervention was too late. Faraday saw the minute tell-tale exchange of glances between Wynne-Thomas and the ACC when Faraday mentioned the planned holiday. Thorpe, the experienced detective, remained expressionless, but it was too late. Faraday was forewarned.

'Close', he replied briefly.
'What do you mean exactly, close?' asked the detective chief superintendent.

'I rely upon Miss Hart completely'.

'We all rely upon our secretaries, Mr Faraday', he asked reasonably.

'And I rely upon mine'.

'But I gauge from your replies that you rely upon Miss Hart more than I would rely upon mine, for example?' he continued carefully.
'I couldn't say. I would not be sure to what extent you rely upon your secretary'.

'Would you say that you relied upon your secretary more than most senior officers?' blustered Wynne-Thomas to the increasing annoyance of Thorpe, the theme of his questioning interrupted again.

'Probably. It is the way I work'.

'Did her duties include driving you to the airport?' asked the Welshman.

'Jane wasn't *on duty*. She was doing me a favour'.

'But you saw her last night?' asked Wynne-Thomas.

'No'.

'Yes, you did?' persisted Wynne-Thomas.

'I have just told you', he replied slowly. 'I did *not* see Miss Hart last night'.

'But you were seen to leave your station and follow Miss Hart's car'.

'I didn't *follow* anyone, as you put it. We both drove towards the City Centre, it was our route home. At Whiteladies Road, Miss Hart drove towards her home in Redland and I drove on to my home in Stoke Bishop'.

'So you didn't have coffee, for example, with her last night?' continued Wynne-Thomas.

'No'.

'And you went straight to your home?' interjected Thorpe.

'Yes'.

'And for the remainder of the evening and that night, what did you do?' continued the detective chief superintendent.

'I remained in my apartment'.

'And is there anyone who could confirm that?'

'Yes. At about seven-thirty, I called into my next door neighbours'.

'Seven-thirty, you say,' interrupted the Welshman with a grin as if he was about to unravel a lie. 'Why?'

'Because I had run out of milk'.

'You ran out of milk!' the Welshman remarked as if this explanation was totally improbable and added to his triumphant expectation of exposing Faraday's explanation as an untruth: 'Why didn't you go out and get some?'

'I had already had a glass of wine'.

'So, gone for just a few minutes, then', continued Wynne-Thomas. 'What about the remainder of the evening?'

'It wasn't for a few minutes at all. It was probably about forty minutes'.

'Forty minutes to collect some milk! I don't think so'.

'You must speak to my neighbours. You obviously don't intend to rely upon my explanation,' observed Faraday. 'Maybe you would be prepared to believe my neighbours, both of whom are doctors.'

'Mr Faraday', asked Thorpe reasonably. 'We only have a few more questions, but, I think you will agree that forty minutes does seem a rather long time to collect some milk?'

'One of my neighbours had had a slight accident in her BMW and needed some advice about making the sketch plan for the insurance claim'.

'And the remainder of the evening?' asked Thorpe.

'In all night', replied Faraday, adding: 'Will you tell me what these questions are in aid of?'

Thorpe had hoped to conduct the interview without confrontation, to seek to establish the extent and nature of Faraday's relationship with his secretary and to obtain a greater understanding of the life of a murder victim, but his efforts where dashed by Wynne-Thomas whose objective was to use the opportunity to crush Faraday as quickly as possible.

'The view is that your relationship with Miss Hart wasn't one usually associated with that of a secretary and senior officer?' interrupted Wynne-Thomas. 'I put it to you that your relationship had been more intimate, sexually intimate?'

He knew now for certain, but simply replied: 'Nonsense'.

'But you have been seen to kiss her, you have been seen to hug her on more than one occasion', countered Wynne-Thomas.

'What has happened to Jane?'

'Why should you think that something has happened to Miss Hart?' said Thorpe, as Wynne-Thomas nodded eagerly.

'Because Mr Wynne-Thomas has used the past tense at least three or four times during this interview'.

Although prepared, the confirmation of her death was devastating. Faraday felt light-headed. He thought of her neat, modest apartment now desecrated by her death. He thought of how he relied upon her, the custodian of his private secret. Visions of her wide eyes and infectious smile, thoughts of her gentleness and kindness, flashed through his mind. He slumped back into his chair. He looked up at the men in the room. Wynne-Thomas, Thorpe and the ACC were looking at Faraday intently, trying to get the measure of his reactions. That was understandable. It was what police officers do. But anger replaced his distress as he saw the gloating delight upon Wynne-Thomas' face.

'I have kissed her on the cheek, as you say', he replied with difficulty, tears beginning to dim his eyes. 'I have hugged her, particularly … particularly over the last few months. It has been a terrible time for her'. He paused for a moment and cleared his throat. 'Her friend … in fact … in fact, her lover, had been dying of cancer'.

'A lover!' exploded Wynne-Thomas with delight. 'So you had competitor', he said pointing an accusing finger directly at Faraday.

'You imbecilic buffoon', said Faraday contemptuously before he had time to restrain himself. 'Her lover was another woman'.

When Faraday had finished describing the interview, Kay Yin asked: 'Did they ask if you were with anyone last night?'

'No. The whole interview degenerated into an incompetent farce. Thorpe obviously saw me as a useful witness who might be able to provide some insights about Jane, although, knowing him as I do, he would have had not the slightest compunction to change my status from helpful witness to prisoner, if he thought it appropriate. But, Wynne-Thomas saw me as an irritant whom he could finally crush. There were too many people present, all with totally different agendas and no one leading the interview'.

'Did anyone interview Richard and Heather?'

'Oh yes. I was kept waiting with Jarrett when Thorpe sent DCI Dufty to the hospital. Heather was apparently in theatre but Richard was in A&E and was able to confirm my visit'.

'Richard made a statement then?'

'Yes, but DCI Dufty confined the content of the statement to my visit between 7.30 and 8.30 to collect some milk', he replied. He raised his left eyebrow towards her as he added: 'Nothing else'.

The phone rang and she leant across the breakfast bar counter and checked the caller's number before she took the phone from the wall.

'Hi, Mum. Can I call you back, please?' she said.

There was a slight pause as her worried mother, having heard the evening news, offered her condolences and enquired if her daughter was in any sort of danger.

'That is kind of you Mum, but I'm quiet safe. Mark's here'.

Chapter 30

Thursday 11th October.

Bristol, England.

IN THE public foyer of the district headquarters, a framed photograph of Jane Hart had been placed on a side table. By 7.15am, flowers had already begun to arrive. The first had been left by a road sweeper. His note read: *'I didn't know your name but, if you saw me outside the station, you always had time for a word or a wave. I'll miss your smile. Bob'*. The second note was from a taxi driver. Soon the number of flowers became too much for the little table, but DI Yin and DC Pau were able to make enough room for their spray of white lilies.

***

Superintendent Faraday and Detective Constable Pau were parked in the unmarked Vauxhall Vectra near the Texaco garage. Both were in plain clothes, Pau seated behind Faraday who was in the driver's seat. They had already been there for an hour, the inside of the car littered, deliberately, with carpet pattern books in the manner of a salesman's car.

They had discussed the plan, a plan that seemed very vague and unusually disjointed to DC Pau, although he was aware that DI Yin had driven straight to the little stockroom of Gray, Wedge and Hodge in her own VW Golf TDI.

'I noticed you left some white lilies in the foyer, Sam. That was kind of you', remarked Faraday, almost absentmindedly.

'Miss Yin and I thought they would be nice', he said, then continued so as to interrupt the silence. 'White lilies, it's what the Chinese would do'.

He didn't reply immediately. 'Jane would have like that', he said eventually, unshed tears stinging his eyes again. 'It was thoughtful of you, Sam'.

'It was the DI as well, sir', said DC Pau. Faraday nodded in acknowledgement, not daring to speak of Jane Hart, one of the few people he had been able to trust completely, the Jane Hart who had covered for him so often and shared the secret of his dyslexia.

***

DI Yin called Faraday at ten past nine on channel 12, the secure channel allocated to the district for restricted operations, her commentary punctuated by pauses pregnant with expectation. 'The Mondeo has arrived …… the usual two male occupants …… Mondeo parked as if waiting …… blue door rolling up'.

'Roger', replied Faraday, knowing that an update was likely to follow immediately.

'The Merc is rolling'.

'OK. It's yours, Kay'.

DI Kay Yin drove along St Andrew's Road and onto the M5 motorway. It was an easy task to remain in contact with the large Mercedes-Benz, its bulk constantly coming into view, particularly as it reached the brow of the bridge over the River Avon.

As DI Yin was driving her VW Golf towards the bridge, Faraday saw the black Audi emerge from the residents' car park at Penpole Court. He started the Vauxhall's 2.2-litre engine.

'Kay, we are on the move', reported Faraday.

The Audi drove unhurriedly down Lower High Street, through the traffic lights towards the roundabout and took the M5 lane, exiting onto the motorway slip road. As it did so, both Superintendent Faraday and DI Yin providing the other with a commentary via their covert mikes and earpieces.

'DI and both targets at Junction 19, turning off towards the Royal Portbury Docks'.

'Roger. Now on M5 south', detailed Faraday.

'Both targets entering Royal Portbury Docks. Will take up usual OP'.

'Roger', acknowledged Faraday as the Audi swept up the slip road at Junction 19.

'Faraday to DI. The Audi appears to be heading for the docks', he said as he too swept up the incline. 'If he enters the docks I shall return to Penpole Court. Do you copy?'

'Roger that'.

Faraday carefully cruised onto the roundabout above the motorway, exiting at 3 o'clock along West Dock Road. At the next roundabout, the Audi exited at 12 o'clock directly towards the dock's main entrance. Faraday did not screech around the roundabout to retrace his steps but carefully took the next exit into Gardner Way and pulled into the side of the road. A few moments passed, occupied by DC Pau clambering over into the front passenger seat. Once the DC was seated, Faraday turned the Vectra around and headed back towards the motorway, activating the blue strobe lights hidden behind the grille.

On the short stretch of motorway between Junctions 18 and 19, Faraday's car was a blur as it reached 92 mph only for him to drop the speed dramatically to 51, the disc breaks sucking in the cooling air and the dampers and tyres straining on the exit curve. By the time the Vecta had approached Avonmouth Road, the vehicle's speed complied strictly with the statutory limits and the blue strobe lights were turned off. Reassuringly, DI Yin provided an update.

'Sir. All three trucks now lined up like good boys and waiting to be loaded onto the *Santo Stefano*'.

'Mondeo?'

'Parked. Occupied by both drivers. Engine appears to be switched off'.

'OK. I'm going to view properties. Tell me immediately if the Mondeo men move or the Audi appears'.

'Roger that'.

Faraday drove past Penpole Court and was able to reverse park outside of Nails Excreta in the High Street.

'You have your pocket book on you, Sam?'

'Always, sir'.

'Good. And your bunch of keys?'

'Bunch of keys, sir?' he asked innocently.

'Yes, Sam. That bunch of keys you carry which will help us get into a car, a house, a bungalow, an apartment, a toilet or a letter box', said Faraday with a knowing grin.

'Oh, *that* bunch of keys', he said, pulling them from his anorak pocket.

'I need to get into the flat used by the Audi driver. We know the number, DI Yin's little computer provided us with that. Are you game?'

There was a pause as DC Pau considered the legal implications, but then answered firmly. 'I'm with you, sir'.

'Good. Then let's get on with it'.

The two officers, carrying samples of carpet patterns, made their way to the sturdy metal gates that protected the residents' car parking area and also gave access to the front doors of all the apartments. To the right of the double gates was another, smaller gate and an intercom. This gate was secured by a lock. Faraday made a pretence of looking at some papers as DC Pau selected an appropriate key. The first key failed to turn in the lock but the second didn't and the gate opened.

'I must speak to them about security', he said as he stepped through the opening.

As both officers mounted the external staircase, DI Yin called them.

'OK', replied Faraday as if talking to DC Pau.

'Audi on the plot. Driver spoke to the two men in the Mondeo', reported DI Yin succinctly. 'Mondeo has just driven off with the two men. Audi and driver now parked up'.

'Excellent. Stay there', said Faraday as they stood outside of number four. He taped on the door. There was no response.

'Open it', he said, as he started to turn some of the patterns over in his hands effectively blocking the surreptitious activities of his junior colleague from the possible prying eyes of others.

As the locked clicked open, Faraday pressed his shoe against the door and pushed it open slightly, at the same time speaking into the empty hallway. This exhibition was concluded by nodding and smiling, and then both officers entered the building and closed the door behind them.

'Wait here and keep your hands in your pockets or glove-up', said Faraday as he quickly checked each room. Then he called DC Pau into the lounge/diner from the small hallway. The room was large and bright; a typical let property with comfortable but rudimentary furniture, a room devoid of personal or family items. Faraday spoke as he stood in the middle of the room surveying every item of furniture, cardboard boxes, a brief case, a shredder, discarded clothing and waste paper bin. Nothing escaped his attention, including the unease of DC Pau.

'You are concerned that we are here, Sam?' he asked with one of his level stares.

'Not sure that we should be here, sir?'

'Is it or has it been your intention to commit the offence of theft, criminal damage or rape here?'

'No, sir', he replied with a frown.

'There we are them. You can now rest easy as you have not committed the offence of burglary', he replied as he took a pair of latex gloves from within his blazer pocket and pulled them on. He searched through each room, the kitchen, bathroom, two bedrooms and the lounge/diner, leaving some of the drawers and cupboard doors open. The few documents he found, Faraday read quickly. Nothing yielded any useful information as to the identity of the occupant. His rapid search concluded, he took the top off the electric shredder and tipped the shreddings onto the carpeted floor and picked up the brief case from the side of an easy chair. He opened the case and emptied the contents, a large AA road atlas, an 'A to Z' map of Bristol, a pocket calculator, some blank sheets of papers and a mobile phone charger, onto the dinning table.

'Can you write in Chinese?'

'Cantonese, sir'.

'Good. That's a bonus', he said. 'Using one of those blank pieces of paper, please write the following in English but as a Chinese woman would whose knowledge of English would be poor'.

'Right, sir', said DC Pau with an amused smile, collecting up a piece of paper in his gloved hand.

As DC Pau began to write the note in response to Faraday's dictation, DI Yin called.

'Go ahead, Kay'.

'Audi man joined by another male in a Rover 75. Hand shaking and smiles all round. Now talking'.

'Remain where you are. Give me a heads-up when the Audi moves'.

'Roger that', she said as DC Pau finished writing the note and handed it to Faraday who placed it in the middle of the table.

'Come on, Sam. We are off', said Faraday to the relief of DC Pau.

Both men left the apartment, returning to the police Vauxhall and drove a short distance to the Shirehampton Golf Club car park.

'We'll be undisturbed here for a few minutes', said Faraday. 'Give me your pocket book please'.

The officer produced a soft-backed book, numbered in the top right hand corner with a unique reference number printed in red ink. Faraday flicked through the pages and came to the page endorsed with today's date under which was the neat entry:

> *'0730: Commenced duty at District HQ.*
> *Reported to Supt MF',*

followed by:

> *'0740: With Supt MF to Shirehampton, obs*
> *on Penpole Court'.*

'Now write the following', ordered Faraday, returning the book to DC Pau. '0955: On the direct instructions of Superintendent

Faraday, entered the premises of 4 Penpole Court with him by means of a key. Occupants not present. Nothing removed by police. 1012: Left premises'.

'Let me sign it, Sam', he said as the officer finished writing his note.

'Thank you, sir', he said as Faraday endorsed the official note book with his elegant signature and returned the book to a much more comfortable officer. 'Although, still not sure about the legality of it, sir'.

'If I had to put forward an argument in court, Sam, it would be this. Whilst we had no lawful authority to enter Penpole Court, it does not automatically follow that what we did was illegal. A mute point, I agree. For now, I must make a call and then we must wait and allow human nature to take its course'.

Faraday removed his mobile phone from his pocket and tapped in an eleven digit number. Almost immediately Winston Langston answered.

***

Captain Chappell opened the front door of 4 Penpole Court but left the door ajar as he froze, his eyes darting rapidly down the hallway and to the right into the single bedroom and to the left into the kitchen, the former with two drawers pulled open, the latter with some of its unit doors open. Satisfied that he wasn't in immediate danger, he balanced on one foot and kicked the door shut with his other foot, at the same time drawing his service automatic. He crouched in the hallway alert for any movement, any noise that would indicate the presence of others. There was none. He moved cautiously forward, checking the master bedroom and bathroom as he went, then entered the lounge/diner. He was incandescent with range, particularly when he read the note.

He screwed up the note in his first and threw into a corner and stomped into each room slamming shut drawers and cupboard doors. He angrily looked through the minor amount of paperwork he had left in the apartment, then sat heavily into a chair, head in his hands. He couldn't work it out. He got up and retrieved the crumpled note and sat at the dining table. He smoothed out the paper and read the message again. He couldn't believe it. He looked at his watch: 1120 hours. He knew that some of the apartments employed cleaners, but he hadn't. He was sure that he had been careful about not leaving anything about that could give the slightest indication or his real identity or the operation. But he also knew that a 'clear desk' policy was not fool-proof and that he may have left a note in one of the compartments of his briefcase.

He began to panic. Hadn't the colonel told him not to expose himself in this way. He thought of the RAF wing commander who had had a laptop stolen from his car containing the plans for the recapture of the Falkland Islands and the army major whose lost plans for the Royal Family's tour had been found on a rubbish tip.
The scribbled note could be a hoax, he reasoned, but then, the cleaner must know something although he was certain that any notes he had made in the last six weeks would have been methodically shredded. Chappell walked into the kitchen, confident that the demand from 'a poor Chinese cleaner woman' for the return of 'much important paper' was a hoax, but, as the kettle boiled, he thought of the thousands of women employed by the North Vietnamese to piece together successfully all the shredded paper taken from the US embassy when Saigon fell.

He checked his watch and then his wallet. The Chinese cleaner wanted to meet him at 3pm outside the post office in West Street with £50. He picked up the 'A to Z' guide, turning to the index, then to page 70. He found West Street between Old Market Street and Clarence Road, and a little black star denoting a post office. He decided. He would be in position by 2pm.

***

Old Market Street is a continuance of West Street, one of the busiest arterial roads in the city, bringing commuters into the heart of Bristol from St George, Kingswood and Hanham and the City of Bath beyond. The junction is intersected by Midland Road that carries heavy traffic from the commercial estates towards the M32 motorway. In the rush-hour these roads are gridlocked, but even at quieter times, the volume of vehicular and pedestrian traffic remains heavy.

Captain Andrew Chappell had parked his Audi in the nearby cobbled Waterloo Street and stood at the bus stop across the road from the post office. He was surveillance-aware and arrived in ample time. He was absolutely sure that he was not compromised as he spotted, fifty minutes after his arrival, the huddled figure, clad in a pale blue and white stripped cleaning company jerkin. Her steps were short and hurried, her black hair tucked under a white cap with a pale blue peak. Her arms were wrapped around her body as if she was cold or clutching something under her clothes.

He had hoped that he would be able to approach the Chinese woman and simply pay her off, but Old Market Street and West Street are run-down and scheduled for redevelopment. He had to assume that there could always be some sort of argument or confrontation with accomplices in an area that was potentially hostile to him. And, any such confrontation would undoubtedly be witnessed by drivers in the constant stream of traffic that passed along the three lanes of this one-way street.

DI Yin continued to play her part as the cleaning lady, looking furtively about, placing her weight firstly on one leg then on the other. As planned, at 3.15pm, she looked up at the Victorian clock above the post office and shuffled off towards Old Market Street to cross the road at the junction with Midland Road. A few yards further on, DI Yin walked into the narrow and cobbled Jacob Street, old terraced houses on one side and gaunt warehouses on the other. Outside of number 11, DI Yin removed a set of car keys from her pocket, fumbled with the driver's door lock of an old Ford Escort and, as she opened the door, Captain Andrew Chappell struck.

His grip around her slender neck was like a vice. She winced with the pain as she put her left hand on the roof above the opened door and drove her right elbow into Chappell's chest just below his sternum repeatedly like a piston. As Chappell fell back, Kay Yin span on the ball of her foot and drove a small knuckled fist into his throat. He stumbled back into Superintendent Mark Faraday who had quickly been followed out of the front door of number 11 by DC Yin.

Faraday grabbed Chappell's right arm, pinning his wrist in a disabling swan-neck hold and forced his face into the grimy gutter. DC Pau swiftly produced handcuffs as DI Yin patted him down.

'He's carrying', she rasped as her hands felt the automatic pistol at his belt, her throat still paining from his violent grasp. Expertly she removed the weapon from its holster as DC Pau fixed the handcuff securely in place.

Faraday pulled Chappell to his feet and held him facing the Ford Escort as DI Yin searched him more thoroughly, removing a wallet and car keys from his pockets. 'He's clean', said DI Yin.

'Officer', said Faraday formally to DC Pau, 'get the car'.

The young detective ran along Jacob Street and into Hawkins Street. When he returned with the police Vectra, Faraday had already been joined by a marked police car, answering his urgent summons.

'Detective Inspector Yin', said Faraday addressing her formally. 'I think you need to say the magic words to this man'.

'Certainly, sir', she replied and, turning to face a still coughing Chappell, said: 'You are under arrest'.

As Chappell was placed into the rear of the Vectra, Faraday turned towards the two unformed officers of the marked car. 'Thank you, gentlemen'.

'That's alright, sir', they said, both grinning.

'I have one task for you', he said as he handed the Audi car keys to one of the uniformed officers. He had seen that the rear window of the Vectra was lowered by about an inch and so did not reveal that he knew the colour or model of the Audi: 'See if you can find this guy's car. It must be about here somewhere'.

'Don't worry, sir, we'll find it for you', one said, eager to prove their worth.

'Just one other thing, gentlemen. This', said Faraday pointing towards the black man standing in the doorway of number 11, 'is

Mr Winston Langston. He's a friend of mine and has been very helpful to us today'.

***

Detective Inspector Kay Yin had recovered from her assault and was now dressed elegantly in a moss coloured Merino roll neck tunic and blue stretch denim jeans. She had up-dated the dry-wipe board in Faraday's office and arranged a series of photographs on his desk. Now she sat at the side of his desk as Faraday, seated in his chair, stared out across the harbour as the afternoon drew to a close.

'The question as always is motive', he said almost to himself.
'Or motives'.

'Yes, you are right, always multiple motives', replied Faraday reflectively. 'However, it's not so much a question of why he was outside the post office, more why should he have responded to the note, why was he so eager to meet you, why so determined to put his hands on you and what did he believe you had discovered that was so important to him?'

'We know that he and his mates have got themselves involved in something more than just motor mechanics and the key might be the chemicals transported by the vehicles, the possible military connection or the disappearance of Barry Atkins'.

Faraday swung around in his chair. 'Let's jot this on the white board', he said.

Gradually headings appeared, including: 'Chemicals', 'Mercedes-Benz', 'military', 'Royal Portbury Docks', 'Barry Atkins', '3rd September', 'Audi', 'Ford Mondeo', 'Rover 75', 'Penpole Court' and

'*Santo Stefano*'. A series of coloured lines began to connect these headings and little notations appeared.

'The essentials in any criminal investigation is to remain objective and logical', mused Faraday. He felt her looking at him and turned to admire Kay Yin. He thought of her first day on the district when he had looked at her and found her instantly compelling. Now she smiled and, in response to her quizzical look, added: 'OK, in this case, I will agree that I am finding it difficult to be completely objective and logical'.

He stood up from his desk and stepped past her towards the white board. As he did so, he kissed her on the head, the perfume of *Amor Amor* assailing his senses.

'Everything, or at least everything we have at the moment, points towards a military connection'. He fixed his eyes on the edge of his desk so as not to be distracted and counted off on his fingers salient points. 'We have David Taylor's ex-army view, his perceptions; the deferential conduct of the two mechanics towards chummy in the cells; the tyres. I say connection ...' he said as he occupied one of the chairs opposite Kay Yin. 'The connection, the connection could be ex-forces who have met up to engage in crime, may be theft of vehicles, shipping prohibited good, weapons, anything. They could, of course, be serving military personnel who are illegally shifting military goods, there's always a market. Or they are serving military, maybe intelligence people, but I can't see it, I can't see the link'.

'The link could be Barry Atkins', suggested DI Yin. 'He had a Mercedes-Benz. What if they were using Atkins as a conduit in some way, to move drugs, stolen goods? What if Atkins asked for a bigger cut and they got rid of him?'

Faraday sat quietly, eyes closed. DI Yin broke the silence.

'How much longer can you keep him incommunicado?'

'A little longer', he said, then seemed to plunge into deep thought and, like many dyslexics, vividly began to recall events in startling detail.

'Mark?'

'It's bugging me'.

'What is?'

'When he was booked in, he didn't ask for a solicitor. He asked if he could telephone his wife or his managing director. If I had been arrested for assaulting a policewoman and possession of a firearm, the last person I would want to tell would be my boss. And I wouldn't be too keen to blurt everything out to my wife'.

'You mean that most men would not want their wives and children to know that they had hit a policewoman?'

'Exactly. But maybe that's it. Maybe he did want to tell his boss', he suggested. 'Maybe his boss is involved'.

'Always a very definite possibility if trafficking of some sort is involved'.

'We need to get a feel of this fellow before we interview him properly', determined Faraday. 'If he is military, he is likely to hold or have held rank. It will be interesting to see how he reacts to police ranks'.

They discussed what points they should, at this stage, put to the prisoner, what should not be disclosed to the prisoner and who should conduct the interview. DI Yin dialled out. Five minutes later, there was a gentle tap on the closed door.

'Come in', called Faraday and Miss Cousins, the temporary secretary, opened the door.

'Detective Constable Pau', she said formally and stood to one side to allow the officer to enter.

'Thank you, Mavis', he said to the 53 year old spinster, hair already greying, the fawn cardigan seeming to mirror her personality.

'Thank you, Mr Faraday' she said stiffly.

'Mavis', said Faraday. 'Thank you for your help today. I haven't been as attentive as I should have been, but one difficult day seems to follow another', adding lightly: 'I will try and improve tomorrow, Mavis'.

'The agency called and asked how I was coping. I said that I was managing, Mr Faraday. So I shall be back tomorrow if that suits?'

'That will be fine, Mavis. It's time you were off home anyway. I'll see you tomorrow'.

Mavis Cousins closed the door quietly, tidied her desk and went home as DC Pau took a seat with his two senior officers.

'You sat with the prisoner on the way to the station and was present when he was booked in', said Faraday. 'What do you think of him?'

'I think his arrest was a shock to him and he spent most of the time tense as if he was struggling to resolve his situation'.

'Did he say anything?'

'Nothing'.

'And in the station?' continued the superintendent.

'He seemed ... funny really. He seemed more relaxed', replied Sam Pau, trying to make sense of the prisoner's reaction. 'More comfortable. Sounds silly, sir'.

'When exactly, Sam?' asked DI Yin. 'When he entered the station or the custody suite; his reaction to the custody sergeant or when something happened specifically?'

'He seemed to be very comfortable in the presence of the sergeant. Probably he thought he was going to get a beating but found the presence of the sergeant reassuring'.

Faraday and Yin exchanged glances as she persisted: 'Was that the only time you sensed any change in his behaviour?'

'He seemed to relax a bit when the traffic lads came in with his car keys. They'd found it two blocks away. Expensive car, so I assumed he was pleased it was safe'.

'OK, Sam', said Faraday. 'What I want you to do is to interview the prisoner, confining your questions to completing his antecedents and descriptive forms. Deal with him casually as if this was the usual routine bureaucracy at work. You know, what's on the forms, details of where he lives, his occupation, the nature of his occupation, his salary, expenses, company car, scars, tattoos, colour of eyes, nick names, medical conditions – the usual. OK?'

'Yes, sir'.

'You are probably wondering what this is all about, Sam. You know some detail, but not all of it by any means. Don't be offended. We are deliberately leaving you in the dark so that you don't inadvertently disclose sensitive details to him'.

'That's fine, sir'.

'You will introduce yourself as DC Pau of the Vice Squad. Take another Vice Squad colleague into the interview with you. If the prisoner asks what DI Yin and you were doing in the area, you can quite honestly say that you were engaged in an undercover operation involving a black man. Under no circumstances at all will you mention Penpole Court. In particular, ask him about his high powered car. Forensics are looking at it now but they have already told me that they don't hold out much hope of anything useful being found because it has clearly been subject to an extremely thorough Spring clean.   Thoroughly cleaned cars always ring warning bells for me, so just ask him if it's a pool car or his, but don't make a big issue of it. Any questions?'

'No, sir'.

'Good. DI Yin and I will be monitoring the interview from her office, but there will be no need for your earpiece. We don't want to spook him into thinking that you are receiving directions and that we are all eager to hear everything he has to say'.

'One last thing, Sam', said DI Yin. 'I don't want the prisoner to see your writing'.

'It's OK, ma'am', he replied with a huge conspiratorial smile. 'I used a blue pen for the note. I shall use a black biro and the writing will be quite different'.

As DC Pau made his way to the ground floor, Faraday turned to DI Yin. 'I'm sure he is very pleased we have his car. That Audi was fitted with GPS. If he is military, they will know where he is now'.

***

D I Yin's office was on the top floor, looking directly over towards the Hole-in-the-Wall restaurant and Redcliffe Bridge. Her desk was immediate opposite the door to the side of which were two cabinets. One cabinet was filled with manuals, legal reference books and drop-files, the other clothes, including body armour and a police baseball cap. In the gap between this cabinet and the window wall was hung, discretely, a photograph of her mother and father, the latter in the uniform of an assistant commissioner. Below this photograph was a framed picture consisting of Chinese writing, indecipherable to the uninitiated but of meaning to her. Her office was business-like, a computer screen on her desk and a video/DVD monitor on a side table. She pressed the controls. The screen rapidly illuminated to show DC Howard sitting with the prisoner in Interview Room 5. As the two senior officers settled into their seats they saw Sam enter the interview room. Kay Yin adjusted the volume as DC Pau switched on the tape recorder.

'I am DC Samuel Pau of the Vice Squad', he said.

'And I am DC Quinton Howard of the Vice Squad', said the other officer, leaning forward.

'You are Andrew Charman?'

'Yes', replied Andrew Chappell.

'Do you have any middle names, Mr Charman?'

'No'.

'Can you confirm your date of birth, please?

'9th January 1955'.

'And your place of birth?'

'Stafford'.

'OK. Thank you, Andrew. My job is to take all your details that will be provided to the court. Your home details, financial situation, employment, that sort of thing, as well as to fill out a descriptive form'.

'How long am I going to be kept here?

'That's up to the custody sergeant and the superintendent, Andrew. I just do the admin. DI Yin will be in to speak with you soon', said the DC. 'Now, your home address in Reading is where exactly?'

'23 Cromwell Road?'

DC Pau continued to ask his questions, mostly routine, as DC Howard looked increasingly bored, unwittingly but authentically adding to the illusion of two detectives burden with red tape.

The detective disarmingly asked not one question regarding the assault upon DI Yin, the unlawful possession of a Part One firearm, nor the reason why the prisoner was in the Old Market Street area of the city. Instead, DC Pau continued to ask the dozens of listed questions and to methodically fill out the pages of yellow coloured forms.

'Mr Andrew Charman' gave his occupation as 'director' with a salary of £56,000, adding unnecessary: 'plus expenses'.

DC Pau saw the opportunity. 'And the, what was it? The Audi? Company car is it?'

'Yes'.

'Right', said DC Pau as he feigned confusion as he looked down the yellow form and added: 'I'll put it down as a pool car'.

'It isn't a pool car?' interjected Chappell in an offended tone.

'I'm sorry. But it's not yours is it, Andrew?' he said, deliberately provoking the prisoner.

Chappell was becoming increasing annoyed at the use of his first name and loss of what he viewed as status in the presence of the lowest rank in the police service. His response was unnecessarily pretentious.

'The Audi wasn't purchased by me if that's what you mean, constable, but it is allocated exclusively to me', he replied with a superior air.

'That's the sort of detail the court needs to know, Andrew. They take that sort of thing into account when determining any financial penalty', said DC Pau dismissively as he continued to fill out the forms.

The tedious process concluded, the prisoner was returned to his cell as DC Pau joined Faraday and Yin in the DI's office.

'Very nicely done, Sam', said DI Yin as Faraday spoke to the Force's Communication Centre.

Faraday replaced the receiver. 'Well done, Sam'.

'But I didn't do much, sir'.

'Yes you certainly did, Sam', said Faraday his arm across the young officer's back. 'The Electoral Register confirms his address but I have a motorcyclist en route to Reading. We can't progress too much for a while and so I think we should all go to the canteen and eat whilst our Mr Andrew Charman stews for a little longer'.

They sat in a quite corner of the canteen, the only other people present being two uniformed constables finishing a late meal whilst playing the gaming machine. Faraday explained that he and DI Yin would conduct the next phase of the interview with Andrew Charman whilst DC Pau worked on the prisoner's mobile phone.

Superintendent Faraday and DI Yin determined their interview strategy and agreed that during the forthcoming interview, no reference would be made to Inspector David Taylor and his enquiries; any suspicions that they may have of a military connection; their observation upon or knowledge of the three Mercedes-Benz tankers and the Audi filmed on the Portway road or observed at Avonmouth. As they pushed aside their plates, DC Pau asked Faraday what would be the specific objectives of the forthcoming interview.

'Is this for your workplace development or just out of curiosity, Sam?'

'Both, sir', he replied eagerly.

'OK. Andrew Charman will know that some enquiries have been made by the police, but he will not know the extent of those enquiries or how much of the information has been shared. I want him to torment himself over what we might know and what we don't know. I believe him to be a dishonest man. An honest man would, as often as not, answer all reasonable questions. The dishonest man will get himself engaged in mental gymnastic, his brain knowing full well what actually happened and these thoughts will be in direct conflict with what his dishonesty will compel him to say. In short, there will be inconsistencies in what he will say that we will be able to probe. He will lie, Sam. I want him to lie because by lying he places himself under even more pressure. In these circumstances he will confuse himself and, hopefully, say something that places him in jeopardy or reveal details that could only be known to the offender'.

'You will try and trick him?'

'Oh no, Sam', he answered reasonably and patiently. 'You see, it is not difficult to trick even an honest person into saying something that is not accurate or entirely true, only for the trick and the real truth to be established later. This is often the basis for the good-humoured hoax or prank at a Christmas or birthday party. No, I want the prisoner to either tell me lies which I will be able to disprove or for him to tell me the truth. I hope to do this by placing him in such a position that truth is the only way forward for him'.

***

'And I am Superintendent Mark Faraday', he said for the benefit of the interview room tape as he pulled his chair into the green topped table and looked across to Mr Andrew Charman, deliberately wearing his superintendent's uniform with his MBE medal ribbon. 'It has already been explained to you why, in compliance with Sections 56 and 58 of the Police and Criminal Evidence Act, I have authorised your detention here and have denied you contact with anyone'.

'You have no right to do this to me, superintendent', replied Chappell, as if speaking to an equal, a fact not lost upon Faraday.

'Fortunately, parliament doesn't share your view and our enquiries so far indicate that the courts will endorse my decision. You were arrested, Mr Charman, for an assault upon this undercover officer', he said, gesturing to DI Yin seated to his left. 'During the course of this assault you were found to be in possession of a firearm as described in Part One of the Firearms Act 1968. Do you have an explanation for your possession of this loaded weapon?'

'I'm saying nothing to you until I have phoned my solicitor and my wife'.

'Well, that will be an interesting exercise, Mr Charman'.

'What do you mean?' demanded Chappell.

'The home address provided by you does exist, but the curtains are drawn and no one appears to be at home'.

'My wife must be out' he protested.

'She pops in and out does she?'

'That's what wives do'.

'Not your wife, Mr Charman. Neighbours haven't seen you for weeks and they haven't seen … ', DI Yin pointed to the name printed on her note pad. 'Maureen, at all'.

'My neighbours can't be as nosey as yours', he remarked as Faraday, seemingly ignoring the remark, accepted a plastic card from DI Yin.

'The Royal Automobile Club have you listed as living at 23 Cromwell Road', said Faraday fingering the plastic membership card, 'with Maureen also listed'.

'There you are then'.

'What I find a little strange is that you have never called upon the services of the RAC since you signed up with them eleven years ago', observed Faraday, hoping to draw the questioning in the direction of the ownership of the Audi.

'You need to get a quality car, superintendent', he said.

'Yours is an Audi 2.7?'

'The Avant. That is correct', he said in a confident manner.

'A very nice car. The top of the range but not yours, of course, Mr Charman', he said, not as a direct question but simply to goad.

'It is in the sense that, as a director, the Audi is allocated to me personally', replied Chappell, maintaining his *short-term cover*, the use of which would have been completely adequate when attention was unlikely.

'Top of the range and not for use by the minions then', Faraday remarked, almost casually as he fumbled in his tunic pocket.

'Certainly not', replied Chappell briskly.

'You will know, Mr Charman, that the courts do not look favourably upon those who assault police officers, particularly, female officers', said Faraday, deliberately changing tack.

'I had no idea that she was a police officer. I have already apologies. I thought that she was trying to break into a car'.

'And what explanation do you have for possession a loaded firearm?'

'I found it', he said without thought, caught unawares by another change of tack.

'Where?' the superintendent asked rapidly.

'In the road'.

'Which road?'

'In one of the side streets. I don't know exactly'.

'When?' His questions following in quick succession.

'A few days ago'.

'Were you in Bristol a few days ago?'

'Yes', he replied, a hesitancy in his voice.

'And what were you doing on that day? En route to a restaurant? Leaving a business meeting? On your way home?

'I was driving through Bristol. Well, in a Bristol car park'.

'Which car park?'

'I'm not familiar with Bristol. It was a municipal car park'.

'And you found it?'

'And I didn't know what to do with it'.

'I've been interviewing prisoners for many years, Andrew. Thieves will tell me that they bought stolen goods from a man in the pub or the stolen item fell off the back of a lorry, but to find a dangerous and loaded weapon in the street and to keep it because you didn't know what to do with it beggars belief'.

'Well I did. I found it in the street'.

Faraday chose to ignore the fact that he was now fully aware of the journeys made by the prisoner as he change tack again. 'I am wondering whether you have a more plausible explanation regarding your possession of the Audi?'

'I've told you that the car is mine'.

'I'm not convinced it is. I'll tell you what I think, Mr Charman', said Faraday in a deliberately patronising way. 'You came into this station with a pretence of airs and graces, describing yourself as a director who drives an executive car but your address at Cromwell Road isn't quite so executive is it. I don't think you are the director of bugger all and as far as that Audi is concerned, you've probably taken it from the pool, pretending to us that it is for your exclusive use'.

Chappell could hardly control himself. What he had seen of Faraday, how he acted, how he spoke, reminded him of House-Layton and other senior army officers, officers whom he resented. 'Who do you think you're talking to, you stuck up bastard', he shouted standing up, 'that car is for my exclusive use'.

Faraday said and did nothing. He let Chappell stand there hyper-ventilating until he slowly lowered himself into his chair, then he spoke again quietly and in a matter-a-fact way. 'You were, Andrew, in what President Ronald Reagan once referred to as "deep, deep do-do". I say "where" because in your case, the "do-do" has got very much deeper'.

'What do you mean?' Chappell said, rising to the mocking yet worrying comment.

Without instructions, but on cue, DI Yin handed Faraday a large envelope from under her pad. Faraday opened the end carefully and removed three pieces of A4 stapled in the left-hand corner.

'This report is from our forensic people', he said, scanning each page slowly in turn. 'They have been very busy examining your Audi. You said a few moments ago that you were not familiar with Bristol. But you are'.

He paused as Chappell became more uncomfortable.

'You are very familiar indeed with this city, aren't you?'

'I've driven through a few times. I've had business calls to make'.

'Did you have business calls to make in Avon Street, Oxford Street and Gas Lane in the early morning of …'. He glanced at Kay Yin's pad again. '… the 3rd September?'

'I don't know what you are talking about', he replied, perspiration forming on his top lip as he began to think of the death of Barry Atkins.

'Your Audi is fitted with a GPS system, a feature of which is an internal memory that automatically stores "waypoints" or grid references at five minute intervals. I know exactly where you have been, Mr Charman'.

Chappell, unaware of the traffic camera records or the observations conducted by DI Yin and DC Pau, continued to bluff. 'I can't be expected to know ever road I travel on, can I?'

Faraday ignored his response as he continued his questioning: 'Your Audi has recently been subject to a very thorough clean as you know, Mr Charman. But not thorough enough'.

Chappell thought of Corporal Mooney, that bloody fool Mooney, as Faraday drew Chappell's attention back to his questioning.

'Mr Charman, you will know that the boot cover of your Audi is on a sprung-loaded roller. The scientist pulled it across and, whilst the top was spotlessly clean, the underside hadn't been cleaned at all. On the underside of the cover were discovered traces of blood, traces that match perfectly with this man'. He pulled out a photograph of Barry Atkins from the large envelope and turned it to face the prisoner.

'I know nothing about it', he replied, blood draining from his face and, realising that his hands had started to trembled, he quickly hid them from view as he blurted out: 'Other people drive my car'. 'Do they? You told the Vice Squad detectives on at least three occasions that the Audi was for your exclusive use. You told me the same a matter of minutes ago in response to very specific questions, all of which has been recorded on the tape here', replied Faraday, gesturing towards the whirling tape machine.

Chappell looked at the black box. He could see the cassettes turning, the red light mocking him. 'I am telling you that others have access to that car', he replied, panic in his voice.

'Give us their details, Mr Charman, and maybe some of your problems can go away'.

'I'm saying nothing', replied Chappell defiantly, sitting back in his chair and folding his arms across his chest.

'I don't think that any judge would see that as a very reasonable response, nor will the twelve men and women of his jury', said Faraday pointedly, adding in a reasonable tone: 'Provide us with the details of these individuals and we can quickly interview them'.

'I'm saying nothing', he replied as he realised that his *short-term cover* could not cope with his predicament.

'You are not very good at providing details, are you, Andrew?' Chappell sat silently.

'You have told the custody sergeant, the two Vice Squad detectives, the detective inspector here and myself, that your name is Charman?'

'What point are you trying to make?' challenged Chappell nervously as perspiration mounted under his arms.

'The point I am making is that Charman isn't your name, is it?'

His first reaction was to remain silent as the walls seemed to close in around him. 'It is my name', he said, but the words were distorted by acute panic.

'No, no it's not'. Faraday paused for effect. 'Your name is …' DI Yin passed Faraday a descriptive sheet of paper containing a photograph – all theatre. 'Andrew Chappell'.

'You've made a mistake'

'No. You made a mistake, Andrew. You made a mistake many years ago when, as a young soldier, you broke some light fittings on a London underground station. A bit of a lark with the lads that resulted in your arrest by the British Transport Police. They charged you with malicious damage and fingerprinted you. Those fingerprints match the fingerprints all over your Audi. You *are* Andrew Chappell'.

'I'm saying nothing more to you'.

'Well, let me say something more to you, Andrew Chappell. I believe that Barry Atkins was attacked and killed in his garage. *You* were party to that death and his body was transported in *your* Audi by *you* to Dartmoor'.

Chappell felt as if the walls and the ceiling of the interview room where now closing completely in upon him. His heart rate increased as he grasped at straws. 'You don't have a body do you?' he said, anxious hope in his voice.

'No I don't', replied Faraday as if without a care in the world. 'But a body isn't essential in a trial for murder. Criminals are regularly convicted without a body'.

'You'll never make it stick without a body', replied Cappell defiantly, a strained smile appearing on his face, his head nodding from side to side.

'James Camb thought that too'.

'James Camb? Who in the bloody hell is James Camb?'

'He was a steward on the *Durban Castle*, a luxury cruise liner sailing off the coast of West Africa. He murdered Miss Gay Gibson in her cabin and then pushed the body of this beautiful actress out through the porthole. Miss Gibson's body was never found but James Camb was subsequently convicted of her murder and sentenced to death'. Faraday stood up. 'You see, Andrew, I don't need the body of Barry Atkins. I just need you'.

Superintendent Faraday slowly adjusted his tunic and pushed his chair back carefully under the green-toped table. He leant forward towards the microphone. 'This interview is terminated at 2107' and turning towards DI Yin ordered: 'Return the prisoner to his cell'.

Chapter 31

Friday 12th October.

Bristol, England.

DETECTIVE CONSTABLE Samuel Pau had obtained useful data from the SIM card in Chappell's mobile phone, but this could not be expanded upon until a print-out was forwarded by the service provider.

DI Kay Yin had charged Andrew Chappell with unlawful possession of a firearm and prepared the papers for his appearance before the magistrates at 10am. Meanwhile, Faraday had been able to convince Detective Chief Superintendent Thorpe that they be allowed to pursuit the enquiries in respect of Barry Atkins, although Thorpe had insisted upon a meeting with the Crown Prosecution Service at 9am, firstly to ensure that any bail application by Chappell was opposed and, secondly, to seek guidance regarding preferring a charge of murder.

Mark and Kay had reached his apartment at twenty past midnight.

***

The call came at 04:11. Kay Yin was quickly wide awake. Mark Faraday wasn't. She woke him with difficulty. Once awake, he sat on the end of the bed as she walked towards to the kitchen, opening the left hand door of his wardrobe as she went.

He picked up the cordless phone. 'Faraday', he said scratching is head.

'I'm sorry to trouble you, sir', said a voice devoid on any personality at all. 'It's Sergeant Metherill here, but I thought I should ring you'.

'It's not a problem, John. Go ahead', he said to the well-intentioned but pedantic sergeant.

'Would you like me to give you a few moments to collect your thoughts, sir?' he said frustratingly.

'No, no. You go ahead, John', said Faraday, conscious that his impatience was showing through again. 'I'm wide awake. Go on'.

'I thought I should call you and tell you that Andrew Charman, or Andrew Chappell as we now know him to be, has been taken to hospital'.

'Which one?' asked Faraday knowing that certain city hospitals specialised in severe head injuries, burns and so on.

'A&E at Bristol Royal Infirmary', the sergeant replied as Kay re-entered the room and Faraday pointed his index finger towards items of clothing in his wardrobe.

'Why?' asked Faraday violently nodding the affirmative as Kay pointed to herself and mouthed 'And me?'

'Head injuries, sir'.

Faraday was immediately on his guard. He knew that patients with serious head injuries would normally be taken to the hospital at Frenchay. 'How were these injuries caused?

'He apparently banged his head against the cell wall ...'

Faraday interrupted the sergeant and, putting his hand across the mouthpiece, said to Kay Yin: 'Get Sam on the road', then returned his attention to the caller. 'Sergeant, wait a minute', he said sharply. 'Were any other persons involved?'

'No, sir'.

'Self-inflicted then?'

'Apparently so, sir'.

'How bad did these injuries appear to be?'

'Forehead all red and bruised, blood from the ear'.

Blood from the ear would normally indicate a fracture of the base of the skull and so Faraday probed again.

'But not so bad an injury so as to be taken to Frenchay Hospital?'

'No, sir. The BRI'.

'How long ago?'

'They left here about ten minutes ago in an ambulance, sir'

'Who has gone with him?'

'PC Anderson'.

'Preserve the cell', said Faraday, as he struggled into a blue and white striped shirt. 'Send another PC to the BRI and I am en-route'.

'A bit stretched at the moment, sir'.

'Look, Chappell would only self-inflict for one reason', he said as Kay Yin laid his dark blue pullover on their bed, 'and that is to get out of his cell. I must have someone else at the hospital'.

'Sorry, you'll have to wait a moment', said the sergeant abruptly and the line went dead.

Faraday climbed into his Armani jeans and Kay Yin pulled up his fly zip, with her mobile still under her chin.

DC Pau answered her call and Kay Yin went out into the hall, tossing Faraday his black leather moccasin shoes as she went. After what seemed like an age, Kay Yin returned to the bedroom and, pulling a pale pink, short sleeved cable jumper over her head gave Faraday another thumbs up, confirming that Sam Pau had be raised.

'I'm sorry about that, sir', said Sergeant Metherill coming back on-line. 'There's something I need to tell you, sir. There has been a call to say that a parcel bomb has been placed on the approach road at Temple Meads rail station'.

'Any code word used in the call?' asked Faraday, nodding again to Kay Yin who was dangling a police baseball cap from her finger.

'No, sir'.

'Then speak to BTP and confirm that they will be dealing, but send a sergeant and a PC to assist. Meanwhile, speak to FCC and get two ARVs to respond to the BRI, one to St Michael's Hill, the other to St James' Barton. Tell them: "silent approach". I shall be on channel 12 en-route to the BRI. DI Yin and DC Pau will also be attending. Do you have that?'

'I have it, sir. Do y...' said the sergeant but Faraday had replaced the receiver and was already at his front door, Kay Yin in pale blue jeans and suede loafers.

'Your car', he said, tossing her keys to her.

En route, Faraday attempted to call PC Anderson at the Bristol Royal Infirmary without success. He did raise DC Pau and directed him to the security control room at the hospital then contented himself with fiddling with the strap on his baseball cap.

They sped down Druid Hill, tyres screeching on the severe bend as they approached Stoke Hill, the 1.9 engine responding to every touch of her tiny shoe on the pedal, slackening speed only slightly as they approached red traffic lights.

'Clear. Clear both', called Faraday, a perfect team in intuitive harmony as they darted across Saville Road and onto Durdham Downs. They took the bus lane as they passed the water tower, the rev counter needle bouncing as gears dropped from 4th to 2nd, exiting the roundabout at 3 o'clock.

When the Force Communication Centre had contacted the two nearest Armed Response Vehicles, Tango Eight had been cruising on the M5 north of Clevedon, whilst Tango Three had been mobile on the Keynsham bye-pass west of the city of Bath.

Faraday picked up the locations of the ARVs as they entered the city. He called both units and directed the RV point for Tango Eight as St Michael's Hill, just below the maternity hospital.

'See if you can tuck yourself out of sight in Park Place. No lights', requested Faraday, a deployment that allowed for coverage of anyone exiting the BRI to the west or north.

Tango Three's approach from the east allowed for deployment at St James' Barton, providing coverage of east and south-east exits, whilst both deployments did not necessitate actually entering the roads that immediately abutted upon the hospital.

Faraday briefed the ARVs' crews as to the potential threat level, details of the Ford Mondeo and Rover 75 and use of Channel 12.

Kay Yin pulled her Golf into the drop-off/pick-up bays immediately outside the main entrance of the hospital, an ultra modern six storey building of unattractive stained concrete. Both Faraday and Yin noticed and acknowledged the Chinese girl seated in the passenger seat of Sam's battered Marina TC parked across the road. They didn't know the girl but assumed her to be Pau's girlfriend. As they approached the front entrance, DC Pau walked towards them.

'You were quick, Sam?' said Faraday.

'Just arrived, sir. We were in a club in Frogmore Street'.

'Where is the security office?'

'Just inside the main entrance', he said, gesturing towards a set of automatic doors, outside of which were a small collection of people, patients' relatives and friends Faraday thought, smoking cigarettes, all looking preoccupied with varying degrees of private concerns.

The security office was a few paces from Information and across from Admissions. The briefest of introductions were made to the two security officers on duty.

'I need you', said Faraday to one of the men, 'to run all of your external discs back to cover the last 30 minutes'. Without waiting for an agreement, he spoke to DC Pau. 'You know what we are looking for, Sam. A Mondeo or the Rover'.

Then, turning his attention to the other security man, he asked: 'Have you a camera covering A&E?'

'There are three', he said, pleased to be able to confirm this level of cover.

'Put them up now, please'.

The guard pressed a number of keys and pointed to one screen divided into three segments.

'There should be a uniformed constable with an injured prisoner', said Faraday. They all looked at the screens. Faraday leant forward, both knuckles planted on a desk, deep in thought. 'A possible fracture to the base of the skull', he said to himself and, turning to the guard, snapped: 'Give me a view of X-Ray'.

The guard pressed one key. In the reception area of the X-Ray department was a man in a wheel chair with an injured leg and a uniformed constable standing guard at a door.

'Where does that door lead?' Faraday asked pointing at the screen.

'The X-Ray suite. Patients and authorised persons only'.

'Right, you show me where the X-Ray department is', commanded Faraday.

As Faraday, DI Yin and the guard were about to leave the office, DC Pau, who had been scanning the frames, spoke: 'Nothing in the car parks, sir, but the Rover drove slowly up Horfield Road, 16, 17 minutes ago'.

'Keep on it, Sam', he said and they were gone, along the corridor, through a swing door to their right and up the stairway, their footsteps, hollow echoes. They pulled open the door which gave access to A&E reception to the right, but the trio turned to the left and followed the red line marked 'X-Ray' painted into the floor. Faraday's radio crackled.

Tango Eight braked sharply and, as if in one movement, reversed into Royal Fort Road. The observer, PC Dave Wood, calling Faraday, 'Tango Eight to Alpha Charlie One, we have sighted the Rover 75 parked outside the Robin Hood PH, St Michael's Hill'.

'Alpha Charlie One to 'Tango Eight', replied Faraday. 'Noted, wait one'.

They ran on, Faraday's heart pumping, imagining what might lie ahead, juggling with the possible courses of action open to him. As they approached the department, Faraday's radio bleeped. It was DC Pau.

'Yes, Sam?'

'They're on the fire escape outside X-Ray', he said as he saw the grey figures of two men jumping down the external fire escape to run through the maze of alleys and service roads at the rear of the hospital.

'Stay there, Sam, and track 'em for me', he said. He looked around for Kay Yin. She was there.

Simultaneously, they burst through the doors into the restricted area of the X-Ray department, followed by the guard and observed by a startled PC Anderson. They found the X-Ray technician unconscious, sprawled on the floor.

'I have it', she said kneeling at the figure on the floor as Faraday went to the fire escape door.

'Alpha Charlie One to Tango Eight, there are two men, both possibly armed, making their way towards you on foot. Direction of approach uncertain'. Once acknowledged, Faraday called Tango Three: 'Proceed to St Michael's Hill and deploy 200 yards below Robin Hood PH'.

As two nurses arrived, Faraday's instinctive reaction was to chase the two men down the stairs and through the alley ways. But he knew better. 'Keep talking to us, Sam, you are my eyes'.

'Concussion only', reported DI Yin as they both ran along the red line back towards the main entrance of the hospital, radios held close to their ears.

DC Pau commentary was punctuated by frustrating silence.

'Both men', said DC Pau. 'skirting the ambulance bays and now on car park steps leading up towards Horfield Road. Wait one'. There was an agonising pause. 'Lost to sight amongst trees', he said, then confirmation. 'Still no contact'. Faraday and Yin waited tensely until Pau broke the silence. 'Got them again', said DC Pau. 'Approaching hospital's rear entrance in Horfield Road. It's a steep climb and neither seems to be tiring'. There was another pause, thankfully much shorter this time. 'Crossing Horfield Road and … wait one … up the steps into Robin Hood Lane'.

'Tango Eight', said the armed officers. 'We copy and now deploying on foot immediately outside St Michael's Hospital, 30 yards above and on the same side of the road as PH'

'Roger', said Faraday quickly, knowing that the other ARV would call instantly.

'Tango Three, now deployed on foot, opposite and across the road from PH behind parked vehicles. We have visual on Tango Eight'.

'Completely lost to sight', reported DC Pau. 'They're in Robin Hood Lane. It's a dark, narrow lane with high walls'.

'I see them', reported Tango Three. 'Two men in lane approaching'.

'Wait, wait', said Tango Eight.

The two men walked swiftly towards the Rover, the remote control unlocking the doors, amber lights blinking, smiles creasing their faces, caution evaporating.

'Armed police, armed police …..' the officers bellowed, their disorientating cries breaking the stillness of the night.

***

Colonel House-Layton had mixed feelings – mostly bad. True, the *Santo Stefano* had already entered the Bristol Channel steaming towards to the Mediterranean. His arrest had not compromised

Operation Dragonfish as such, but his arrest would be an embarrassment. He knew only too well that embarrassing his superiors would be a career-stopper. House-Layton would need to salvage what he could.

He sat in the interview room. In front of him was Superintendent Mark Faraday. He was wary of him. He already knew something of him. He was a danger and the colonel knew that he needed to focus on his two main objectives. Firstly, he needed to alert his superiors. Secondly, he needed to know what the police knew without revealing to them what they did not already know. But he found himself being distracted by Detective Inspector Kay Yin. She had said nothing, other that to introduce herself for the purpose of the tape, but the intensity of her beautiful brown eyes and the way in which she seemed to read the superintendent's requirements, handing him a piece of paper, silently dealing with DC Pau who brought an envelope into the room or simply pointing to a line on the clipboard notes, he thought was either theatre or the very neat workings of a complimentary pair of competent professionals. He found himself wondering whether DI Yin's presence was a deliberate ploy so as to distract him as he found that he could not ignore her alluring face with its petite nose, perfect mouth and teeth, all framed by raven black hair that shimmered in the light as she moved her head. He speculated that if she was to crook her delicately exquisite index finger at him, her request would be difficult to ignore. He noticed that neither police officer wore wedding rings and also wondered if there was more to their relationship than simply a pair of interrogators.

The closing of the door as DC Pau left the room, restored House-Layton's attention as Faraday continued the interview.

'You told the custody sergeant that your name was Jeremy Lawrence?'

'It is, superintendent'.

'I'm not so sure that is correct'.

'Why not?'

'It's very simple, really. Witnesses tend to give the same range of responses to questions. And so it is with prisoners. Their responses, reactions, manner and behaviour will be different, of course, but it will be within a reasonably predictable range. I've spoken to the arresting officers and the custody staff and I've reflected upon my short time with you. You are *not* Jeremy Lawrence, nor do I believe this man', said Faraday as DI Yin, on cue, selected and presented a photograph of Andrew Chappell, 'to be Andrew Charman as he claims'.

He glanced, but only fleetingly, at the photograph of the man he knew and said: 'I am Jeremy Lawrence and that fact can be confirmed by my solicitor', he replied, adding with a challenge, 'Have *you* contacted my solicitor as is my right?'

'At the moment, your rights begin and end with me', replied Faraday definitively. 'As far as your solicitor is concerned, we have checked and I can confirm that John Trimble is a partner with Stone Trimble Guinan. However, as I am uncertain as to your identity and believe that other persons unknown are involved in the death of a certain Barry Atkins, your request for others to be informed of your detention is denied'.

'Who is Barry Atkins?' asked the colonel innocently, whilst not challenging his detention *incommunicado*.

DI Yin pushed forward the copy of the photograph of Barry Atkins with Anna Manin.

'I don't understand', he said, his eyes loitering over the photograph of the man he had not seen before. 'I've never met this man', he said.

Faraday rapidly, almost unthinkingly, absorbed his prisoner's reaction to both photographs and his last answer. House-Layton's inner mind had answered accurately. He had never met Barry Atkins. But an innocent man's response would ordinarily have been that he did not *know* Barry Atkins but, of course, House-Layton did *know of* Barry Atkins.

'I think you do. This man was murdered, murdered by *your* friend', said Faraday pointing directly at House-Layton, 'Andrew Charman'.

'All I can do is repeat that I have never set eyes on this man before', protested House-Layton.

'Maybe you can tell me when you first set eyes on Andrew Charman?'

'I am ashamed to say that I was duped', he said a little too eagerly, pleased that he was now able to recount his *snap cover*, a story adopted quickly and without preparation. 'I was driving through Bristol and my heart began to race. I realised that I didn't have my tablets with me and stopped near a hospital. I went into A&E. I saw a constable there talking to a doctor and Mr Charman called out that he had been beaten up by the police. When he was being wheeled to X-Ray in a chair, he passed me and mouthed "can't you help me?" I just followed him. On reflection, it was a very foolish thing to do. Then, in the X-Ray department, he punched the technician. I just panicked and went along with him'.

'But your car was parked well away from A&E?'

'Yes, it was. You see, I saw a hospital and stopped only to discover that it was a maternity hospital but they kindly directed me to the A&E'.

'Why didn't you drive?'

'Because I wasn't comfortable driving in case I took a turn for the worst'.

'But prepared to walk?'

'The doctor tells me that I need to exercise as much as I can'.

'So you have never met this man before?'

'Never'.

'So how is it that you appear on this photograph with him?' asked Faraday taking the photograph from Kay Yin and holding it up in front of the prisoner.

House-Layton starred at the photograph clearly picturing him with Chappell at the Royal Portbury Docks. A little tic danced at the corner of his mouth. He looked ahead, his eyes fixed on the photograph as he began to grapple with the implications. He needed, he knew, to contact his superiors. The second emergency number would have to be used. He started to blink rapidly and put his right hand to his forehead as if in distress.

'I think I do need my heart tablets now, superintendent'.

'And what tablets are they?' asked Faraday without emotion.

'I can never remember the brand name', he said with a pained expression on his face. 'You will need to ring my doctor. You have his number, I gave it to the desk sergeant'.

Faraday turned to DI Yin. She understood and got up from the table and walked to the wall phone, dialled out and spoke quietly to the custody sergeant.

DI Yin returned to the table and said to Faraday: 'The doctor will be called, sir'.

Faraday noticed that the prisoner, instead of relaxing chose to confirm his 'medical condition' by a performance of make-believe gratitude and relief. Faraday gathered the papers together as the custody sergeant knocked on the interview room door and entered with a plastic cup of water.

'Trying to get the doctor as requested, sir. Thought the prisoner here might like some water'.

'Thank you, Derek', replied Faraday as the cup was handed to the prisoner who drank the water slowly. 'Maybe, whilst we are waiting, Mr Lawrence should be returned to his cell'.

'Right you are, sir. Come along then, Mr Lawrence'.

***

Forty minutes later, House-Layton was brought from his cell to the interview room. He sat at the table, a uniformed constable his only companion standing silently at the door, until Superintendent Faraday and Detective Inspector Yin entered.

'Mr Lawrence', opened Faraday. 'I think I should tell you of my concerns. You see, I intend to prove that Mr Charman killed Barry Atkins and transported and disposed of his body on Dartmoor. You know Charman and, I believe, that you were involved in the murder of Atkins'.

'This is preposterous', said House-Layton with a chuckle, confident in the knowledge that he had not been involved in the death or transportation of Barry Atkins. However, he was not so confident regarding his present position. He had assumed that the 'doctor' had been called and thus his superiors alerted. He had assumed that contact with an ACC, if not the chief constable himself, would have been made by the Home Office, that his release would be immanent and that he would shortly be spirited away. These accusations and the line of questioning were unexpected.

'Where is my doctor?' he demanded. Faraday looked towards DI Yin.

'DI Yin leaving the interview room in order to enquire regarding the progress in contacting the doctor', she said for the benefit of the tape and left the room.

Faraday continued. 'Do you have a mobile phone?'

'I have one at home'.

'But you had one this evening?'

'No I didn't', he replied, tension effecting his voice as Faraday removed from a large brown envelope a clear plastic exhibit's bag containing a silver Nokia mobile phone.

'Where did you find it?' he asked. Wrong question thought Faraday.

'I didn't find it. A police dog called Bonnie found it in Robin Hood Lane. She became very interested in what was under a drain cover'.

'Well, it isn't mine'.

'How do you explain the fact that it is covered in your fingerprints, and none other?'

'You don't have my fingerprints', he said, the tick appearing at the corner of his mouth again.

'Yes we do', said Faraday and reached for another exhibit bag containing the aluminium dusted photograph of Barry Atkins and Anna Manin, handled by House-Layton during the previous interview.

'You didn't find my finger prints on that mobile'.

'Not on the mobile, Jeremy, but we did find your prints on the SIM card and battery'.

DI Yin silently reappeared with a man wearing civilian clothes and carrying a large black case. 'DI Yin entering the interview room', she said, placing another ominous-looking envelope on the table.

'And I am Doctor Donald Stevens, a police surgeon', said the man in civilian clothes.

'I asked for my own doctor', protested House-Layton, realising that no contact had been made with his superiors and that his arrest was still known only to the police and Chappell.

'Oh, I think you will find that this doctor is well able to cater for your medical needs. Doctor Stevens will examine you now. Whilst you are being examined, you may wish to consider an explanation as to why we now know that Charman has made many, many calls to your mobile phone. And you may wish to explain how it is that your phone is registered in the name of Jeremy House-Layton?

'I told you that the phone is not mine. Clearly it belongs to this House-Layton fellow and not to me, Jeremy Lawrence'.

'You are related to House-Layton then?'

'Related? What do you mean related?' he said impatiently.

'You must be his twin brother', said Faraday as DI Yin pulled a copy of a *Daily Telegraph* article with photographs from the envelope. 'This article details The Queen's Birthday Honours' List of three years ago. You are in fact Colonel House-Layton and a recipient of the OBE and Mr Charman is actually Andrew Chappell'.

There was utter silence until House-Layton, inhaling through his nose, declared with as much authority as he could muster: 'I don't have to make an explanation to you, superintendent. I would not have thought it necessary to remind you that, in cases of national security, the designated officer is your ACC (Crime). I suggest you call him now and use the code words "blue oak".'

'You seem to have made a full recovery, Jeremy?' observed Faraday, unfazed by his arrogance.

'I don't need your bloody doctor. I need you to get on and tell your ACC'.

'I will contact the Assistant Chief Constable, as you suggest', said Faraday. 'But not yet. When I do telephone him I will tell him that I have charged you with the offence of Misfeasance in a Public Office and that you will be appearing before the court later this morning with Andrew Chappell'.

'What are you talking about?'

'What I am talking about is the fact that you assisted a prisoner, a prisoner arrested in connection with a murder, to escape from lawful detention. What I am talking about is the Common Law offence committed by you, as the holder of a public office, who has conducted himself in such a way as to abuse the trust placed in him'.

Faraday stood up from the table and, collecting his papers together, continued: 'You will now be taken back to your cell'.

Superintendent Faraday turned towards DI Yin, nodded and spoke again to House-Layton.

'This type of accommodation will soon become very familiar to you, Jeremy, as this Common Law offence is punishable by an unlimited term of imprisonment'.

Chapter 32

Sunday 2nd December.

HMP Bristol, England.

PRISONS ARE very much like a hospital wards – they are never quiet. The gangling of keys and clanging shut of heavy metal doors reminds the prisoner of his incarceration; the heavy footsteps of the guards reminds him of the guards' authority and the austere prison furnishings reminds the prisoner of comforts so recently lost.

The two men pulled out the metal chairs and sat opposite Andrew Chappell in the bare prison interview room. They were lawyers, military lawyers, and this was their second visit.

'Have you considered our proposition?' said the senior of the two, a lieutenant-colonel.

'I want it in writing', said Chappell.

'Nothing will be in writing, Andrew', replied the major. 'However you want to excuse or justify your position, the bottom line is that the Crown has ample evidence of your implications in the murder of this lorry driver. Plead guilty to manslaughter and their interest in the murder of the superintendent's secretary will wane'.

'That bloody Faraday won't let that drop'.

'I think he will'.

'Why are you so sure? He found Mad Mike Mason's number on my mobile?'

'But he won't find Mason, well, not alive that is'.

'What do you mean?'

'Our information is that he's dead. His death will be confirmed by the French authorities when we ask them to do so and Faraday will then be informed'.

He thought for a moment longer. 'And the deal?'

'You are aware of the case in which members of the DGSE', said the lieutenant-colonel, referring to the French secret service, 'sank Greenpeace's *Rainbow Warrior* in Auckland harbour?' asked the lieutenant-colonel.

'Yes. They were arrested by the New Zealand police'.

'Two of them, Major Mafart and Captain Prieur, were arrested and charged with murder and arson', he explained. 'They pleaded guilty to manslaughter and in less than two years were free. Major Mafart has since been promoted to colonel and as far as Prieur is concerned, she now holds the rank of commandant'.

'And both received the Legion d'Honneur', added the major.

'The deal is this', continued the lieutenant-colonel. 'Because of the secret nature of the operation, your trial will take place in camera. You will explain that you discovered this Atkins fellow stealing a top-secret lorry and accidentally killed him in a fight. You panicked and disposed of his body, laying a false trail in an attempt to confuse the police. You plead guilty to manslaughter and you will receive ten years but will be out, like the French officers, in six, nine months at the most. You will also be promoted to the rank of major and posted to Germany. That's the only deal'.

'The alternative?'

'The alternative is that you are convicted on murder and, with Faraday running around with his sniffer dogs straining on their leashes, I suspect he will link you with the suicide of one of his inspectors and the murder of his pretty secretary. I don't think you would be out for 25 years'.

'I need more time to think'.

'That's one commodity you don't have', concluded the lieutenant-colonel. 'We need to know now if you are going to accept this deal with the guarantee of promotion to the rank of major within a matter of months?'

Chapter 33

Bristol, England.

SIR HASTINGS Perry had died suddenly in his office of a heart attack. His death was unexpected to some but not so to his family. High blood pressure and long hours had taken their final toll.

The Perry family had sought to keep the funeral as much of a family affair as tradition and protocol allowed, although Sir Hasting's memorial service at Bristol Cathedral would be a very formal affair. The service would be attended by the Lord Lieutenant and the High Sheriff of Bristol. Lord Mayors and Mayors of cities and towns in the force area had been invited to attend, as had representatives of the Metropolitan, Merseyside and Lancashire forces in which Sir Hastings had served with distinction during the last 42 years. The service would be conducted by the dean and would be a dignified affair.

Less dignified were the Byzantine antics being played out at force headquarters. Quickly, the DCC assumed the role of Acting Chief Constable. As this quite proper transition took place, lower ranks began to jostle for preferment and position. Phone calls were made and private meetings held. In this process, Chief Superintendent Wynne-Thomas bubbled upwards, not on the basis of ability but as a move designed by others to block a competitor. In his new found role as Acting Assistant Chief Constable, Wynne-Thomas summoned Mark Faraday.

'Come in, Faraday', said Wynne-Thomas now wearing the insignia of an ACC on his uniform. His new cap, resplendent with a row of silver oak leaves, was placed prominently on his desk for all to see. Faraday was not invited to sit.

'It has been necessary in the light of Sir Hastings' tragic death', said Wynne-Thoma, 'to make some changes. These changes need to be undertaken swiftly so as to eliminate uncertainty. You will know that Superintendent Oliver Richardson has taken up an appointment in Kent and therefore a vacancy now exists in Operational Planning. It has been agreed that you will be posted to HQ accordingly'.

'Are you in a position to tell me who will take over Bristol Central?' Faraday asked in a dignified manner that disguised his anger.

'Yes', he replied with ill-disguised glee in his voice. 'Mary Craven. She has performed in a very promising fashion in the short time she has been in command of the South Gloucestershire District'.

Faraday knew that protest was completely futile and simply enquired: 'And when will these changes be announced?'

'Later this afternoon'.

'And the date?'

'Monday the 28th'.

'I'll carry on then, sir. There will be a good deal to do in the next few days', he said calmly.

Wynne-Thomas had hoped that this meeting would have resulted in Faraday arguing. He had been prepared for such an eventuality, but Faraday did not protest. He would not, however, be denied the opportunity to berate Faraday.

'You are a loose cannon, Faraday. Sir Hastings might well have thought you gifted and imaginative. We consider that you need to be brought to heel and Ops Planning will serve to kerb your maverick tendencies'.

Superintendent Mark Faraday turned and walked silently to the door. As he did so he thought of Inspector David Taylor and Jane Hart, their faces blocking from his mind the prattling of Wynne-Thomas. He thought too of his father. None compared with him. Faraday opened the door, walked through and closed it quietly behind him.

***

He drove to the top of Lower Redland Road. In the block in front of him was her apartment. He parked in one of the visitor's bays, made his way to the front foyer and opened the door with one of the keys she had given him. Mark Faraday didn't wait for the lift but bounded up the stairs, twenty-three steps in eight strides, practiced to perfection. He was not out of breath until he opened her apartment door, then his breath was taken away.

There were two rows of lighted candles in the hallway, like the lights on a runway guiding a lone pilot to safety.

Her bedroom was an oasis bathed in subdued brightness, perfumed by a peaceful blend of jasmine and sandlewood, in the middle of which was a bed with pristine pillows and sheets. Kay Yin uncurled her almond legs, stepped down from the bed and walked towards him. She looked so petite and quite perfect, with the coy brown eyes of a fawn, a wide mouth with exquisite teeth that burst into an irresistible welcoming and seductive smile. Her dainty feet seemed to sail silently across the carpeted floor. All she wore was a black cheong sam.

She stretched up on tiptoe and gently kissed him on the lips, then took his hand and led him to the bed.

Chapter 34

Thursday 7th February.

Whitehall, London, England.

COLONEL JEREMY House-Layton disliked the somewhat intimidating office and disliked its occupant even more. He had assumed that he was to meet with an officer from personnel regarding his posting, not this short, rather rotund brigadier seated behind a splendid desk.

'I absolutely agree with you, colonel', said the brigadier. *'Operation Dragonfish* was a tremendous success. Opium production has been reduced by 72%. That's excellent, of course. However, the real benefit is that many of the drug lords either ran off or have killed each other. More importantly, those that remain have been discredited. Unfortunately, Jeremy, you have also been discredited.'

'I don't believe that to be case at all', he protested.

'The view', replied the brigadier, 'of those who walk the corridors of power is that you failed to grip the situation, that you failed to keep your finger on the pulse of events'.

'Are you giving me the brush off?'

'You will not be going to DC, Jeremy'.

House-Layton had thought as much weeks ago, but he was oblivious as to what the future held for him.

'Where am I going?'

'Into quiet retirement', replied the brigadier with an expressionless face. There was a moment's silence as anger welled up.

'I shall not go quietly, at all', said House-Layton, venom in his tone only to be matched by the harshness in the brigadier's voice.

'Yes you will. You are lucky not to be spending a significant part of that retirement in prison, along with Chappell, and … without your pension, of course'.

'But the operation was a success. You said so yourself and local leaders sympathetic to the West are now beginning to replace the drug lords. The irresponsible and unofficial actions by that idiot Chappell didn't compromise the operation one jot, and you know it'.

'But *you* have been compromised, Jeremy. You've been arrested and been in prison, for God's sake. The Americans won't tolerate you in DC …'

'But …'

'Do *not* interrupt me, Jeremy', the brigadier said, getting up from his chair and walking to the tall windows overlooking Victoria Embankment, the bright daylight serving to silhouette him completely against the window. 'The American's won't tolerate you in Washington any more so than we would tolerate Oliver North in London'.

'I will take this higher', he responded defiantly.

'No you won't. I'm as high as you go. As far as those higher up are concerned, you are a retiree on probation'.

'A retiree?' he said indignantly. 'What do you mean a retiree?'

'Your pension and your freedom are secure, conditional upon you retiring quietly. And if you want to take up a security post somewhere in civvy-street, you will receive a glowing reference from us. Meanwhile, as from midnight *last* night, you were no longer a serving officer in the British army.'

House-Layton stood up angrily and snatched up the discharge papers from the desk, then stormed towards the door.

'Jeremy', snapped the brigadier. House-Layton turned.

'Yes?' he asked equally curtly.

'Chappell did the right thing. He pleaded guilty. *You* need to do the right thing. Certainly not the *wrong* thing'.

'What do you mean, not the *wrong* thing?'

'You might foolishly consider that an army pension is a small reward in comparison to the royalties you might be able to command from selling your story to the English tabloids or to an Australian publisher. You have relatives in Australia don't you?'

'Yes, I certainly do', he said smugly.

'And you have relatives here too?'

House-Layton tried to distinguish the expression on the brigadier's face, but his silhouette was jet-black against the window, his tone ice-cold.

'What are you getting at?' he demanded, the smugness gone.

'You have a son and a daughter, both of whom are serving commissioned officers, are they not?'

'Don't you dare threa……'.

'If you betray your country', interjected the brigadier deliberately, all compromise gone from his voice, 'you will, at the very same moment, betray the aspirations and the futures of your son and your daughter … and then you will go to prison. I guarantee it'.

For a moment Colonel Jeremy House-Layton (Retired) reflected. Gradually his head bowed, only slightly, but bowed as if in submission. He turned and left the office closing the door quietly. Now alone, the brigadier walked away from the window towards the grey filing cabinet with the combination lock. He twirled the dial right, then left and right again. Unlocked, he pulled the top drawer towards him, fingered through the A to E files and extracted one marked 'Captain Andrew Chappell'. He opened the file on the top of this opened drawer. The standard content, personal and service records, course reports and posting, he left to one side. What commanded his attention were the statements from House-Layton, Collins and Mooney, an operational order, details of the closure of International Bodyworks of Swindon, details of rented properties in Bristol and Reading, the reports by the two military lawyers, the receipt for the destruction of a phantom black 2.7 Audi and other papers that would be certain to facilitate the early release of Andrew Chappell.

These papers he carefully removed. He carried them to his desk and placed them all into a black burn-bag which he secured with a numbered tag. Satisfied, he pressed a key on his desk intercom. 'Sergeant Tomlinson', he said quickly and, without waiting for a response, returned to the filing cabinet. He replaced the now much thinner file into the top drawer, pushed it closed and flicked the combination lock between finger and thumb. There was a knock on the door.

'Enter'.

Sergeant Tomlinson entered.

'Ah. A safe pair of hands, sergeant', he said, then pointing to the open book on his desk, added: 'Sign there'.

Sergeant Tomlinson, checked the date and then the number on the burn-bag's security tag against the number listed in the dark green covered book. The contents of the burn-bag were listed as 'Operation Dragonfish – Superfluous Documents'. Satisfied, he signed the book accordingly.

'I'll take the bag to the furnace immediately m'self, sir'.

'That's a good chap'.

coming soon

The third *Mark Faraday Collection* crime novel

Treachery casts a long and deadly shadow

Darker than DEATH

by Richard Allen

THE DEATH OF A RESPECTED BRISTOL ARTIST is written-off as the unfortunate consequences of an apparently bungled burglary by an unknown opportunist. But at police headquarters, Superintendent Mark Faraday is not so easily convinced.

As Faraday, with DCI Kay Yin, investigate the death, he begins to uncover a web of betrayal and dishonesty that stretches from the battlefields of the Great War and an abattoir in the small Belgian village of Boesinghe in November 1914 to the very heart of present-day British government and the headquarters of the United Nations in New York, oblivious to the betrayal and dishonesty that stalks him with his own headquarters, where loyalty by many is fleeting and deceit by some corrupting.

Available as eBook or paperback direct from
www.amazon.com or www.amazon.co.uk

39183096R00195

Printed in Poland
by Amazon Fulfillment
Poland Sp. z o.o., Wrocław